Rachel Gibson's first two romance novels – *Simply Irresistible* and *Truly Madly Yours* – were named among the Top Ten Favourite Books of the Year by the membership of the Romance Writers of America. She is married and lives with her husband and children in Boise, Idaho.

The Trouble with
Valentine's Day

Rachel Gibson

little
black
dress

First published in the USA in 2005
by AVON BOOKS
An imprint of HARPERCOLLINS PUBLISHERS

This edition published in Great Britain in paperback in 2006
by LITTLE BLACK DRESS
an imprint of HEADLINE BOOK PUBLISHING

A LITTLE BLACK DRESS paperback

2

9 780755 334049 (ISBN-13)

Typeset in Transit511BT by Avon DataSet Ltd,
Bidford-on-Avon, Warwickshire

Printed and bound in Great Britain by Clays Ltd, St Ives plc

Headline's policy is to use papers that are natural, renewable and
recyclable products and made from wood grown in sustainable
forests. The logging and manufacturing processes are expected to
conform to the environmental regulations of the country of origin.

HEADLINE BOOK PUBLISHING
A division of Hodder Headline
338 Euston Road
London NW1 3BH

www.littleblackdressbooks.co.uk
www.hodderheadline.com

With much love and appreciation to
Betty Gregorie: an avid reader, mad recycler,
and a huge influence in my life

Valentine's Day sucked the big one.

Kate Hamilton lifted a mug of hot buttered rum to her mouth and drained the last drop. On the 'things that suck' scale, it ranked somewhere between falling on her face in public and her great-aunt Edna's bologna pie. One was painful and embarrassing, while the other was an abomination in the eyes of the Lord.

Kate lowered the mug and licked the corners of her mouth. The hot rum heated her up from the inside out, warmed her skin, and cast the room about her in a nice, cozy glow. Yet it did nothing to lift her mood.

She was feeling sorry for herself, and she hated that. She wasn't the sort of woman to sit around and get all weepy. She was the sort to get on with life, but there was nothing like one whole day devoted to lovers to make a single girl feel like a loser.

A whole day of hearts and flowers, chocolate candy and

naughty undies delivered to someone else. Someone undeserving. Someone who wasn't her. Twenty-four hours to remind her that she slept alone, usually in a sloppy T-shirt. A whole day to point out that she was just one bad relationship away from throwing in the towel. From giving up her Fendi pumps for Hush Puppies. From driving to the animal shelter and adopting a cat.

Kate looked around the Duchin Lounge, where she sat on a barstool inside the Sun Valley lodge. Shiny heart garlands decorated the brass rails, while roses and flickering candles sat on each tabletop. Red and pink hearts were taped up behind the bar and on the big windows looking out at snow-covered pines, groomed runs, and night skiers. Spotlights poured down the slopes, washing them in white gold and darker shadow.

Those inside the Duchin were decked out in the latest skiwear chic. Ralph Lauren and Armani sweaters, UGG boots and Patagonia fleece vests. Kate felt a bit like a poor relation in her jeans and dark brown sweater. Her sweater fit well and matched her eyes, but it wasn't a brand name. She'd bought it at Costco, along with a bag of bikini-cut Haines Her Way, a gallon of shampoo, and about five pounds of margarine.

She turned sideways on her stool, and her gaze moved to the big windows across the bar. When had she started buying her underwear in bulk at a warehouse instead of at Victoria's Secret? When had her life become that pathetic? And why had five pounds of margarine ever seemed like a good idea?

Outside the Duchin's windows, downy snowflakes drifted past the outside lights and softly touched the ground. It had started snowing earlier that afternoon, shortly after Kate had hit the Idaho/Nevada border, and it hadn't let up. As a result of all that snow, the drive to Sun Valley from Las Vegas had taken her almost nine hours instead of the usual seven.

Normally, she would have driven straight through without stopping, but not when it was snowing so hard. Not when it was so dark that one wrong turn in the Sawtooth Wilderness could land a girl in one of those tiny towns where men were men and sheep were nervous. The next morning she planned to drive the last hour to the small town of Gospel, Idaho, where her grandfather lived.

Kate ordered her third hot buttered rum and turned her attention to the bartender. He looked to be in his late twenties with curly dark hair, and he had a wicked little glint in his brown eyes. He wore a white dress shirt and black pants. He was young and cute and wore a wedding ring, too.

'Can I get anything else for you, Kate?' he asked through a smile that oozed boyish charm. He'd remembered her name, a quality that made him a good bartender, but the foremost thought in Kate's head was that the man probably had a few girlfriends on the side. Men like him usually did.

'No thank you,' she answered and purposely shoved her cynical thoughts to the back of her mind. She didn't like that she'd become so negative. She hated the pessimist who'd taken up residence in her head. She wanted the other Kate back. The Kate who wasn't so cynical.

At the tables and booths, couples laughed and talked

and shared kisses over bottles of wine. Kate's Valentine's Day blues sank a little lower.

This time last year, Kate had been having dinner in Las Vegas at Le Cirque with her boyfriend, Manny Ferranti. She'd been thirty-three, Manny thirty-nine. Over shrimp cocktail she'd told him she'd booked them a suite in the Bellagio. Over roasted veal she'd described the crotchless panties and matching cutout bra she was wearing beneath her dress. Over dessert she'd brought up the subject of marriage. They'd been together for two years, and she'd thought it was time to talk about their future. Instead of talking, Manny had dumped her the next morning. After he'd put the hotel suite and those panties to good use.

At the time, Kate had been a little surprised at how fine she'd been with the breakup. Well, maybe not *fine*. She'd been plenty ticked off, but her world hadn't fallen apart. She'd loved Manny, but she was also practical. She didn't know why she hadn't seen it before, but Manny was commitment phobic. Thirty-nine and never married? The man obviously had serious issues, and she didn't wanted to waste her time with a man who couldn't commit. She'd been there before, with other boyfriends who'd wanted to date for years but never quite commit to more. Good riddance to bad relationships.

At least that's what she'd told herself, until a few months ago when she'd seen Manny's wedding announcement in the newspaper. She'd been in her office, thumbing through the *Las Vegas Review-Journal*, looking for the vital records section, seeing if any of her missing persons had turned up dead, and there it'd been. A nice little announcement with a photo. Manny and some brunette looking in love and happy.

Manny had found someone and married her in less than eight months after breaking things off with Kate. Someone he'd dated for less than eight months, too. He hadn't been opposed to a commitment. Not at all. He'd just been opposed to a commitment with *Kate*. Which hurt more than she'd ever thought possible. More than the breakup. More than him walking out on her after a night of hot sex. It made her chest tight and throat squeeze and confirmed something she could no longer ignore.

There was something wrong with her.

Something more than her height of five-eleven. More than her size ten feet and straight red hair. She was a private investigator. She made a living digging into people's personal lives, seeking motives and agendas. Peering into their backgrounds and private and social patterns, but she'd never stopped to dig into her own life.

Seeing Manny's wedding announcement in the paper had changed that. It had forced her to examine her own life, something she'd always avoided if at all possible. What she'd discovered was that she was drawn to unattainable men. Men with roving eyes or hidden girlfriends or commitment fears.

Maybe she didn't think she deserved better, or maybe she liked the challenge. She didn't know for certain why she always picked unavailable men, but one thing was for sure, she was tired of bad relationships and a broken heart.

The day after seeing Manny's announcement, she'd sworn off bad relationships. She'd vowed to date only *available*, nice guys without any issues. She'd thrown herself into her work. A job she'd always loved and was damn good at doing.

She'd worked for Intel Inc., one of the most prestigious investigating firms in Vegas. She'd enjoyed everything about being a PI. Everything from spying on lowlifes out to defraud insurance companies or the casinos, to reuniting long-lost loves or separated family members. If she'd had to follow cheating boyfriends or girlfriends or spouses, that had been okay too. Hey, if a man or woman was cheating, then they deserved to get caught. If they weren't (which was *never* the case), then no harm done. Either way, it had not been her problem. Kate had gotten paid for her time and walked away . . .

Until the day Randy Meyers had come to her fourth-floor office. There hadn't been anything remarkable about Randy. He'd been neither handsome nor ugly. Short nor tall. He'd simply been.

He'd come to Intel Inc. and to Kate because his wife had disappeared with their two children. He'd shown Kate the typical family photo. The kind taken at the mall for around thirty bucks. Everything about that photo had been ordinary. Everything from the matching sweaters, to the boy's crew cut and the little girl's missing front tooth.

And everything about Randy had checked out. He'd worked where he'd said he did. He'd had no criminal record. No history of abuse. He'd sold cars at Valley Automall and had been his son's Cub Scout leader. He'd been his daughter's soccer coach, and he and his wife, Doreen, had taken classes together at the community college.

His wife and the children hadn't been hard to find. Not at all. They'd fled to Waynesboro, Tennessee, to stay with Doreen's sister. Kate had given Randy the information, signed off on the case, and never would have given it a second thought if Randy hadn't made the national news twenty-four hours later. The things he'd done to his wife and children before he'd killed himself had stunned the country. It had shocked Kate to her core.

This time, she hadn't been able to remain detached. This time she hadn't been able to tell herself that it wasn't her problem, that she'd just been doing her job. This time she hadn't been able to move on.

A week later, she'd resigned from her job. Then she'd called her grandfather and told him she was coming to visit him for a while. Her grandmother had died two years earlier, and Kate knew that her grandpa, Stanley, was lonely. He could use her company, and she could use a breather. She didn't know how long she would stay, but long enough to figure out what to do now. To take a step back and figure out what she wanted to do next.

She faced the bar and took a drink. The rum slid down easy and added a little kick to her growing buzz. With single-minded determination, she pushed thoughts of the Meyers family from her head and concentrated on the hearts strung along the bar. It was Valentine's Day, and that reminded her that she hadn't been on a good date in months. No sex since the Bellagio and Manny. And while she really didn't miss Manny, she did miss intimacy. She missed the touch of a man's strong hands. Sometimes she wished she were the sort of woman who could pick up a man in a bar. No regrets. No recriminations. No wanting a criminal background check first.

Sometimes she wished she was more like her friend, Marilyn. Marilyn's motto was, 'If you don't use it, you'll lose it,' as if her vagina had an expiration date.

She looked at her reflection in the mirror behind the bar and wondered if losing the desire for sex was like losing a sock at the Laundromat. Did it just disappear without a trace? By the time you noticed it was gone, was it too late? Was it gone for good?

She didn't want to lose her desire for sex. She was too young. For just one night, she wished she could turn off the interrogator in her head and find the sexiest guy around, grab him by the front of his shirt, and lock lips. For just one night, she wished she were the type of woman who could gorge on wild sex with a man she'd never met and would never see again. His touch would burn her alive, and she'd forget about everything but his mouth on hers. She'd take him to her hotel room, or perhaps they wouldn't even make it to the room and they'd have to do it in the elevator, or a service closet, or maybe she'd do him in the stairwell.

Kate took a drink and turned her attention to the good-looking bartender. He stood at the end of the bar laughing and joking and shaking up martinis. She might have become cynical about people and especially men, but she was still a woman. A woman with dozens of secret fantasies spinning about in her head. Fantasies of being swept up into big strong arms. Of eyes meeting across a crowded room. Of instant attraction. Remorseless lust.

Since her breakup with Manny, all her fantasy men

were the complete opposite of her old boyfriend. They were all bad boys with big hands and bigger . . . feet. The star of her current fantasy was a blond badass with size thirteen biker boots. She'd picked him from a Dolce & Gabbana ad in *Cosmo*, looking all cool and unkempt with his bad self.

Sometimes her fantasy involved him tying her to the back of his Harley and absconding with her to his love shack. Other times she'd see him in different dive bars with names like The Brass Knuckles or Devil's Spawn. Their eyes would meet and they'd only make it as far as the alleyway before they tore at each other's clothes.

Someone took the stool beside Kate and bumped her shoulder. Her drink sloshed, and she cupped her hands around her warm mug.

'Sun Valley Ale,' a masculine voice next to her ordered.

'Draft or bottle?' the bartender asked.

'Bottle's fine.'

As much as Kate would love to live out one of her fantasies, she knew it would never happen because she could not turn off the PI in her head. The one that, at a crucial moment, would decide she needed a background check first.

The scent of crisp night air suddenly surrounded her head, and she slid her gaze from her mug to the green plaid flannel rolled up thick forearms. A gold Rolex was strapped around his left wrist, and a thin silver band circled his middle finger.

'Do you want this on your room tab?' the bartender wanted to know.

'Nah, I'll pay for it now.' His voice was low and a little

rough as he reached for his wallet in the back pocket of his Levi's. His elbow brushed hers as she ran her gaze up the green flannel of his arm to his big shoulders. The ceiling lights above shone down on him and picked out variegated gold in his brown hair. Unruly and finger-combed, his hair covered his collar and the tops of his ears. A Fu Manchu mustache framed his wide mouth, and he'd grown a soul patch just below his full bottom lip.

Her gaze continued upward to a pair of deep green eyes staring back at her across his broad shoulder, past all the greens on his shirt. His lids looked a little heavy, like he was tired or he'd just gotten out of bed.

She swallowed. Hard.

'Hello,' he said, and his voice just seemed to pour through her like her hot buttered rum.

Holy Mary mother of God! Had thinking about her badass fantasy man conjured him up? He wasn't blond, but who cared? 'Hello,' she managed, as if the hair on the back of her neck hadn't started to tingle.

'It's a beautiful night to hit the slopes. Don't you think?' he asked.

'Spectacular,' she answered, although her mind wasn't on skiing. This guy was big. The kind of big that came from genetics and physical labor. She'd guess he was in his mid to late thirties.

'Lots of new powder.'

'That's true.' Kate pressed her fingertips into the warm porcelain mug and fought the urge to play with her hair like she was in the eighth grade. 'Gotta love all that fresh powder.'

He turned on his stool to face her, and her heart just

about stopped. He was even better than her fantasy man, and her fantasy man rocked.

'So why aren't you out there?' he asked.

'I don't ski,' she confessed.

Surprise lifted one brow and the corners of his mouth. 'You don't?'

You'd never mistake this man for a male model. Never see his face pushing Dolce & Gabbana or him lying on the beach in a Gucci suit. He was too big. Too masculine. Too male. The full impact of him all too real. 'No. Just passing through. It's been snowing so hard, I had to stop for the night.' He had a tiny white scar just below his soul patch, and his nose looked like it had been broken. It was hardly noticeable really, but Kate was trained to notice everything about a person's face. And studying this man's face was pure pleasure.

'Hope it clears up.' He snagged the beer bottle in his right hand. 'I'm heading out for Bogus Basin in the morning.'

'Are you a ski bum?'

'During the winter months, pretty much. After Bogus, we'll hit Targhee and Jackson Hole before heading to Colorado.'

We'll? 'Are you here with friends?'

'Yeah, my buddies are still out on the slopes.' He hooked the heels of his boots on the bottom rung of his stool, and his wide-spread knees brushed the outside of her thigh.

The casual touch did something to her insides. It wasn't exactly instant, remorseless lust, but it was something. 'Why aren't you out there with them?' Buddies. As in male friends. Men didn't generally refer to female friends as buddies.

He raised the beer to his lips. 'Knees acting up,' he answered and took a long drink.

But there was little doubt in her mind that this guy had a woman in his life. Probably more than one. 'Skiing with buddies on Valentine's Day?'

He watched her through those green eyes of his as he lowered the bottle. 'Is it Valentine's Day?' he asked and sucked a drop of beer from his top lip.

Kate smiled. The fact that he didn't know meant he probably didn't have anyone serious in his life right now. 'Every year on the fourteenth of February.'

He looked about the room as if really seeing it for the first time. 'Ahh. That explains the hearts.'

Her gaze lowered past the mustache framing his mouth and chin, down the wide column of his thick neck to the hollow of his tan throat. 'I think we're the only two in here who aren't a couple.'

'Don't tell me you're here alone?'

Kate returned her gaze to his and laughed. She liked the way he'd said that, as if he found it hard to believe. 'Yeah, go figure.' In her favorite fantasy, she was trapped with a hunk of man in Nordstrom's shoe department. 'How about you? Anyone going to be angry with you for forgetting Valentine's Day?'

'Nope.'

She'd never set a fantasy in a ski lodge, but she was thinking about it now. She couldn't help it. The man was throwing off pheromones like he was a nuclear reactor at Chernobyl. Sitting so close to ground zero, the fallout was lethal.

He pushed up the sleeves of his flannel shirt and

exposed what appeared to be the tail of a snake or some sort of reptile on his thick left forearm. 'Is that a snake?'

'Yeah. That's Chloe. She's a sweetheart.'

Right. The tattoo was dark gold with black-and-white bands and appeared so real she leaned in for a closer look. The scales were perfectly defined, and without giving it a thought, Kate reached out and touched his bare arm. 'What kind of snake is she?' She half expected to feel cool scales instead of warm, smooth flesh.

'An Angolan python.'

Python. Yikes! 'How big?' Kate looked back up into his face. Something hot and sensual shimmered within the green depths of his eyes. A need that made her pulse jump and tingles spread up her wrists.

He raised the beer to his mouth and looked away. 'Five feet.' He took a long drink, and when he returned his gaze to her, that flicker of that something was gone, as if it had never been there.

She dropped her hand. 'Are all five feet of her tattooed on your body?'

'Yeah.' He pointed to his forearm with the mouth of the bottle. 'Her tail ends here. She's wrapped around my arm, down my back, and is coiled around my right thigh.'

Kate looked down at his thigh and straight at his groin. Soft worn Levi's covered his legs and cupped the bulge in his crotch. She quickly looked away before he caught her staring. 'I have a tattoo.'

He laughed. A low rumble in his chest that did funny things to *her* chest. 'What? A heart on your ankle?'

She shook her head and took a long drink from her mug. Her temperature shot up and her face felt flushed.

She didn't know if it was the rum or the testosterone cocktail sitting next to her, but she was starting to feel a little light-headed. Not the kind of light-headed that made you faint, but the kind that brought a grin to your face even when you didn't feel like smiling.

'Hmm?' He lowered his gaze down the side of her throat. 'A rose on your shoulder?'

The kind of light-headed that made a girl think of hot sweaty things. Hot sweaty *naked* things she probably shouldn't act upon. 'Nope.'

He looked back into her eyes and speculated, 'A sun around your navel.'

'A moon and a few stars, but not around my navel.' Hot sweaty naked things that no one else would ever know about.

'I knew it would be something girly,' he scoffed as he shook his head. 'Where?'

It couldn't be just her. He had to feel it too, but what if she did proposition him and he turned her down? She didn't think she could handle that kind of humiliation. 'My butt.'

Smile lines crinkled the corners of his eyes, and he laughed again. 'Full or half?'

Wait, he's a guy, she thought as she polished off her drink. Guys were guys were guys. He wouldn't turn her down. 'Crescent.'

'A moon on a moon.' He cocked one brow and leaned to one side and looked at her butt as if he could see through her clothing. 'Interesting. I've never seen that before.' He took a drink of his beer and straightened.

Maybe it was the rum and her hot sweaty naked

thoughts. Maybe it was because it was Valentine's Day and she was lonely and didn't want to wear Hush Puppies yet. Maybe for just once she wanted to act on an impulse. Maybe it was all of those things, but before she could stop herself, she asked, 'Wanna see?' The second the words left her lips, her heart seemed to stop along with her breath. Oh God!

He lowered the bottle. 'Are you propositioning me?'

Was she? Yes. No. Maybe. Could she really go through with it? *Don't overanalyze it. Don't think it to death,* she told herself. *You'll never see this guy again. For once in your life, just go for it.* She didn't even know his name. She guessed it didn't matter. 'Are you interested?'

Slowly, as if to make sure he understood her perfectly, he asked, 'Are you talking sex?'

She looked into those eyes staring back at her and tried to breathe past the sudden constriction in her chest. Could she use and abuse him? Could she twist him into a sexual pretzel then toss him out the door when she was through? Was she that kind of person? 'Yes.'

There it was again. That hot, sensual need that flickered and burned. Then in the blink of an eye, his features hardened and his gaze turned cold. 'Afraid not,' he said as if she'd offered him up a fate worse than death. He set his beer on the bar and rose until he towered over her.

Kate managed a stunned, 'Oh,' just before her cheeks caught fire and her ears started to buzz. She raised a hand to her numb face and hoped she didn't pass out.

'Don't take it personal, but I don't fuck women I meet in bars.' Then he walked away, moving from the lounge as fast as his big boots could carry him.

2

By thirteen, Kate had become an infrequent visitor to Gospel, Idaho. As a kid, she'd loved hiking in the wilderness area and swimming in Fish Hook Lake. She'd loved helping out at the M&S Market, her grandparents' small grocery store. But once she'd entered her teen years, hanging out with her grandparents hadn't been cool any longer, and she'd only visited on rare occasions.

The last time Kate had been in Gospel had been to attend her grandmother's funeral. Looking back, that trip had been a short, painful blur.

This trip was less painful, but the moment she lay eyes on her grandfather, she knew there would be nothing short about her stay.

Stanley Caldwell owned a grocery store filled with food. He butchered fresh meat and bought fresh produce, yet he ate TV dinners every night. Swanson Hungry Man. Turkey or meat loaf.

He kept his house clean, but after two years, it was still cluttered with Tom Jones memorabilia, which Kate thought odd since her grandmother had been the Tom Jones fanatic, not her grandfather. In fact, he'd gone out of his way to indicate that her obsession was something he supported but did not share. Just as she had not shared his love of big game hunting.

Of the two, Melba Caldwell had been more devoted to Tom than Stanley had been to hunting. Every summer Kate's grandfather had driven her grandmother, like a pilgrim journeying to holy sites, to Las Vegas and the MGM Grand to worship with the faithful. And every year, instead of bits of paper or teaspoons of milk, Melba had carried an extra pair of panties in her handbag.

Kate had accompanied her grandmother to one of Tom's shows a number of years ago. Once had been enough. She'd been eighteen, and seeing her grandmother whip out a pair of red silkies and toss them on stage had scarred Kate for life. They'd sailed through the air like a kite and had wrapped around Tom's mic stand. Even now, after all these years, the mental picture of Tom wiping sweat from his brow with her grandmother's panties disturbed her and caused a deep groove in the center of her forehead.

Kate's grandmother had been gone for two years, but nothing of hers had been packed up and put away. Tom Jones chotchkes were everywhere. It was as if her grandfather kept the memory of her grandmother alive through sex bomb ashtrays, Delilah shot glasses and pussycat bobble heads. As if to lose those things would be to lose her completely.

He refused to hire more day help in the grocery store,

even though he could certainly afford it. The Aberdeen twins and Jenny Plummer rotated the night shift. The store was closed on Sundays, and the only real difference was that now Kate worked with him at the M&S instead of Melba.

He was so old-fashioned that he still did the book-keeping by hand in a big ledger. He kept track of his sales and inventory in different color-coordinated books just as he had since the 1960s. He absolutely refused to step into the twenty-first century and didn't own a computer. The only piece of modern office equipment he owned was a desk calculator.

If things didn't change, he was going to work himself into an early grave. Kate wondered if that was what he secretly hoped. She'd come to Gospel for a break, to get away from her life for a short while. One look into her grandfather's sad face and even sadder existence, and she'd known there was no way she could leave him until he was living again. Not just going through the motions.

She'd been in Gospel for two weeks now, but it had only taken her two days to see that Gospel really hadn't changed that much since she was a kid. There was a sameness about Gospel, a day-to-day predictability, that Kate was surprised to discover appealed to her. There was a certain peace in knowing your neighbors. And even though those neighbors were all locked and loaded, there was comfort in knowing they weren't likely to go on some wild killing spree.

At least not until spring. Like the black bears that roamed the wilderness area, the town pretty much hibernated during the winter months. Once the regular hunting season was over in the late fall, there wasn't a lot to do until the snow melted.

As far as Kate could tell, the townspeople had a love/hate relationship with tourists and were suspicious of anyone without an Idaho 'famous potatoes' license plate bolted to their bumper. They had a distrust of California and felt a superiority over anyone not born and raised in Idaho.

After all these years, Gospel still had only two diners. At the Cozy Corner Café, the specials of the day were still fried chicken and chicken fried steak. The town had two grocery stores. The M&S was the smaller of the two, with only one checkout. On the outskirts of town, two different churches lined the same street. One nondenominational, the other Mormon. Gospel had five bars and four gun and tackle shops.

The only new business in town was a sporting goods store located in what had once been the pharmacy right across the parking lot from the M&S. The old log building had been refurbished and restored, and big gold letters spelled out SUTTER SPORTS just above the stained-glass fish in the huge front window. It had a green tin roof and awnings, and a Closed Until April sign hung on the double glass-and-brass doors.

According to Stanley, Sutter's didn't sell guns. No one knew why. This was Gospel after all, gun-nut capital of the world. A place where kids got their NRA membership cards before their driver's license. A place where all pickup trucks had gun racks and THEY CAN HAVE MY GUN WHEN THEY PRY IT FROM MY COLD DEAD FINGERS bumper stickers. People slept with handguns stuck in the headboards of their beds and stashed in panty drawers. And they took it as a matter of pride that no citizen of Gospel had been killed with a gun since the turn of the century, when two of the Hansen boys had shot it out over a whore named Frenchy.

Well, there *had* been that incident in '95 when the old sheriff of the town had taken his own life. But that didn't count since taking your own life really wasn't a punishable crime. And no one really liked to talk about that particular chapter of the town's history anyway.

Most everything inside the M&S Market was the same as Kate recalled from her childhood. The antlers of the twelve-point buck her grandfather had blown away in '79 were still on display above the old battered cash register. Around the commercial coffeemaker, conversation ranged from the mysterious owner of Sutter Sports, to Iona Osborn's hip replacement surgery.

'You can't weigh that much and *not* have hip problems,' Ada Dover said as Kate punched the keys of the cash register, then hit Add with the side of her hand.

'Uh-huh,' she responded as she set a can of cling peaches in a plastic grocery bag. Even the sounds inside the store were the same. From the back room, she could hear the whine of the meat slicer, and from the speakers overhead, Tom Jones sang about touching the green grass of home. Melba's presence was still everywhere in the M&S, from the horrible music to the velvet Tom painting hung in the back office. About the only thing that had really changed inside Melba Caldwell's store since her death was the stream of widows trolling for her husband, Stanley.

'Iona should have gone on Weight Watchers years ago. Have you ever tried Weight Watchers?'

Kate shook her head, and the end of her ponytail brushed the shoulders of her black shirt. Last week she'd substituted Tom Jones with *Matchbox Twenty*. But halfway into the second verse of 'Disease,' her grandfather had ejected her CD and plugged Tom back in. As Ada rambled and Tom crooned, Kate felt a slight brain bleed coming on.

'It really keeps my figure trim. And Fergie's too. Being that I'm Iona's good friend, I tried to get her to at least check out a few meetings over at the grange.' Ada shook her head and her eyes narrowed. 'She said she would, but she never did. If she'd listened to me, she'd have lost that weight huckity-buck and there would've been no need to have that hip replaced.'

What the heck was a huckity-buck? Fearing the answer, Kate pointed out instead, 'It could be that Iona has a low metabolism.' According to her grandfather, Ada Dover arrived every day around noon, coifed, decked, and doused in Emeraude. No doubt about it, she was looking to make Stanley Caldwell husband number three.

'She should buy one of those mountain bikes from over there at the sports store.'

Now that Kate was here, her grandfather always found something to do in the back room to avoid Ada and the widow posse who had him in their sights. He also made her do the home deliveries the widows called in on a regular basis. Kate didn't appreciate it either. She didn't like getting pumped for information about her grandfather, and she had better things to do than listen to Myrtle Lake rattle on about the horrors of heel spurs. Better things – like giving herself a lobotomy. 'Maybe Iona should just start out walking,' Kate suggested as she rang up a box of Wheat Thins and placed it in the sack.

'Of course, even if Iona wanted to buy one of those bikes, she can't. The owner of that store is probably in the Caribbean, sunning himself like a lizard. His mama is the nurse over there at the clinic. She's not from around here. Minnesota, I think. Tight-lipped as Tupperwear.' Ada dug into her huge purse and pulled out her wallet. 'I don't know *why* he opened his store in Gospel in the first place. He'd probably sell more bikes and what-nots in Sun Valley. He doesn't sell guns over there. Don't know why, but that's a Minnesotan for ya. Liberal and contrary.'

Kate wondered what being a Minnesotan had to do with not selling guns or being contrary, but she was too busy fighting the shudder passing through her to ask. *Sun Valley*. The scene of the greatest humiliation of her life. The place where she'd gotten drunk and propositioned a man. The one time in her life when she'd managed to suppress her inhibitions and go for it, she'd been shot down by a man who'd practically run from the room to get away from her.

'He's handsome as sin but doesn't park his boots under anyone's bed. Everybody knows Dixie Howe's been trying her best to hook him, but he isn't interested. 'Course I don't blame him for avoiding Dixie. Dixie's got a gift for hair dye, but she's been rode hard and put away wet more often than Aunt Sally's mule.'

'Maybe he doesn't like women,' Kate said and hit Total. The guy in Sun Valley hadn't liked women. He'd been a misogynist. At least, that's what Kate liked to tell herself.

Ada sucked in a breath. 'Homosexual?'

No. As much as Kate would have liked to believe the jerk had been gay, and that's why he hadn't taken her up on her proposition, she really didn't think so. She was too good at reading people to miss those signs. No, he was just one of those men who liked to degrade women and make them feel really bad about themselves. That, or he had erectile dysfunction. Kate smiled, maybe both.

Ada was silent a moment, then said, 'Rock Hudson was gay, and that Rupert Everett fella too. Regina's son Tiffer is gay, but he isn't good-looking. He was in one of those gay pageants down in Boise. He sang "Don't Rain on My Parade," but of course he didn't win. Even drag queens have their standards.' She pulled out a pen and began writing out a check. 'Regina showed me the pictures. I swear, Tiffer in a wig and rouge looks just like his mama. And Regina looks more like Charles Nelson Riley than Barbra Streisand. Seems a waste and a shame if that Sutter fella is gay, though. But it would explain why he isn't married and never dates.' Ada ripped out the check and handed it to Kate. 'And Myrtle Lake's granddaughter, Rose, is after him, too. Rose is young and cute as they come, but he's never parked his boots under her bed neither.'

Kate wondered how Ada knew so much about the owner of the sporting goods store. Kate could have found out the same information easily enough, but she was a licenced private investigator. Ada was the manager of The Sandman Motel and obviously a very busy body.

After Ada left the store, Kate locked the cash register and walked to the back. The room smelled of fresh meat and the bleach her grandfather always used to sanitize his equipment and cutting boards. At the far end of the room was the store's small bakery, where her grandmother had made cakes and cookies and homemade bread. The equipment was covered, and no one had used it in over two years.

Stanley sat at a long white table, having finished packaging T-bone steaks in six blue Styrofoam trays and plastic wrap. On the wall above him hung the same meat-cutting charts that Kate remembered from her childhood. Other than the deserted bakery, it appeared as if nothing had changed in a few decades, but it had. Her grandfather was older and tired easily. Her grandmother was gone, and Kate didn't know why he didn't sell the store or hire someone to run it for him.

'Ada's gone,' Kate said. 'You can come out now.'

Stanley Caldwell looked up, his brown eyes reflecting the dull sadness of his heart. 'I wasn't hiding, Katie.'

She folded her arms beneath her breasts and leaned a shoulder into boxes of paper products that needed to be carried into the storage room. He was the only person in the world who called her Katie, as if she were still a little girl. She continued to simply look at him until a slight smile lifted his white handlebar mustache.

'Well, maybe I was,' he confessed as he stood; his pot-belly pushed at the front of his bloody apron. 'But that woman talks so much, she makes my head hurt.' He untied his apron and tossed it on the worktable. 'I just can't take a woman who talks too much. That's one thing I liked about your grandmother. She didn't talk just to hear her own voice.'

Which wasn't entirely true. Melba had loved to gossip as much as anyone else in town. And it had taken Kate less than two weeks to discover that Gospel included gossip in their daily diet like it was a fifth member of the food groups. Meat. Vegetable. Bread. Dairy. All served alongside a healthy portion of 'Vonda's youngest was caught smokin' behind the school.'

'What about the woman who works for the sheriff? She seems nice and doesn't talk as much as Ada.'

'That's Hazel.' Stanley picked up the packages of T-bones, and Kate followed as he carried them through the store to the display case. The worn wood floor still creaked in the places Kate remembered as a child. The same Thanks for Shopping Here sign still hung above the door, and candy and gum were still sold on the first aisle. These days, though, the penny candy was ten cents and the owner's steps were slower, his shoulders more hunched, and his hands were gnarled.

'Hazel's an okay gal,' her grandfather said as they stopped at the open refrigerated case. 'But she isn't your grandmother.'

The meat case had three decks and was split into four sections: chicken, beef, pork, and prepackaged, which her grandfather always called the 'hanging meat.' In Kate's sick mind, 'hanging meat' had an entirely different connotation. She was from Vegas, where you could find Mr Hanging Meat 'dancing' at the Olympic Gardens five nights a week.

'Have you thought about retiring, Grandpa?' Kate asked as she straightened packages of Ballpark Franks. The subject had been on her mind, and she'd been waiting for the right moment to bring it up. 'You should be having fun and taking it easy instead of cutting meat until your hands swell.'

He shrugged one shoulder. 'Your grandma and me used to talk about retiring. We were going to buy one of those motor homes and travel the country. Your mother's been nagging me about it, too, but I can't do it just yet.'

'You could sleep as late as you wanted and not have to worry about getting Mrs Hansen's lamb chops exactly an inch thick or running out of lettuce.'

'I like providing the perfect cuts for people. I'm still good at it, and if I didn't have someplace to go every morning, I might never leave my bed.'

Sadness tugged at Kate's heart, and together she and Stanley returned to the back room, where her grandfather showed her how to load the pricing gun with a roll of stickers. Every item got a sticker, even if the price was clearly marked by the manufacturer. She'd pointed out the redundancy, but he was too set in his ways to change. His dreams for the future had died with Kate's grandmother, and he hadn't replaced them.

The bell above the front door rang. 'You go this time,' Kate said through a smile. 'It's probably another one of your women coming to flirt with you.'

'I don't want women flirting with me,' Stanley grumbled as he walked out of the room.

Want the attention or not, Stanley Caldwell was bachelor number one with the senior women in Gospel. Maybe it was time for him to stop hiding from his life. Maybe she could help him let go of old dreams and create new ones.

Kate opened a case of beets with a box knife and picked up the pricing gun. She'd never really been much of a dreamer. She was a doer. Instead of dreams, she had full-blown fantasies. But, as she'd learned recently, her fantasies were better left safely guarded in her mind, where they couldn't be crushed by rejection.

She was probably the only woman in history to be turned down in a bar, and she hadn't been able to work up a good fantasy in her head for two weeks now. No more badass biker dude tying her to the back of his hog. No more fantasy men at all. Not only had the jerk in Sun Valley humiliated her but he'd also killed her fantasy life.

She stuck a test sticker on the box flap, then went to work on the first row of cans. From the speakers bolted to the walk-in freezer, Tom Jones belted out a crappy rendition of 'Honky Tonk Woman,' which Kate figured was an abomination on so many different levels. One of which was that, at the moment, a song about a honky-tonk woman taking a man 'upstairs for a ride' was her least favorite topic on the planet.

'Katie, come here,' her grandfather called out to her.

Not since the twelfth grade, she thought as she finished putting stickers on the last row of cans, when her boyfriend had asked someone else to the prom, had Kate suffered such a mortifying blow to her self-esteem. She was long over it now, and she would get over what had happened in Sun Valley, too. At the moment, though, her only consolation was that she'd never have to lay eyes on the jerk from the Duchin Lounge again.

She moved from the back room toward her grandfather, who stood at the end of a produce bin talking to a man with his back to Kate. He wore a blue ski parka with black on the long sleeves. He held a half gallon of milk in one hand, and a box of granola was stuck under one arm. Messed brown hair brushed the collar of his coat, and he was taller than her grandfather's six-two height. He tipped his head back and laughed at something her grandfather said, then he turned, and his laughter died. Across the too short distance, his deep green gaze met hers, even more brilliant in the light of day. His brows lowered, and within the perfect frame of his Fu Manchu, his lips parted.

Kate's footsteps faltered and stopped. Everything within her seemed to stop, too. Except for her blood, which drained from her head and made her ears buzz. Her chest got tight, and just like the first time she'd seen him, she wondered if thinking about the man had conjured him up. Only this time, there were no warm tingles. No urge to flip her hair. Just that funny feeling in her head like she might faint.

At the moment, Kate wished she would just faint dead away and wake up somewhere, but she just wasn't that lucky. And while she stood there wishing she *could* faint, she was sure he was recalling every detail of the night she'd propositioned him. The night he'd made his rejection of her look like the easiest thing he'd ever done.

'This is Rob Sutter. He owns the sporting goods store where the old pharmacy used to be. Rob, this is my only granddaughter, Katie Hamilton. I don't believe you've met.' That's what her grandfather was saying, but over the buzz in Kate's ears, and Tom Jones growling about the Honky Tonk Woman, she heard something else. *Don't take it personal, but I don't fuck women I meet in bars*, shot through her brain like a thousand pin pricks. The silence between them seemed to stretch forever as she waited for him to inform her grandfather that they *had* already met. To tell him his granddaughter was a drunk and a slut. The pricing gun fell from her hand and hit the floor with a thud.

He glanced across his shoulder at Stanley. 'No. We haven't met,' he said. When he returned his attention to Kate, the surprise she'd seen on his face was gone, replaced by a curious smile that turned up the corners of his mouth. 'It's nice to meet you, Katie.'

'It's Kate,' she managed past the constriction in her chest. 'Only my grandfather calls me Katie.'

He stepped toward her and bent to pick up the pricing gun. The overhead light filtered through the hair on the top of his head and picked out the gold. The rasp of his jacket sleeve filled the silence between them. 'How long have you been in town?' he asked, his voice as deep and smooth as she remembered, only this time it didn't pour through her like hot buttered rum.

He knew how long she'd been in town. What was he up to? 'A couple of weeks.'

'Then we just missed each other. I've been on a ski trip with my buddies the last couple of weeks.'

She knew that, of course. And he knew that she knew it, too. But if he wanted to pretend they'd never met, that was more than fine with her. She looked down at his hand holding the sticker gun toward her. The brand name Arc'teryx was spelled out in white on the Velcro cuff that wrapped around his wrist.

'Thank you,' she said as she took the sticker gun from him. The tips of her fingers inadvertently brushed his and she took a step backward, dropping her hand to her side. Her gaze slipped up the zipper closing the front of his coat.

'It's a real surprise to walk in here and see anyone but Stanley working,' he said.

She blinked and stared into his green gaze. Nothing. Not a hint of mockery or a flicker of recognition. At first he'd looked surprised. Now nothing, and she couldn't tell if he was pretending or not. Was it possible that he didn't recognize her? No, that was probably just wishful thinking on her part. She'd never been that lucky.

'It's about time he got some help.'

'Ah, yes,' she murmured, distracted by her thoughts. She'd been drunk. He'd probably been drunk too. Perhaps the surprise she'd seen on his face a few moments ago had been nothing more than surprise at seeing someone besides her grandfather working in the M&S. Lord knew the rest of the town had been shocked to see her.

'She's come to help me out in the store.' Stanley moved to stand beside her and patted her shoulder. 'She's such a good girl.'

Rob Sutter glanced at her grandfather, then slowly he returned his gaze to her. She waited for him to laugh or at least crack a smile. He didn't, and she relaxed a fraction. Maybe this Rob guy was a total boozer. Could she be that lucky? Some men beat their wives and shot up the house. When they woke up in jail, they didn't have a clue why they were incarcerated. They sat with their head in their hands and didn't remember a thing. Being a person who remembered everything, Kate had never believed in alcohol amnesia. Maybe she'd been wrong. Maybe the owner of the sporting goods store had it. Maybe he was a blind drunk.

Perhaps she should feel a bit irritated that she was so

utterly forgettable. At the moment all she felt was a glimmer of hope that she'd lucked out and he was a raging alcoholic.

Good girl, my ass. With his free hand, Rob Sutter unzipped his coat and shifted his weight to his left foot. Good girls didn't get wasted and pick up men in bars.

'How long do you plan to stay in Gospel?' he asked. The last time he'd seen her, she'd had her hair down. Smooth and shiny, like liquid fire. He liked it better down.

Color returned to her pale cheeks, and she tilted her head to one side. He could practically read her mind. She was wondering if he remembered her. 'As long as my grandfather needs me.' She turned her attention to Stanley. 'I'm going to finish pricing the beets. If you need anything, holler.'

As if Rob *could* forget her offer to show him her bare butt. As she walked away, Rob's gaze slid down the ponytail that hung below her shoulders, past the tight black shirt to her rounded behind in black pants. No, he hadn't forgotten her. The image of her within the soft lighting of the Duchin Lounge had stayed with him long after he'd left the bar. That night he'd dreamed of soft auburn hair and eyes the color of rich earth. Of long legs and arms entwined with his. Of sex so intense, so real, that he'd just about climaxed in his sleep. That hadn't happened to him in a long time. A man didn't tend to forget a thing like that. At least not right away.

'I really don't need her help,' Stanley said, 'but it's nice to have her around, just the same.'

Rob returned his gaze to the grocery store owner. He

wasn't certain, but he thought he detected a light in Stanley's eyes when he spoke of his granddaughter. A little light that he'd never seen there before. He liked Stanley Caldwell, and he respected him, too. 'Is she living with you?'

'Yeah. She pampers me, but I try not to get too used to it. She can't stay with me forever. She'll have to get back to her own life one of these days.'

Rob grabbed an apple and moved toward the front counter. 'Where's home?' he asked. He'd been living in Gospel long enough to know it didn't take much to get a person's life story, whether you were interested in hearing it or not. And in this particular case, he was mildly curious.

'Katie's from Las Vegas,' Stanley answered as he moved behind the counter and rang up the milk, granola, and apple.

As Rob dug out his wallet, he wondered if Kate Hamilton was a dancer in one of the casinos. She was certainly tall enough. She had the breasts for those skimpy costumes, too. Back in his hell-raising days, she would have been just the sort of woman he would have gone for. Tall. Built. Easy.

'She's a private investigator,' Stanley provided while he placed the box of granola in a plastic bag.

That announcement surprised Rob. Almost as much as when he'd turned around and seen her standing a few feet from him, looking as stunned as he'd felt.

He handed Stanley a ten. 'She doesn't look like any investigators I've ever met,' he said, and he'd known a few.

'That's what makes her so good,' Stanley bragged. 'Women talk to her because she's one of them, and men talk to her because we just can't resist a beautiful woman.'

Rob had been doing a pretty good job of resisting women for a while now. Beautiful or otherwise. It wasn't easy, never that, but he'd thought he'd gotten over the worst of it. The constant craving – until a certain redhead had propositioned him. Walking away from Kate Hamilton had been one of the hardest things he'd done in a very long time.

He put the bills in his wallet and shoved it in his back pocket.

'Here's the key to your place,' Stanley said and shut the cash drawer. 'A couple of boxes from UPS came while you were gone. And yesterday, I picked your mail up off the floor for ya.'

'You didn't have to do that.' Rob took the key to his store and put it back on his key ring. Before he'd left for his ski trip, Stanley had offered to accept freight for him. 'I appreciate it, though. I made you something for your trouble.' He unzipped the breast pocket on the inside of his jacket and pulled out a fishing fly. 'This is a bead-head nymph I tied just before I left. Rainbows can't resist these guys.'

Stanley took it and held it up to the light. The ends of his handlebar mustache lifted up. 'It's a beauty, but you know I don't fly-fish.'

'Not yet,' he said and grabbed his bag of groceries. 'But I'm planning your introduction.' He headed for the door. 'See ya, Stanley.'

'See ya. Tell your mother I said hello.'

'Will do,' Rob said and walked from the store.

The midmorning sun bounced off snow banks and

blinded him with white, stabbing rays. With his free hand, he dug around in the pocket of his heavy coat for his sunglasses. He shoved the Rēvos on the bridge of his nose, and instantly the deep blue polarized lenses eliminated the glare.

He'd parked his black HUMMER in the first slot, and he slid easily into the front seat. He didn't care what anyone thought about his HUMMER. Not his mother and certainly not environmentalists. He liked the leg room and the shoulder room too. He didn't feel so huge in the HUMMER. Cramped. Like he took up too much space. He liked the storage capacity and the fact that it plowed through snow and climbed over rocks with grit and spit and enough pure muscle to spare. And yeah, he liked the fact that he could climb over the top of the other cars on the road if he had to.

He fired up the vehicle and reached into the grocery bag to pull out the apple. He took a bite and put the SUV in reverse. From within the M&S, he caught a glimpse of red ponytail and black shirt.

Her name was Kate, and the night he'd walked out of the Duchin Lounge, he never thought he'd see her again. Not in a million years, but here she was, living in Gospel. Stanley Caldwell's granddaughter was working right across the parking lot from Rob, pricing cans and looking better than he remembered – and what he'd remembered had been pretty damn good.

Rob shoved the HUMMER into gear and drove around to the back of his store. She hadn't been pleased to see him. Not that he could blame her. He could have let her down easier that night. A lot easier, but being propositioned had pissed him off. It had reminded him of a time in his life when he would have taken her up on the offer. When he wouldn't have even hesitated before he kissed her mouth and tangled his fingers in her hair. A time when he would have stared into her liquid brown eyes as he had sex with her all night long. A time in his life when women had been within easy reach and he'd never gone without.

Back then, his life had been fast and furious. Full tilt. Balls to the walls. Everything he'd ever expected and could ever want. Yeah, he'd been blindsided and slammed in the corners more times than he could count. He'd made mistakes. Done things he wasn't proud of, but he'd loved his life. Every damn minute of it.

Right up to the second it had been blown all to hell.

Rob opened the back door to Sutter Sports and pushed his sunglasses to the top of his head. He took the stairs up to his office and bit into his apple. The sharp crunch joined the sound of his footsteps, and he wiped the back of his hand across his mouth. He flipped on the light switch with his elbow and headed toward the open end of the loft, which looked down into the dark store below.

A tandem canoe and nine-foot kayak were suspended from the ceiling beams and cast shadows across a row of mountain bikes. With Sun Valley sixty miles away, and several gun and tackle stores within the city limits of Gospel, Sutter's didn't sell winter sporting goods. Instead he concentrated on summer recreational equipment, and last summer he'd made a nice profit off the rental side of the business.

The temperature in the building was sixty-five and felt warm in comparison to the biting chill outside. He'd lived

in every time zone and climate in North America. From
Ottawa to Florida, Detroit to Seattle, and several stops in
between, Rob Sutter had been there and done that.

He'd always preferred the four distinct seasons of
the Northwest. Always enjoyed the radical change in
temperature and scenery. Always loved the raw, in-your-
face wilderness. And there weren't many places more raw
or in-your-face than the Idaho Sawtooths. His mother had
lived in Gospel for nine years now. He'd lived here not
quite two. It felt like home, more than any other place he'd
lived.

Rob turned away and headed for his desk in the middle
of the large room. A carton of Diamondback fly rods and a
box of T-shirts with his store's name and logo on the front
leaned against his workbench on the far side of the room.
His vise and magnifier competed for space with intricate
tools, spools of thread, tinsel, and wire.

On top of Rob's desk, Stanley Caldwell had neatly
stacked his mail. Rob had liked Stanley the moment he'd
met him a year ago. The old guy was hardworking and
honest, two qualities Rob respected most in a man. When
Stanley had offered to 'look after' the sporting goods store
while Rob was out of town, Rob hadn't thought twice
before he'd handed over the key.

Rob took one last bite of his apple and tossed the core
into the garbage can. He sat on the corner of his desk and
kept one foot planted on the floor. Beside the mail sat the
latest issue of *The Hockey News*. On the cover, Derian
Hatcher and Tie Domi duked it out. Rob hadn't seen the
game, but he'd heard that the Dominator had gotten the
better of Hatcher.

He picked up the magazine and thumbed through it, past the ads and articles, to the game stats in the back. His gaze skimmed the columns, then stopped halfway down the page. One month to the play-offs and the Seattle Chinooks were still looking good. The team was healthy. The goalie, Luc Martineau, was in his zone and veteran sniper Pierre Dion was on fire, with fifty-two goals and twenty-seven assists.

The last year Rob had played for the Chinooks, they'd made it to the third round of the play-offs before the Avalanche had narrowly defeated them by one goal. It was the closest Rob had come to getting his name inscribed on Lord Stanley's cup. He'd been bummed about it, but he'd figured there'd always be next season. Life had been good.

Earlier that same year, his girlfriend, Louisa, had given him a child. A six pound, green-eyed, beautiful baby girl. He'd been there at her birth, and they'd named her Amelia. The baby had brought him and Louisa closer, and a month after Amelia's birth, he and Lou had gotten married in Las Vegas in between road games.

Before the baby, the two of them had been together off and on for three years, but they'd never been able to make it work for more than a few months at a time. They'd fought and made up, broken up and gotten back together so many times that Rob had lost count. Almost always over the same issues – her insane jealousy and his infidelity. She'd accuse him of cheating when he wasn't. Then he would cheat and again they'd break up only to get back together a few months later. It had been a vicious circle, but one each had vowed to stop once they were married. Now that they had a baby and were a family, they were determined to make it work.

They'd made it five months until the first major blowup.

It was the night he'd gone out with the guys and come home late, and Louisa had been waiting up for him. He'd spent most of the night playing bad pool and decent darts in winger Bruce Fish's game room. Fishy was a damn good hockey player, but he was also a notorious womanizer. Louisa had flipped out and refused to believe that they hadn't been at a strip club getting lap dances and worse. She'd accused Rob of cheating with a stripper and stinking of cigarettes. That had set him off. He didn't have sex with strippers anymore and hadn't for a few years. He'd smelled like cigars, not cigarettes, and he hadn't cheated with anyone. For over five months he'd been a damned saint, and instead of yelling at him, she should have been taking him to bed and rewarding his good behavior. Instead, they'd slipped back into their past behavior of fighting. In the end, both agreed that Rob should leave. Neither wanted Amelia exposed to their contentious relationship.

By the beginning of hockey season that October, Rob was living on Mercer Island. Louisa and the baby were still living in their condo in the city, but she and Rob were getting along again. They were talking about a reconciliation because neither wanted a divorce. Still, they didn't want to rush things and decided to take it slow.

He'd just signed a four-million-dollar contract with the Chinooks. He was healthy, happier than he'd been in a while, and was looking forward to a kick-ass future.

Then he fucked up big time.

The first month into the regular hockey season, the Chinooks hit the road for a nine-day, five-game grind. Their first stop was Colorado and the team that had put an end to their chances at the cup the prior season. The Chinooks were fired up and ready for another run at it. Ready for another go in the Pepsi Center.

But that night in Denver, the Chinooks couldn't seem to get their game together, and in the third frame the Avalanche was up by one with twenty-five shots on goal. What no one talked about, what no one even dared to whisper out loud, was that losing their first road game by one point to the Avalanche once again could jinx the rest of the season. Something had to change – fast. Something had to happen to knock Colorado off their game. To slow them down. Someone had to fix the situation and create a little chaos.

That someone was Rob.

Coach Nystrom gave him the signal from the bench, and as Avalanche Peter Forsberg skated across center ice, Rob charged him and knocked him on his ass. Rob received a minor penalty, and as he served out his three minutes kicking back in the sin bin, Chinook's sniper, Pierre Dion, shot from the point and scored.

Game on.

Five minutes later, Rob was back at work. He checked Teemu Selanne in the corner and gave him a glove rub for good measure. Denver defender Adam Foote joined the action along the boards, and while the Denver fans cheered on their man, Rob and Adam dropped gloves and had a go. Rob had two inches and thirty pounds on the Denver player, but Adam made up for it with incredible balance and a right uppercut. By the time the referees stopped the fight, Rob could feel his left eye swelling, and blood streamed from a cut on Adam's forehead.

Rob put ice on his knuckles and once again kicked back in the penalty box. This time for five minutes. The fight had been a good one. He respected Foote for standing up for himself and his team. What few people outside of hockey understood was that fighting was an integral part of the game. Like puck handling and scoring.

Fighting was also a part of Rob's job description. At 6'3" and two hundred and thirty pounds, he was good at it too. But he was much more than an enforcer. More valuable to the team than just the guy who burst the other team's bubble while racking up penalty minutes. It wasn't uncommon for him to put up twenty goals and thirty assists in one season. Impressive stats for a guy who was known mostly for his solid right hook and lethal haymakers.

When the final whistle blew that night in Denver, the game ended in a respectable tie. Afterward some of the guys celebrated in the hotel bar, and after a quick call to Louisa and Amelia, Rob celebrated with his teammates. A few beers later, he struck up a conversation with a woman sitting alone. She wasn't a puck bunny. After twenty years in the NHL, he could identify a hockey groupie a mile away. She had short blonde hair and blue eyes. They talked about the weather, the slow hotel service, and the black eye he'd gotten from fighting with Foote.

She was nice enough looking, but in an uptight schoolteacher way. She really didn't pique his interest . . . until she leaned across the table and put her hand on his arm. 'Poor baby,' she said. 'Should I kiss it all better?'

Rob knew exactly what she was really asking, and he was about to laugh it off when she added, 'Should I start with your face and work my way down?' Then the woman who looked like an uptight schoolteacher proceeded to tell him all the naughty things she wanted to do. She followed that up by telling him all the things she wanted *him* to do to *her*.

She invited him up to her room, and looking back on it, he was a little embarrassed that he hadn't even hesitated all that much. He followed her to her room and had sex with her for several hours. He'd had a good time, and she'd had three good times. The next morning he caught a flight to Dallas with the rest of the team.

Like all other sports, hockey had its share of players who indulged in road sex. Rob was one of them. Why not? Women wanted to be with him because he was a hockey player. He wanted to be with them because he liked no-strings sex. They both got what they wanted.

When it came to road sex, management looked the other way. A lot of wives and girlfriends looked the other way, too. Louisa wasn't one of them, and for the first time, he felt the weight of what he'd done.

Yeah, he'd always felt bad when he'd cheated before, but he'd always told himself that it didn't count because he and Louisa were either broken up or not married. He couldn't say that now. When he'd taken his wedding vows, he'd meant them. It didn't matter that he and his wife weren't living together. He'd betrayed Louisa, and he'd failed himself. He'd messed up, had risked losing his family for a piece of ass that meant nothing. He'd been married nine months now. His life wasn't perfect, but it was better than it had been in a while. He didn't know why he'd risked it. It wasn't as if he'd been extremely horny or even looking to hook up. So why?

There wasn't an answer, and he told himself to forget about it. It was over. Done. It would never happen again. He meant it, too.

When the plane landed in Dallas, he'd managed to put the blonde with the blue eyes out of his mind. He never would have even remembered the woman's name if she hadn't somehow gotten his home telephone number. By the time he returned to Seattle, Stephanie Andrews had left more than two hundred messages on his answering machine. Rob didn't know which was more disturbing, the volatile messages themselves, or the sheer volume of them.

Although it was no secret, she'd discovered he was married, and she accused him of using her. 'You can't use me and throw me away,' she began each message. She screamed and raged, then cried hysterically, as she told him how much she loved him. Then she always begged him to call her back.

He never did. Instead, he changed his number. He destroyed the tapes and thanked God Louisa hadn't heard the messages and would never need to know about them.

He never would have remembered Stephanie's face if she hadn't found out where he lived and been waiting for him one night after he returned home from a Thanksgiving charity auction at the Space Needle. Like a lot of nights in Seattle, a thick misty rain clogged the black sky and smeared his windshield. He didn't see Stephanie as he drove his BMW into the garage, but when he stepped from his car, she walked inside and called out his name.

'I will not be used, Rob,' she said, her voice raising above the sound of the door slowly closing behind her.

Rob turned and looked at her beneath the light of the garage. The smooth blonde hair he remembered hung in soggy chunks at her shoulder, as if she'd been standing outdoors for a while. Her eyes were a little too wide, and the soft line of her jaw was brittle, like she was about to shatter into a million pieces. Rob reached for his cell phone and dialed as he moved backward toward the door. 'What are you doing here?'

'You can't use me and throw me away as if I am nothing. Men can't use women and get away with it. You have to be stopped. You have to pay.'

Instead of boiling a rabbit or pouring acid on his car, she pulled out a .22 Beretta and emptied the clip. One round hit his right knee, two bullets hit his chest, the others lodged in the door by his head. He'd almost died on the way to the hospital from his injuries and blood loss. He spent four weeks in Northwest Hospital and another three months in physical therapy.

He had a scar that ran from his navel to his sternum and a titanium knee. But he'd survived. She hadn't killed him. She hadn't ended his life. Just his career.

Louisa didn't even come to see him in the hospital, and she refused to let Amelia visit. Instead, she served him with divorce papers. Not that he blamed her. By the time he was through with therapy, they'd hammered out visitation, and he was allowed to visit Amelia at the condo. He saw his baby on weekends, but after a short time it became clear to him that he had to get out of town.

He'd always been strong and healthy, ready to take

names and kick ass, but suddenly finding himself weak and reliant on others had kicked *his* ass. He fell into a depression that he fought against and denied. Depression was for wussies and women, not Rob Sutter. He might not be able to walk without help, but he wasn't a weeny.

He moved to Gospel so his mother could help him with his rehabilitation. After a few months, he realized that he felt like a weight had been lifted. One he'd been refusing to acknowledge. Living in Seattle had been a constant reminder of everything he'd lost. In Gospel, he felt like he could breathe again.

He opened the sporting goods store to take his mind off his troubled past and because he needed something to do. He'd always loved camping and fly-fishing, and he'd figured it would make a good business move. What he discovered was that he really enjoyed selling camping and fishing equipment, bicycles and street hockey gear. He had a stock account that allowed him to take the winter off. He and Louisa were getting along once again. After he'd sold his house on Mercer Island, he'd bought a loft in Seattle. Once a month he flew to Washington and spent time with Amelia there. She'd just turned two and was always happy to see him.

The trial of Stephanie Andrews had ended within a few short weeks. She'd received twenty years, ten fixed. Rob hadn't been there at the sentencing. He'd been fishing in the Wood River, whipping his Chamois Nymph across the surface of the water. Feeling the rush and pull of the current.

Rob picked the mail off his desk and walked toward the door. He turned off the lights and headed down the stairs.

He'd never been the kind of guy to overanalyze his life. If the answer didn't come easy, he forgot about the question and moved on. But getting shot forced a man to take a good hard look at himself. Waking up with tubes stuck in your chest and with your leg immobilized gave you plenty of time with nothing to do *but* think about how your life got so screwed up. The easy answer was that Rob had been stupid and had had sex with a crazy woman. The harder answer was the *why*.

With his mail in one hand, he locked the store behind him. He shoved his sunglasses on the bridge of his nose and headed for the HUMMER. Once inside, he tossed his mail on the passenger seat beside his groceries and fired up the vehicle. He still didn't know the answer to the last question, but he figured it didn't matter now. Whatever the answer, he'd learned the lesson the hard way. He was a poor judge of women, and when it came to relationships, he was a bad bet. His marriage had been painful, the divorce an inevitable slam to the ice. That's all he needed to know to avoid a repeat of his past.

He would like a girlfriend, though. A girlfriend in the sense of a girl who was a friend. A friend who came over to his house and had sex with him a couple of times a week. Someone who just wanted to have a good time and ride him like a hobbyhorse. Someone *not* crazy. But there was the rub. Stephanie Andrews hadn't *looked* crazy – not until she'd shown up in Seattle with a grudge and a gun.

Rob hadn't had sex since he'd been shot. Not that he wasn't able or had lost his desire. It was just that every time he saw a woman he was interested in, and who seemed interested in him, a little voice inside his head always put a stop to it before it even got started. *Is she worth dying for?* it asked. *Is she worth your life?*

The answer was always no.

As he pulled out of the parking lot, he glanced in the rearview mirror at the M&S Market. Not even with a gorgeous redhead with long legs and a nice ass.

Across the street, Rob stopped at the self-serve Chevron and pumped gas in the HUMMER. He leaned his hip into the side of the car and prepared for a long wait. Once again his gaze was pulled to the front of the grocery store. Whoever had come up with the maxim that the more you went without sex, the less you wanted it, was a moron. He might not think about sex all the time, but when he did, he still wanted it.

A Toyota pickup pulled in behind Rob, and a short blonde got out and made her way toward him. Her name was Rose Lake. She was twenty-eight and built like a little Barbie doll. In the summer she liked to wear tank tops without a bra. Yeah, he'd noticed. Just because he didn't have sex didn't mean he wasn't a guy. Today she wore tight Wranglers and a jean jacket with that fake white fur on the inside. Her cheeks were pink from the cold.

'Hey there,' she greeted as she stopped in front of him.

'Hey, Rose. How're things?'

'Good. I heard you were back.'

Rob pushed his sunglasses to the top of his head. 'Yeah, I got back last night.'

'Where'd you go?'

'Skiing with friends.'

Rose tilted her chin and looked up at him out of the corners of her light blue eyes. 'What are you doing now?'

He recognized the invitation, and he shoved his fingers into the front pockets of his Levi's. 'Pumping gas in the HUMMER.'

Yeah, she was cute, and he'd been tempted more than once to take what she was offering. 'What about when you leave here?' she asked.

He was tempted even now. 'I've got a lot of work to do before I open the store in a few weeks.'

She reached out and tugged at the front of his coat. 'I could help you out.'

But not enough to drown out the warnings in his head. 'Thanks, but it's the sort of paperwork I have to do myself.' Still, there was nothing wrong with chatting up a pretty girl while filling his HUMMER with fuel. 'Anything interesting happen while I was gone?'

'Emmett Barnes got arrested for drunk and disorderly, but that's not anything new or interesting. The Spuds and Suds got a health code violation, but that's nothing new either.'

He pulled his hand from his pocket and reached for his sunglasses.

'Oh, and I heard you're gay.'

The pump shut off, and his hand stopped in midair. 'What?'

'My mom was at the Curl Up & Dye this morning getting her roots done, and she heard Eden Hansen telling Dixie Howe that you're gay.'

He dropped his hand. 'The owner of Hansen's Emporium said that?'

Rose nodded. 'Yeah. I don't know where she heard it.'

Why would Eden say he was gay? It didn't make sense.

He didn't dress like a gay guy, and there wasn't a rainbow sticker on his HUMMER. He didn't like to decorate or listen to Cher. He didn't give a crap if his socks matched; as long as they were clean, that's all that mattered. And the only hair care product he owned was a bottle of shampoo. 'I'm not gay.'

'I didn't think so. I'm usually pretty good at sensing something like that, and I never got the gay vibe from you.'

Rob removed the gas nozzle and shoved it in the pump. Not that it mattered, he told himself. There was nothing wrong with being homosexual. He had a few friends in the NHL who were gay. He just didn't happen to be one of them. To him, it was just a matter of sexual preference, and Rob loved women. He loved everything about them. He loved the scent of their skin and their warm, wet mouths beneath his. He loved the heated look in their eyes as he seduced them out of their panties. He loved their soft, eager hands on his body. He loved the push and pull, give and take of hot sex. He loved it fast and he loved to take his time. He loved everything about it.

Rob clenched his jaws and screwed on the gas cap. 'See ya around, Rose,' he said, then opened the door to his vehicle.

In the beginning it had been extremely difficult to go without sex, but he'd kept himself active and busy. When a sexual thought had popped into his head, he'd just thought of something else. If that hadn't worked, he'd tied flies, losing himself in nymphs and tung head zug bugs. He'd concentrate on mastering the perfect wrap, and eventually going without had got easier. Through force of will, and over a thousand flies later, he'd gained command of his body.

Until recently. Until a certain redhead had brushed her fingers across his arm and sent a bolt of desire straight to his groin, reminding him of everything he'd given up.

It wasn't like she'd been the first woman to offer him a good time. He knew women in Seattle and women right here in Gospel who were up for some bed action. She just tempted him more than he'd been tempted in a while, and he didn't know why. But like all the questions in his head for which there were no answers, he didn't have to know why.

The only thing he knew for certain was that that kind of temptation wasn't good for his peace of mind. It was best to steer clear of Kate Hamilton. Best if he stayed on his side of the parking lot. Best to get her completely out of his head.

And the best way to do that was with a seven-foot bamboo rod and an eight-ounce reel, a box of his favorite midges and nymphs, and a river filled with hungry trout.

He drove home and grabbed his rod and reel and waders, then headed to the Big Wood River and the spot just below the River Run Bridge where the big trout fed without fear in the winter. Where only the most dedicated fly fisherman stood knee deep in water so cold it forced its way through Gore-Tex, pile, and neoprene. Where only the hard-core walked cautiously across the frozen ice, stacked like blue cards against the river's steep banks. Where only the obsessed walked into the river and froze their balls off for a chance to battle a twelve-inch rainbow.

Only when he heard the sound of the river tripping over rocks, the swish of his line whipping back and forth, and the steady clicking of his reel could Rob begin to feel the tension ease between his shoulders.

Only when the sight of his favorite nymph kissed the perfect spot at just the edge of a deep pool did his mind finally clear.

Only then did he find the peace he needed to calm the struggle within him. Only then did the loneliness ease. Only then did everything seem right again in Rob Sutter's world.

'There's a group social at the grange tonight,' Regina Cladis informed Stanley Caldwell as he rang up a pound of bologna, a quart of milk, and a can of coffee.

Stanley groaned inwardly and kept his gaze pinned on the keys. He knew better than to look into Regina's thick glasses. She'd take it as a sign of encouragement, and he didn't have an interest in Regina or socials of any kind.

'We're all bringing samples of our poetry. You should come.'

He glanced over at Hayden Dean, Rob Sutter, and Paul Aberdeen, who stood gathered around his coffee machine a few feet away. 'I don't write poetry,' he said loud enough for them to hear, just in case they thought he was the kind of guy who sat around writing poetry.

'Oh, you don't have to write it to enjoy it. Just come and listen.'

Stanley might be old, but he wasn't near senile enough

to get himself shut in a grange with a bunch of poetry reading and writing women.

'Iona is bringing her famous peach thumbprints,' Regina added as enticement.

'I have to work on my accounts books,' he lied.

'I'll do the accounts books for you, Grandpa,' Kate offered as she moved toward the front of the store with a snow shovel in one hand and her coat in the other. 'You should go out with your friends.'

He frowned. What was wrong with her? Lately she'd been pushing him to 'get out of the house,' even though she knew he liked to stay home nights. 'Oh, I think that—'

'I can pick you up at seven,' Regina interrupted.

Finally Stanley looked into Regina's thick glasses and stared at the only thing he feared more than one of those social meetings – riding in a car with a woman who was practically blind. 'That's okay. I can drive,' he said, having absolutely no intention of driving anywhere.

He gazed past Regina's kinked-up hair to his granddaughter, who was walking toward the door. Kate's brows were pulled together like she was irritated. She stopped to lean the shovel against the magazine rack.

'I'll save a chair for you,' Regina offered.

'I'll shovel the snow, Katie,' he said. He set Regina's can of Folgers in a paper bag. 'I need you to take a delivery to Ada over at The Sandman Motel.'

'Ada just wants to pump me for information about you. Tell her she needs to come in and do her shopping like everyone else,' Kate said through a frown. The last delivery she'd made to The Sandman hadn't gone well, and Stanley suspected he'd never get her to go back. Still, he had to try, because the alternative was having to go himself.

'Shoveling snow is man's work.' He glanced once more at the men by the coffee machine. 'Let me finish up here, and I'll go out and do it.'

'There's no such thing as "man's work" anymore,' Kate told him as she shoved her arms into her navy blue peacoat. Stanley took Regina's check and glanced at the men standing around the coffee machine. He prayed his granddaughter wouldn't elaborate. He and Katie had had several arguments concerning men's and women's roles. This wasn't Las Vegas, and she wouldn't win any friends with her women's lib crap.

The good Lord didn't see fit to answer Stanley's prayer. 'Women can do anything men can do,' Kate added, eliciting several raised brows and pointed looks from the men. His granddaughter was a beautiful young woman. She had a good heart and she meant well, but she was too independent, too opinionated, and too vocal. And that was too many things for a man to overlook. After living with her for a month, Stanley could see why she wasn't married.

'Can't make a baby by yourself,' Hayden Dean pointed out, and he topped off his mug.

She glanced down as she buttoned her coat. 'True, but I can go to a sperm bank and pick out the perfect donor. Height. Weight. IQ.' She pulled a black beret out of her pocket and placed it on her head. 'Which, when you think about it, seems a more logical way to conceive than in the backseat of a Buick.'

Stanley knew she meant to be funny, but her humor was lost on the men of Gospel.

'Not as much fun, though,' Hayden added.

She glanced over at Hayden, who stood between the other two men. 'That's debatable.'

She wrapped a black wool scarf around her neck, and Stanley wondered if he should wrap it around her mouth. That Rob was a strapping young fella. He was single, too. He hadn't been in the store for a few weeks now, and if Kate would just keep quiet, she might trick him into a date. And Kate needed a date. Needed something to do, other than fussing at him about his eating habits, rearranging the hygiene aisle, and telling him how to live his life.

'Can't pee standing,' Paul Aberdeen said.

'No lady would consider doing that,' Stanley interceded on Kate's behalf.

'I'm sure if I absolutely had to, I could manage it somehow.'

Stanley winced. That last announcement would scare off any man, but Rob looked more amused than insulted. Laughter shone in his green eyes as he gazed across the candy aisle at Katie. 'But you can't write your name in the snow,' he said and lifted his mug to his lips.

In the flattest voice Stanley had ever heard her use, Kate asked, 'Why would I want to?' Her tone puzzled Stanley. The last time Rob had been in, Kate had gotten all red-faced and flustered. The kind of flustered a woman got around a guy like Rob. The good Lord knew Rob had been flustering the women in Gospel since the day he'd driven that HUMMER of his into town, and his granddaughter had been no exception.

Rob took a drink, then slowly lowered the mug. One corner of his mouth slid up. 'Because you can.'

The other two men chuckled, but Kate looked perplexed rather than amused. The kind of perplexed women got when they didn't understand men. And for all of her years, there was a lot Kate didn't understand about the opposite sex. Like a man naturally wanting to take care of his woman, even if that woman was perfectly capable of taking care of herself.

Stanley handed Regina her bag of groceries, then moved from behind the counter in one last attempt to save Kate from herself. 'Now, let me do that. Your grandmother never lifted a snow shovel in her life.'

'I've lived on my own for a long time,' she said as she grabbed the snow shovel before Stanley could get to it. 'I've had to do a lot of things for myself. Everything from hauling my own garbage cans to the curb to changing the tire on my car.'

Other than wrestle with her, what could he do? 'Well, if it gets to be too much, I'll finish up.'

'Shoveling snow kills more than a thousand men over forty a year,' she informed him. 'I'm thirty-four, so I think I'll be fine.'

With no other choice, Stanley gave up. Kate opened the door and walked outside, leaving a chill in her wake that Stanley wasn't certain had all that much to do with the weather.

A cold morning breeze slapped Kate's left cheek as the door closed behind her. She pulled the frozen air deep into her lungs and let it out slowly. A warm puff of breath hung in front of her face. That hadn't gone well. Her intent had been to get out of the store as quickly as possible, not to upset her grandfather or sound like a man-basher. She didn't even want to contemplate peeing while standing – ever. She'd never actually changed a tire, but she was sure she could do it. Fortunately she wouldn't have to, because like a lot of capable and intelligent women, she belonged to AAA.

Kate leaned the handle of the shovel against her shoulder and took her gloves from her pockets. For the past half hour, she'd felt like she'd been holding her breath. Ever since Rob Sutter had walked into the M&S looking better than she remembered. Bigger and badder. A green-eyed, six-foot-three reminder of the night she'd wanted to live out a fantasy. A night she'd just wanted some anonymous sex and had ended up with a humiliating rejection instead.

She knew the mature thing to do would be to get over that night in the Duchin, but how was she ever going to forget it if she had to see Rob all the time?

Kate wiggled her fingers in her gloves. She hadn't been near Rob for two weeks now, but she'd spotted him a few times across the parking lot or driving that ridiculous HUMMER around town. She hadn't seen him up close and personal, though, until this morning when he'd come in for a granola bar and stayed for a cup of free coffee.

While she'd shelved paper products and listened to Tom Jones moan his way through 'Black Betty' like he was getting blown, Rob had chatted it up with some of the other local men. They'd talked about the freakish snow-storm that had hit the area the night before, and all she'd been able to think about had been details of the Sun Valley debacle. While they'd debated whether the snowfall should be measured in inches or feet, she'd wondered if

Rob Sutter really couldn't recall any of the details – if he was a blind drunk in need of Alcoholics Anonymous. It was a question that had been driving her insane. Not, however, enough to ask.

The conversation had progressed to the mountain goat Paul Aberdeen had blown away that hunting season. Kate had wanted to ask Paul why anyone would fill their freezer with an old goat when there was perfectly good beef at the M&S. She hadn't because she hadn't wanted to draw attention to herself and because she knew her grandfather was already irritated with her for packing away a Tom Jones, The Lead and How to Swing It, poster that had hung over her bed.

Living and working day in and day out with her grandfather was taking a while to get used to. He liked dinner at exactly six. She liked to cook and eat sometime between seven and bedtime. If she didn't have something prepared by six, he just pulled out a Hungry Man and tossed it in the oven.

If he didn't stop it, she was going to have to hide all his Swansons, and if he didn't stop having her do all the home deliveries, she was going to have to kill him. Before she'd moved to Gospel, Stanley had closed the store between 3 and 4 P.M. and done the deliveries himself. Now he seemed to think the job fell on her shoulders. Yesterday she'd delivered a can of prunes, a jug of prune juice, and a six-pack of Charmin to Ada Dover. She'd had to listen to the older woman go on about how she'd been 'backed up for days.' That was just one conversation you didn't want to have with anyone, especially a woman who resembled an old chicken.

Kate feared she was scarred for life now. As soon as she got her grandfather over his depression and she helped him move on with his life, she needed to get her *own* life. One that didn't include home deliveries to man-hungry widows. She didn't have a plan or know how long any of it would take, but if she gave it more effort, gave him a gentle loving push, the sooner it would happen.

Kate grasped the handle and scooped up a big shovelful of snow from the sidewalk. A little grunt escaped her lungs as she tossed the snow into the shrubs. She'd never experienced an Idaho winter and didn't know snow was so heavy. She recalled one year in Las Vegas when it had snowed almost half an inch. Of course it had melted within an hour. No wonder over a thousand people a year had heart attacks.

She placed the shovel's edge on the walk and pushed. The sound of metal scraping along concrete filled the morning air and competed with the occasional sound of traffic. A white curl of snow filled the shovel, and instead of lifting it again, she pushed the pile into the shrubs next to the building. *A much better method*, she thought as she slid the blade down the walk. A lot better than straining her back and flirting with the kind of heart failure that an aspirin a day wouldn't help.

The chilly breeze lifted the ends of Kate's scarf, and she paused to pull her hat over the tops of her ears. Her head was filled with worthless factoids. She knew that an adult brain weighed three pounds and the human heart pumped two thousand gallons of blood a day. She'd spent a lot of time on surveillance reading magazines and general reference books because they weren't all that engrossing and she could easily put them down to tail a suspect. Some of it had stuck. Some hadn't. She'd tried to learn Spanish once, but all she could remember was *Acabo de recibir un envio*, which would come in handy if she ever had to tell someone that she'd just received a shipment.

One side benefit of having a head cluttered with trivia was that she could use it to break the ice, change the subject, or slow things down.

At the end of the walk, she turned and started her way toward the front of the M&S once more. This time she pushed the snow off the curb and into the parking lot. Her toes inside her leather ankle boots were starting to freeze. It was March, for God's sake. It wasn't supposed to be so cold in March.

Just as she approached Rob's HUMMER, he stepped out of the M&S and moved toward her, wearing the same dark blue coat he'd had on two weeks ago when she'd seen him. His hiking boots left waffle tracks, and his heels kicked up the snow. She expected him to step off the curb and jump in his HUMMER.

He didn't.

'How's it going?' he asked as he came to stand in front of her.

She straightened, and her grasp on the handle tightened. His coat was zipped to the middle of his chest, and she fixed her gaze on the black label sewn on the tab. 'Okay.'

He didn't say anything, and she forced her gaze past his tiny white scar, soul patch, and Fu Manchu. His green eyes stared back at her as he pulled a black knit hat from his coat pocket. For the first time she noticed his lashes. They were longer than hers. Lashes like that were a total waste on a man, especially a man like him.

He pulled the hat on his head and continued to study her as if he were trying to figure something out.

'Warn me if you're going to write your name in the snow,' she said to break the silence.

'Actually, I'm standing here wondering if I'm going to have to wrestle that snow shovel out of your hands.' His warm breath hung in the air between them as he added, 'I'm hoping you'll be nice and hand it over.'

Her grasp on the handle tightened a bit more. 'Why would I hand it over?'

'Because your grandfather is in there getting all worked up over you doing what he thinks is a man's job.'

'Well, that's just stupid. I'm certainly capable of shoveling snow.'

He shrugged and slid his hands into the hip pockets of his cargo pants. 'I guess that's not the point. He thinks it's a man's job, and you've embarrassed him in front of his friends.'

'What?'

'He's in there right now trying to convince everyone that you're . . .' Rob paused a moment and tilted his head to one side. 'I believe his exact words were that you're "usually a nice, sweet-tempered girl." And then he said something about you being cranky because you don't ever get out with people your own age.'

Great. Kate suspected her grandfather's nonsense had been directed at Rob and not the other men. Worse, she was sure he suspected it also. The last thing she needed was for her grandfather to interfere in her nonexistent love life. Especially with Rob Sutter. 'I'm not cranky.'

He didn't comment, but the lift of his brow said it all.

'I'm not,' she insisted. 'My grandfather is just old-fashioned.'

'He's a good guy.'

'He's stubborn.'

'If I had to guess, I'd say you're a lot alike in the stubborn department.'

'Fine.' She thrust the shovel toward him.

A smile touched the corners of his mouth as he withdrew his hand from the front pocket of his pants and took the shovel from her. He clamped his bare hand over hers. She tugged, but his grasp tightened.

She wasn't about to get into a tug-of-war with a man built like the Rock. 'Can I have my hand back?' He relaxed his grip finger by finger, and she pulled free.

'Damn,' he said, 'I was kind of hoping I'd have to wrestle you for it.'

She knew that wasn't true. Drunk or sober, he had no interest in 'wrestling' Kate. It wasn't personal. She told herself he had some sort of dysfunction that prevented him from 'wrestling' with any woman. There wasn't anything wrong with her. It was him. She should feel sorry for him.

'I was kinda hoping to get a look at your tattoo while I was at it.'

It took several heartbeats for his meaning to penetrate Kate's brain. When it did, she forgot all about trying to feel sorry for Rob Sutter. Not that it was working, anyway. She sucked in a breath. 'You do remember!'

'What? Your offer to show me your bare ass?' He rocked

back on the heels of his boots and chuckled. 'How could I forget that?'

'But . . .' Her sucked-in breath got caught in her chest, and she had to let it out. 'But you said you'd never met me.' She was starting to see spots and took another deep breath. 'That first day you didn't . . . oh my God!'

'Did you want me to tell Stanley that we'd already met?' he asked as he bent to shovel snow. 'He'd want to know the details.'

Good Lord. She put her gloved hand to the side of her face as thoughts rushed and collided in the middle of her brain. Of all the bad luck, he wasn't an alcoholic. He remembered. How many people had he told about that night? In this town, all it would take was one person, then the news would spread like the West Nile virus. Although she would prefer that the town not know of her humiliation, she really only cared about her grandfather. He went to church every Sunday. He didn't believe in sex outside of marriage, let alone in women propositioning men in bars.

'I don't want to be the one who shatters his illusion of you.' He scooped up the patch of snow between them and tossed it off the curb. 'The truth would probably give him that heart attack you seem so worried about.'

She lifted her gaze to his knit ski cap. His hair curled up like little fishhooks along the back. 'You don't know me, and you don't know anything about my relationship with my grandfather.'

'I know you're right about Stanley being an old-fashioned guy. He probably thinks you're saving it for your wedding night, and we both know you're not.'

If Kate hadn't given him her shovel, she would have beaned him with it.

'I also know you don't want to hear some advice from me, but I'm going to give it to you anyway,' he said as he rested the blade of the shovel on the concrete and hung his wrist over the top of the handle. 'Picking up men in bars isn't smart. You could find yourself in a lot of trouble if you keep it up.'

She didn't care what he thought and didn't feel as if she needed to defend herself. 'I know you're not my father, so what are you? A cop?'

'No.'

'Priest?' He didn't look like a priest, but it would explain a lot.

'No.'

'Mormon missionary?'

He chuckled, and several puffs of air hung in front of his nose. 'Do I look like a Mormon missionary?'

No. He looked like a guy who liked to sin, but he wasn't. She didn't know anything about him at all. Other than the fact that he was a jerk and drove a HUMMER. What kind of person drove an army assault vehicle? A jerk with erectile dysfunction, that's what kind. 'Why don't you drive a human-sized car?'

He straightened. 'I like my HUMMER.'

A cold breeze lifted the tails of Kate's wool scarf, and it danced on the air between them. 'It makes people wonder if you're overcompensating for something,' she said.

Lines appeared in the corners of his eyes, and he reached out to tug at one end of her scarf. 'Are you standing there wondering about the size of my package?'

She felt heat rise to her already heated cheeks, and she was grateful they were already red from the cold. She pulled her scarf out of his grasp. 'Don't flatter yourself. I don't wonder about you at all.' She walked around him and added, 'Let alone the size of your package.'

He tipped back his head and laughed. Deep, satisfied male laughter that chased her all the way to the front of the store. She mumbled a 'Have a nice day' to Paul Aberdeen and Hayden Dean as she passed them on their way out of the M&S. Inside, Regina still hovered near Stanley, going on about the library where she worked, her thick glasses bobbing on the end of her nose as she nodded her head. Stanley busied himself with impulse items near the checkout. Normally Kate would have rescued him from Regina's chatter, but Stanley had sicced Rob on her and she wasn't feeling charitable at the moment.

'I'll be in the back,' Kate told her grandfather as she walked past. She pulled off her gloves and hat and unwound her scarf. She tossed them on the worktable and hung her coat on a hook. An overhead vent blew warm air on the top of her head. She lifted her face and closed her eyes.

He remembered everything about the night she'd propositioned him. The knowledge settled in her stomach like a lead ball. Her hope that he was a blind drunk had been in vain. She'd moved to Gospel for a little break from her life. A little rest, relaxation, and reevaluation.

Kate opened her eyes and sighed. Could her life get much worse? She was lonely and, outside of the M&S, the only conversation she'd had with anyone her own age was with the six-foot-three-inch, green-eyed *a-hole* from across the parking lot. And what had just taken place between them couldn't *really* pass for conversation.

She had to find something to do. Something other than working in the M&S and watching *Friends* reruns at night. The problem was that there were only two things to do in this town – join the Mountain Mama Crafters and knit toaster cozies or hit the bars and get toasted. Neither held the slightest appeal.

The bell above the front door rang, and Stanley called for her to come out front. She wondered if Rob was back and feared yet another transparent matchmaking attempt by her misguided grandfather. But when she moved out front again, thankfully Rob was nowhere to be seen.

Stanley stood at the end of the counter talking to a woman who looked to be in her late fifties, early sixties. Her brown hair was streaked with gray and brushed into a perfect bob. She stood only a few inches shorter than Kate's grandfather, which made her about Kate's height. Between the open zipper of her thick coat hung a red stethoscope. Regina stood with them, and the two women were telling Stanley about their poetry social.

'I hope you'll change your mind,' the taller woman said. 'Our monthly social group could use a few men.'

'What about Rob?' Regina asked.

As Kate approached, the taller woman shrugged and looked up at Stanley. 'I saw you put Rob to work shoveling your walk.'

'He volunteered.' Stanley looked up at Kate, and the corners of his handlebar mustache turned up. 'Grace, I don't believe you've met my granddaughter, Katie Hamilton.'

'Hello.' Kate stuck out her hand, and the other woman took it into hers.

'It's nice to meet you, Katie.' Grace turned her head to the side and looked at Kate for a moment. Age lined her green eyes, and her fingers were still a little cold. 'Where did you get your red hair? It's beautiful.'

'Thanks.' Kate dropped her hand to her side and smiled. 'My father's family has red hair.'

'Grace is Rob's mother,' Stanley told her. 'She works down at the Sawtooth Clinic.'

Kate felt her stomach drop, and she forced her smile to stay in place. Had Rob told his mother about the Duchin Lounge? Did the nice lady with the stethoscope know that Kate had propositioned her son? Did Kate need to explain that she'd been a little tipsy that night? That it had been the one and only time she'd propositioned a man in a bar? That she really wasn't a drunk slut? Not that she didn't have sluttish thoughts sometimes. She'd just never had the nerve to act on them before that night.

Good grief! She was rambling inside her own head. 'It's nice to meet you, Grace.' She took a few steps back before her rambling could make its way out of her mouth, 'I'm going to finish stacking the paper towels,' she said and took off for aisle three. Why should she care what Rob Sutter's mother thought of her? Grace had raised a rude and obnoxious son. She obviously wasn't perfect either.

Just as Kate picked up a roll of Bounty and set it on the top shelf, Grace walked down aisle two, Regina following on her heels.

'I need to talk to you, Grace.'

'I really don't have time to chat. I'm just here long

enough to get some sugar cubes for the clinic,' Grace said.

'It won't take but a minute,' Regina insisted as the two women stopped on the other side of the row of paper towels. 'I was at the Cozy Corner just yesterday, having the lunch special, and Iona told me that your son Rob is gay.'

Kate moved her head slightly to the left, and between the rows, she watched Grace's eyes widen and her lips part. 'Well, I don't think—'

'Now the reason I bring it up,' Regina interrupted, 'is because my son Tiffer is coming up for the Easter weekend. I don't know if you've heard, but Tiffer is a female impersonator down in Boise.' Even Kate had heard that, but she couldn't recall when and where. 'Tiffer doesn't have a partner right now, and I thought that if perhaps Rob is single, we should introduce the two of them.'

Grace fingered her coat collar. 'Well, I don't believe Robert is gay.'

Kate didn't believe so either, and she wondered who'd started the rumor and why anyone would believe it. Not that she felt bad for 'Robert.'

'Sometimes us mothers are the last to know,' Regina assured the other woman.

'He's thirty-six.' A frown pulled Grace's brows together. 'I think I'd know by now.'

'Being a hockey player, I can understand him wanting to keep quiet about his sexuality.'

'He doesn't play hockey anymore.'

'Maybe he's still in the closet. Some men never come out.'

Hockey player? Kate had heard quite a bit of gossip about Rob, but no one had mentioned that he'd played hockey. Although it did explain the knee injury he'd complained about the first night they'd met. It also explained his nasty temperament.

'I assure you, Regina, my son likes women.'

The bell above the door rang, and all eyes turned to the man in question as he walked inside and stamped snow from his boots. He pulled off his cap and shoved it in his coat pocket. His cheeks were red, and his green eyes shone. The overhead light bounced off his silver ring as he combed his fingers through the side of his hair. Somehow, he managed to look big and bad and boyish all at the same time.

Regina leaned in close and said just above a whisper, 'You be sure and talk it over with him. Tell him Tiffer's a good catch.'

The corners of Grace's lips slid up. 'Oh, you can be sure I'll tell him.'

5

'Regina Cladis wants to set you up with her son Tiffer.' Rob reached for the door handle of his mother's Bronco and opened it. In one part of his brain, he knew his mother was talking, but he wasn't paying attention to her. His thoughts were on Kate Hamilton and their conversation. Not only had she wrongly believed he didn't recall the night she'd propositioned him but she also didn't seem to want to talk about it. Not that he blamed her, but he'd tried to give her some good advice about picking up men in bars anyway. He'd tried to joke with her, too. She obviously had no sense of humor.

'Regina thinks you're in the closet.'

That got his attention, and he glanced over his shoulder at his mother. 'What?'

'Apparently Tiffer's taking a break from his career as a female impersonator just long enough to come home for an Easter visit. Regina thinks he's a good catch.'

Rob frowned. 'What does that have to do with me?'

Grace ducked beneath his arm and tossed her grocery bag on the passenger seat. 'Regina just told me that Iona is telling everyone at the Cozy Corner that you're gay.'

It wasn't the first time he'd heard the rumor, but he hadn't given it much thought. He'd hoped that his denial had put out the fire. He should have known better.

With one foot inside the car, Grace paused and looked up into Rob's face. 'Of course if it's true, there's nothing wrong with it. You're my son, and I'll support you no matter who you love.'

Rob sighed. 'For God's sake, Mom, you know I'm not gay.'

She smiled. 'I know. What do you think we should do about the rumor?'

Rob glanced up at the gray clouds and let out a breath as he thought about the ramifications. In a big city the rumor probably wouldn't matter. In a town the size of Gospel, it might hurt his business. If that happened, he'd have to close Sutter Sports and move away, which he didn't want to do. 'I don't know,' he said and returned his gaze to his mother. He felt a bit helpless, but short of grabbing a woman and doing her on Main Street, there wasn't anything he could do.

'Do you think maybe Harvey Middleton started the rumor to hurt your business?'

'No.' He didn't think the owner of Sawtooth Gun and Tackle would spread rumors. Harvey was a good guy and had more business than he could handle.

'Then who do you think started it?'

He shook his head. 'I don't know the answer to that. Why would anyone believe it anyway?'

The question was rhetorical, but Grace thought about it nonetheless. 'Maybe because you don't date anymore.'

Rob didn't want to talk about dating with his mother, not only because they'd had the conversation before but also because talking about dating inevitably made him think of sex. Lack of sex was his real problem, and that was definitely something a man didn't want to discuss with his mother.

'You don't date either,' he pointed out and looked over at the doors to the M&S. There was no sign of a certain smart-ass redhead inside. *Don't flatter yourself. I don't wonder about you at all,* she'd told him. *Let alone the size of your package.* Which didn't seem quite fair, since he'd been giving a lot of thought lately to that tattoo she supposedly had on her rear end.

'I've been thinking that it's time for us both to start dating again.'

He turned back to his mother. 'Is there someone you're interested in seeing?' he asked, half joking. Since the death of his father in 1980, he wasn't aware of his mother dating very much.

She shook her head and sat down in her car. 'No. Not really. I just thought maybe we both need to get out a little more. Maybe get more out of life than work.'

'My life is fine.'

She gave him that 'you can lie to yourself, but you can't lie to your mother' look and reached for the door handle. 'I'm reading my new poem tonight at the grange. You should stop by.'

Oh, hell no. 'I'm leaving this weekend to visit Amelia,' was the best he could come up with on the spur of the moment. It was lame, but it was also the truth.

Grace shut the door and started the car. 'That's not for three days,' she said as she rolled down the window.

He'd read his mother's poetry, and even though he was no great judge of good writing, he knew hers was bad.

Real bad.

'I'm opening the store in two weeks, and I have tons to do to get ready.' Which was also true but was just as lame as his first excuse.

'Fine. I bought Amelia a little something. Come by the house before you leave town.'

He'd hurt her feelings, but he'd rather get puck shot in the nuts than go to a poetry reading. 'I really can't make it tonight.'

'I heard you.' She put the CRV into reverse and said, as she backed out, 'If you change your mind, it starts at seven.'

Rob stood in the empty parking space and watched his mother drive away. He was thirty-six. A grown man. At one time in his life, he'd slammed hockey players against the boards and fed them their lunch. He'd been the most feared player in the NHL and had led the league in penalty minutes. They'd nicknamed him the Hammer, in tribute to the original Hammer, Dave Schultz.

And tonight he was going to a group social that he knew consisted of old women so he could hear his mother's poetry. He only prayed this one wouldn't be as bad as her poem about nut-hungry squirrels.

*

The Gospel poetry social started right at seven with a discussion about binding the group's poems and selling them at this summer's Rocky Mountain Oyster Feed and Toilet Toss. This year's social director, Ada Dover, stood at a pulpit in the front of the grange conducting business.

Chairs had been set up inside the long room. There were about twenty-five ladies . . . and Rob. He'd purposely come in a half hour late and sat in the empty back row by the door. When the time came, he figured he could make a quick getaway.

'We can't afford a booth,' someone pointed out.

From several chairs up, he saw his mother raise her hand. 'We can sell them in the Mountain Momma Crafters' booth. Most of us belong to the Mountain Momma Crafters anyway.'

'I bet the poems will sell faster than last year's Kleenex cozies.'

Rob pushed up the sleeves of his ribbed gray sweater and wondered if a Kleenex cozy was like those knitted things his grandmother used to put on her extra roll of toilet paper. If he remembered right, hers had lots of lace and a doll's head stuck on the top.

The back door by his right shoulder opened and he glanced up to see Stanley Caldwell, looking like he'd come for a root canal. Along with the fridge night air, his granddaughter blew in behind him, looking even less pleased than her grandfather. Stanley spotted Rob and moved toward him. 'Do you mind if we sit next to you?' Stanley asked.

Rob glanced up past Stanley to Kate, at her hair curling about the shoulder of her peacoat and her glossy pink lips.

Her attention was directed at Ada, and she was doing a good job of pretending he didn't exist. 'Not at all,' he answered as he stood.

Stanley moved to the third seat and stopped, leaving the seat next to Rob free. Kate gave her grandfather a hard stare as she stepped past Rob. The shoulder of her coat stirred the air an inch in front of Rob's sweater as she brushed by him. Her white cheeks were pink from the cold, and the scent of her cool skin filled his chest.

For one brief instant, her gaze met his, and the wealth of her dislike for him filled her rich brown eyes. Her obvious feelings toward him should have mattered, but they didn't. For some reason that he couldn't begin to comprehend, he was attracted to Kate Hamilton more than he had been to any other woman in a long time. He didn't kid himself. It was sex. Nothing more, and completely understandable, given the way they'd met. He didn't feel bad about his purely sexual attraction. Not that he would have anyway. Every time he saw her, he saw the woman who'd propositioned him. The woman who'd wanted to show him her bare ass.

They took their seats and Stanley leaned across his granddaughter to say, 'Never thought I'd see you here.'

Rob turned his attention from Kate to her grandfather. 'My mother's reading her poem tonight. I didn't have a choice. What's your excuse?'

'Katie blew my alibi and Regina's been calling all day, threatening to pick me up and drive me here herself.' He pointed to Kate. 'I made Katie come 'cause it's all her fault.'

Kate folded her arms beneath her breasts and her lips pursed a little, but she didn't say anything.

Stanley shrugged out of his shearling jacket and laid it across his lap. 'Have I missed anything?'

Rob shook his head. 'No.'

'Damn.'

Stanley sat back, and Rob took another long look at Kate, starting at the top of her hair. She was clearly irked, but he didn't care. He'd always been a big fan of true redheads, and looking at Kate's hair was like staring into a fire. One of the first things he'd noticed about her the night they'd met in the Duchin Lounge besides her smooth white skin and big brown eyes had been her hair.

Tonight she appeared cool and composed, but the longer he studied her, the more her full lips pulled into an irritated frown. Her arms remained folded across her wool coat, and her long legs were crossed at her knees and seemed to stretch out forever in front of her. She wore black pants and spiky-heeled boots. The kind that most likely came with a matching whip and paddle. Damn was right.

'If I can have everyone's attention,' Ada Dover spoke from the pulpit, drawing Rob's gaze to the front of the room. 'I'd like to welcome everyone to this month's social. Especially the first-timers in the back row.' Stanley cringed while Rob and Kate sank a little lower in their chairs, but both were too tall to disappear completely.

'As everyone knows, this is poetry night. Quite a few of us have brought something to read. After everyone has a chance to share, we'll begin the social portion of the evening.' She glanced down at her notes, then continued, 'I'll be the first to share, followed by Regina Cladis.'

As Ada launched into a long poem she'd written about

her dog, Snicker, Kate's cool composure showed one more sign of cracking. It started with a slightly annoyed sway of her right foot, but after several minutes of Snicker, the little sway worked up to an agitated little kick.

'His eyes are brown,' Ada waxed in the final stanza.

> *'He's the only dog in town*
> *to come when I call Snicker.*
> *His tongue is pink,*
> *his fur is like mink, and*
> *he's one hell of a licker!'*

Kate's foot stopped, and Rob thought he heard her murmur something that sounded like, 'God have mercy.'

Stanley coughed behind his fist, and Rob was grateful that his mother wasn't the only bad poet in the room.

Regina was up next and read a poem about the library where she worked. After Regina, Iona Osborn plugged in a tape player, and the sound of a steady *boom bop-bop boom* filled the grange. Over the drumbeat Iona recited a poem entitled 'If I Were Britney Spears.' It was lighthearted and wasn't half as bad as Ada's dog poem. Kate's foot settled into an easy sway once more, then stopped as her long fingers worked the big buttons on her coat. Her shoulder bumped Rob's as she tried to pull her arms from the sleeves. Watching her was like watching someone try to get out of a straitjacket.

He leaned in and said close to her ear, 'Lift your hair up.'

She stopped her fidgeting and glanced up at him out of the corners of her eyes. She looked like she might argue.

Like she might launch into another 'I can take care of myself' speech. She opened her mouth, closed it, then ran one hand across the back of her neck, twisted her wrist, and gathered her hair. She scooped it up and Rob reached for her coat. He pulled the back of the collar down as she leaned forward. She drew one arm free and straightened, letting go of her hair. It fell in a gentle wave and brushed the back of Rob's hand. A thousand strands of red silk touching his skin and curling around his fingers. If he turned his palm up, he could gather it in his fist. It had been a long time since he'd felt the weight and texture of a woman's hair in his hands or across his chest and belly. Desire both unexpected and unwanted tugged at his lap.

She looked at him and smiled for the first time since the night they'd met in Sun Valley.

'Thank you,' she said as she pulled her other arm free.

'You're welcome.' He turned his attention to the podium and folded his arms across his chest. His life had become pathetic. Her hair had touched his hand, big deal. There'd been a time in his life when he probably wouldn't have even noticed. When his attention would have been focused on how to get her out of her bra, not on her hair.

He didn't know how he felt about Kate Hamilton. Other than her amazing body and dominatrix boots, he wasn't sure he even liked anything about her. There were a few men around town who were intimidated by Kate. Who thought she wanted their ball sack for a change purse. Rob wasn't so sure they were wrong. So why was he thinking about her in ways that put *his* ball sack in jeopardy?

He really didn't know, but perhaps it was because the Kate that everyone knew contrasted sharply with the woman in the Sun Valley bar. That night she'd been soft and warm and inviting. She'd been temptation all wrapped up in one fine package, but she'd been a temptation he'd resisted. A temptation he could still resist.

Is she worth dying for? asked the voice in his head. *Is she worth your life?* Kate was beautiful. No doubt about that, but as always, the answer was no. There was just no telling when a soft, warm, inviting woman would turn into a praying mantis.

Next up, Eden Hansen took the podium. She was dressed from head to toe – literally – in purple, and Rob concentrated on her purple hair and eyeshadow. If anything could scare thoughts of sex from his head, it was Eden. Her poem was entitled 'Ten Ways to Kill a Mangy Rat' and was about her brother-in-law, Hayden Dean. She didn't mention Hayden by name, but anyone who knew her knew she was talking about her twin sister, Edie's, husband. When she was through, people didn't know whether to applaud or search her for hidden weapons.

From a few rows up, Rob watched his mother move toward the front. She set her poem on the podium and began,

> *'Getting old is a drag*
> *you start to wrinkle and to sag*
> *your behind hangs real low*
> *and you begin to move so slow*
> *that you fear someone might put you in a bag.'*

Rob placed his forearms on his knees and gazed down at his boots. His mother had obviously given her rhyming dictionary a workout.

> *'People half your age*
> *earn a better wage*
> *think they're twice as smart*
> *but there's much to take heart*
> *I happen to like this stage.'*

The poem went on for several more minutes. Grace hit the high points of getting older and ended with,

> *'Your life is calm and void of drama*
> *almost as extinct as Mount Fujiyama*
> *but unlike that mountain peak*
> *I'm not dead or even weak*
> *I'm alive and one red hot momma!'*

'Sweet Mary, mother of Jesus,' Rob groaned and stared at the toes of his boots.

He could feel Kate's leg still, and out of the utter silence Stanley Caldwell said just above a whisper, 'That was wonderful.'

Rob turned his head to look at Stanley. The older gentleman appeared to be serious.

'The best so far,' he said.

Kate looked at her grandfather as if he'd lost his mind. 'Better than the Britney poem?'

'Oh yes. Didn't you think so?'

She pushed one side of her hair behind one ear and rather than lie said, 'Not all poetry has to rhyme.'

Stanley frowned, and the ends of his mustache dipped. 'Well, all I know is Grace's poem was about life and what it's like getting older. It's about wisdom and finding peace with yourself. It spoke to me.'

Rob placed his hands on his knees and continued to stare at Stanley. His mom's poem had been about all that? All he'd heard was that his mother was afraid of being put in a bag and that she was 'one red hot momma.' Neither of which a son wanted to contemplate.

Grace smiled as she took her seat, and Rob suffered through three more poetry readings before the 'social' part of the evening began. He excused himself from Stanley and Kate and sought out his mother, who stood next to the refreshment table. He and Stanley were the only males in the grange, and there was no way he was going to stick around and socialize, which in Gospel meant stand around and gossip.

'What did you think of my poem?' his mother asked as she handed him a cookie with some sort of jelly in the middle.

'I thought it was even better than the squirrel poem you read me last week,' he answered and bit into the cookie. He washed it down with the champagne punch she handed him. The fruity liquid burned a path to his stomach. 'What's in this?'

'A little whiskey, a splash of brandy, and some champagne. If you drink too much, we have designated drivers.'

He didn't plan to be around long enough to need a driver.

'You didn't think the line about Mount Fujiyama was too weird?'

Yes. 'No. Stanley Caldwell liked your poem. He said it was wonderful. It spoke to him.'

The corners of her mouth turned up. 'Really?'

'Yep.' If his mother thought shoving cookies and punch at him would make him stay longer, she was mistaken. Just as soon as he could get the dry cookie down, he was gone. 'He thinks it was the best out of all the other poems.'

'He's a nice man,' she said through her smile. The crow's-feet in the corners of her eyes fanned across her temples and touched the roots of her graying hair. 'And he's been so lonely since Melba passed on. Maybe I'll invite him over for supper one of these nights.'

Rob glanced at Stanley, who stood several feet behind him, surrounded by gray-haired single women. The light shone off his bald head like he'd buffed his scalp with Pledge, and his gaze darted about the grange looking for rescue. It landed on Kate, standing further down the refreshment table, downing the spiked punch like a drunk who'd fallen headfirst off the wagon.

'Are you interested in Stanley Caldwell?' he asked, then shoved the last of his cookie into his mouth.

'Just as a friend. He's only six years older than I am.' She took a drink of her own punch and added, 'We have a lot in common.'

Rob drained his cup and set it on the table. 'Gotta go,' he said as he shrugged into his coat, but before he could take even one step toward the door, Regina blocked his escape.

'Has your mother had a chance to talk to you about Tiffer?' she asked him.

'Yes,' Grace answered in a lowered voice. 'I talked to him.'

Rob frowned and glanced behind him to see if anyone had heard Regina. 'I'm not gay.'

For several long moments she stared at him through those thick glasses that magnified her blue eyes. 'Are you sure?'

He folded his arms across his chest. *Was he sure?* 'Yeah,' he answered. 'I'm real sure.'

Regina's shoulders sagged under the weight of her disappointment. 'I'm sorry to hear that. You would have been a good match for Tiffer.'

A good match for a drag queen? This was getting out of hand, and it was beginning to annoy him now.

'Regina, do you know who started this horrible rumor?' Grace asked.

'I'm not sure. Iona told me, but I don't know where she heard it.' She turned to the knot of people standing a few feet behind them. 'Iona,' she called out, 'where'd you hear the rumor about Grace's boy being gay?'

As one, the cluster of people surrounding Stanley turned and looked at Rob. He felt like there was a spotlight on him, and for the first time since hearing the gossip, his temper flared. At this point, he didn't particularly care who'd started the rumor. He just wanted it to stop before it got out of hand. Before he got jumped by a bunch of rednecks out to prove something – not that he couldn't take care of himself.

'I heard it the day when I was getting my hair done at the Curl Up and Dye. Ada told me. I don't know where she heard it, though.'

Ada put a bony finger to her thin lips, and after a few moments of thought, she announced, 'Stanley's granddaughter said you was gay.'

All eyes turned to Kate. She didn't seem to notice until

she set down her empty punch cup and glanced up. 'What?'

'It was you.'

Kate licked the punch from her lips and looked at everyone looking at her. They were staring as if she'd done something evil. Yeah, she'd had a few glasses of punch. So what? She needed it after suffering though a night of bad poetry and Rob Sutter. He'd tricked her into smiling at him, and he was so big and took up so much room that she'd had to hunch her shoulders to keep from rubbing against him. Now her neck hurt. That was worth a glass or two of punch.

'What?' she asked again as everyone continued to stare at her. What was everyone's problem? She'd left some punch in the bowl. 'What did I do?'

'You're the one who first said Grace's son was gay.'

'Me?' She sucked in a breath. 'I did not!'

'Yes you did. You were ringing up my cling peaches and you said he doesn't like women.'

Kate thought back and barely remembered a conversation she'd had with Ada about the owner of the sporting goods store across the parking lot from the M&S. 'Wait a minute here.' She held up one hand. 'I didn't know who you were talking about. I'd never met Mr Sutter.'

The lift of his brow called her a liar.

'I swear,' she swore. 'I didn't know she was talking about you.' The look in his green eyes told her that he didn't believe her.

'That's not right starting a rumor about someone you don't know,' Iona admonished, as if Kate had broken some gossiping rule. Which was just insane. Everyone knew there was only one rule to gossiping, and that was if you weren't in the room, you were fair game.

'Katie,' her grandfather said while he shook his head, 'you shouldn't start rumors.'

'I didn't!' She knew she hadn't started anything, but by the look on everyone's face, no one believed her. 'Fine. Think what you want,' she said as she stuck her arms into her coat. She was innocent. If anything, she thought Rob was impotent, not gay.

This was crazy. She was being chastised for being a gossipmonger in a town that thrived on gossip. She didn't understand these people.

Her gaze moved from Rob, who looked as if he'd like to strangle her, to the rest of those in the grange. They might look somewhat normal, but they weren't. If she wasn't careful, she might become one of them.

Just another cashew in a town of mixed nuts.

6

Kate looked around the living room, then leaned her head back on the sofa. The gentle swoosh of her grandfather's rocking recliner and the sound of a *Golden Girls* rerun filled the small house. It was Saint Patrick's Day, and she was spending it watching television with her grandfather. She was half Irish. Usually this time of year, she and her friends were out drinking and singing 'Too Ra Loo Ra Loo Ra' off key.

Her grandfather also had some Irish blood, and he should have been out living it up. Maybe she should suggest that he call a few of his buddies and at least invite them over for green beer, although the last time she'd pushed him into doing something, he'd forced *her* into going with him to the poetry reading. That night had turned into a disaster.

Growing up, she'd always known Gospel was a little odd, but after that night, she was convinced it was more than odd. She now knew that she was living in an alternate dimension, one that looked fairly normal on the surface but was freaky as hell underneath. Four nights ago, she'd glimpsed the craziness that hid behind normal faces, and it was scary. The only person who hadn't acted like a nut had been Rob Sutter. He'd looked more angry than insane.

'Why don't you go out, Katie?'

She rolled her head to the left and looked at her grandfather. 'Are you trying to get rid of me?'

'Yes. You're wearing me out.' He turned his attention back to his television program. 'I love you, Katie, but I need a break from you.'

She sat up. She was in Gospel to give him a hand in the store and to help him over his grief. She needed a break from him, too, but she wasn't so rude as to tell him. Obviously, he didn't suffer under the same restraint.

'Go have a green beer somewhere.'

She didn't want to drink in a bar alone. There was something a little sad about it, and besides, it hadn't worked out for her the last time. She'd drunk too much and was still paying the price.

'Play a little pool and meet young people your own age.'

Pool. She could play pool. That wasn't sad and pathetic, and if she didn't drink too much, she wouldn't do anything stupid. 'Which bars have tables?' she asked.

'The Buckhorn has a few in the back. I don't believe Rocky's Bar has any, but the Hitching Post might still have a couple.' While Kate tried to recall which was closest to her grandfather's house, he added, 'Of course you should probably stay out of the Hitching Post on account of the restrooms are a little rough.'

Kate looked down at her sweats and Tasmanian Devil slippers. 'Isn't the Buckhorn a little rough?' she asked. She'd driven by the bar several times and thought it looked about a hundred years old. Not falling down, just very rustic.

'Not this time of year. It only tends to get rough when flatlanders come up for the summer.'

'Why don't we go play some pool together? I'll bet some of your friends are there.'

He shook his head. 'I don't want to go anywhere.' Before she could argue, he added, 'I'll call Jerome and see if he wants to come over for a beer.'

She stood. If her grandfather had a friend over, he wouldn't need her company. 'Okay. Maybe I will go play some pool,' she said as she moved into her bedroom. She changed into her strapless bra, then pulled on a black-and-white-striped boatneck sweater and a pair of jeans. She shoved her feet into her black boots and shot perfume on the insides of her wrists. After she brushed her teeth, she combed her hair until it fell in a smooth, blunt line across the middle of her shoulder blades. She didn't waste a lot of effort on makeup, just a little mascara and soft pink lip gloss. Then she grabbed her coat and her small black Dooney & Bourke backpack and headed out.

'I doubt I'll be late,' she told her grandfather as he walked with her past the kitchen table set with Tom Jones place mats.

'You look lovely.' Stanley helped her with her coat. 'If you drink too much, promise to give me a call.'

'Thanks. I will,' she said, but she didn't have any intention of drinking much at all. She fished her keys out of her backpack and reached for the door.

'And Kate.'

She looked up into her grandfather's eyes. 'What?'

'Don't beat all the boys at pool.' He laughed, but Kate wasn't sure he was joking.

The outside of the Buckhorn Bar looked like a lot of the businesses in Gospel, made of split logs, with a green tin roof. But unlike the other establishments, there were no striped awnings or planters to soften the rough appearance. No wooden Indian or gold leaf lettering on the blacked-out windows. The door handle was made from a horn, and a big neon sign with an elk on it hung over the worn porch. Cement patched the holes in the old logs, but slices of dim light and the whine of steel guitar slipped through a few cracks and into the darkness outside.

Walking into the Buckhorn was like walking into a hundred other small-town cowboy bars. It was a second home to the regulars, and anyone new was eyed with suspicion.

The owner of the bar, Burley Morton, weighed in at about three hundred pounds and stood just over six-feet-five. He kept a Louisville Slugger and a sawed-off shotgun behind the long bar. He hadn't used the Slugger since '85, when a flatlander had attempted to rob him of a case of Coors Lite and a pack of beer nuts. He hadn't had trouble of that nature in years, but he kept both items handy just in case. Occasionally, one of the locals got riled up and developed beer muscles, but it was nothing he couldn't handle with a call to the sheriff's office or his own two fists.

The door to the Buckhorn closed behind Kate, and she was reminded of a lot of the older hotels and casinos in

Vegas. The bar smelled of alcohol and old cigarette smoke that had seeped into the wood like varnish. The owner's attempt to cover it up with cherry deodorizer didn't help.

On the jukebox, Kenny Chesney sang about a big star while a few couples danced in the center of the large room. Kate wasn't a huge fan of country music, but Kenny was a big improvement over Tom. Green shamrock garlands decorated the long bar and several of the red booths. A bulletin board filled with multicolored flyers was nailed to the wall to Kate's right.

Kate hung her backpack over her shoulder and moved toward the bar. She wove through a few tables and found a stool near the neon Coor's light.

'What can I get ya?' the owner of the Buckhorn asked around the cigar stuck in one corner of his mouth.

'Do you have a winter wheat?'

Burley's thick black brows pulled together, and he looked at her as if she'd ordered a Shirley Temple with extra cherries.

'I'll have a Bud Lite,' she amended.

'Good choice,' he said, and a thin plume of smoke followed him as he moved away to the beer spigots.

'Aren't you Stanley's granddaughter?'

She turned her gaze to the man on the stool next to her and instantly recognized Hayden Dean, the inspiration for the Mangy Rat poem.

'Yes. How are you, Mr Dean?'

'Good.' He reached for his beer, and his shoulder brushed Kate's. She wasn't so sure it was an accident.

Burley returned and set two glasses of green beer in front of her. 'Two-fifty.'

'I only ordered one,' she said as the song on the juke changed and Clint Black poured from the speakers.

He took the cigar out of his mouth and pointed to a sign behind him. 'Wednesday night is twofer night.'

Wow, twofer night. Kate hadn't enjoyed twofer night since college. These days, pounding beer didn't hold the appeal it had in her early twenties, when she'd been a champion keg stander and beer bonger.

'I haven't been in here before,' she said to Hayden as she dug into her Dooney bag and handed Burley a five. She glanced over her left shoulder toward the back of the bar. Through an opening she could see billiard lights hanging over two pool tables.

She raised a beer to her lips and felt something brush her thigh.

'I love the redheads,' Hayden said.

She looked down at his hand on her leg, then back up into his heavily lined face. It figured that the only man to pay attention to her in a year was a creepy old guy with beer breath and a reputation for low standards. 'Take your hand off my thigh, Mr Dean.'

He smiled, and she noticed that some of his back molars were missing. 'You've got fire. I like that in a woman.'

Kate rolled her eyes. She'd kept up with selfdefense classes since she'd first received her PI license, and if she wanted, she could remove Hayden's hand and pin his thumb to his wrist all in one motion. But she didn't want to hurt Mr Dean. It might make things difficult the next time he came into the M&S for a free cup of coffee. She stood and placed the strap of her backpack on her shoulder. Even though she really didn't want two green beers, she grabbed them off the bar and headed toward the back. As she carefully wove her way through the locals, she sipped out of each glass to keep them from spilling.

In the cramped back room, four players occupied the two tables while several spectators drank beer and loitered under the big No Spitting, No Fighting, No Betting sign.

Within the dusky shadows of the room, Rob Sutter pushed away from the wall and moved to lean over one of the tables. 'Three in the side pocket,' he said over the crack of pool balls from the other table and the sound of George Jones crooning from the juke in the next room.

Kate stood in the doorway and watched him line up the shot. The light hanging directly over the table shone down on his left hand and the silver ring on his middle finger. Blue flannel was rolled up his long arms, exposing the tail of his snake tattoo, and he wore a navy blue ball cap with a fly hook and the words 'Bite me' embroidered on it. He slid the stick between his thumb and first finger and shot. What he lacked in finesse, he made up for in pure muscle. The cue ball hit the solid red ball so hard that it jumped before shooting across the table and falling into the pocket. His gaze followed the ball to the edge of the table, paused for several heartbeats, then continued up the buttons of Kate's coat, passed her chin and mouth to her eyes. Within the shadow of his hat, his gaze met hers, and he simply stared. Then a slight frown pulled at the corners of his mouth. Kate didn't know if he was irritated to see her or bothered because he'd hit the cue so hard that he'd lost control of it. Probably both.

He stood in one smooth motion, and a shadow from the

brim of his cap slid to the end of his nose, leaving only his lips, mustache, and soul patch exposed to the dim light of the room. He wore a white T-shirt beneath the unbuttoned blue flannel shirt. The tails hung loose about the hips and the button fly of his Levi's.

While he stood there looking like every girl's fantasy, she figured she looked like a dork clutching her green beers in her hands.

Kate thought about backing out of the room, but if she left now, he'd think she'd left because of him, which would be the truth, but she didn't want him to know it. He bent over the table once more, all long and lean, his firm butt filling out his Levi's. No doubt about it, Rob Sutter was hot. The kind that made a girl tingle in interesting places. Not Kate, though. He didn't make her tingle. She was immune. He drew the cue back and she turned away.

There were no tables or stools, and Kate set her beers on one of the shelves sticking out of the wall. She hung her backpack and coat on a hook behind her. Next table over from Rob, two of the three Worsley brothers were about to wrap up their game. Kate slid three quarters under the cushion of the table, then chose a nineteen-ounce house cue from the rack on one wall. She held it like she was sighting in a rifle. The shaft was a little warped, but it had a nice, hard tip. She set the butt end by her right foot and waited.

Rob missed his next shot, which wasn't surprising, since he again practically shot the cue ball off the table. He straightened, and a bleached blonde with enormous breasts handed him a bottle of Heineken. Her name was Dixie Howe, and she owned the Curl Up and Dye hair salon. She had long red nails and hooked a finger through Rob's belt loop. She gave it a tug and said something next to his ear. Evidently Dixie didn't know that Rob had a real problem with bold women who made the first move and that he was a total waste of male perfection.

Over the past few weeks, she'd thought about investigating Mr Rob Sutter. Besides being rude and obnoxious, all she really knew about him was that he drove a HUMMER, used to play hockey, and had a knee injury. She assumed the injury had ended his career, but she didn't know that for certain. She could ask her grandfather, but he'd think her interest in Rob was a romantic one. If she wanted to know more, she'd have to drag her laptop out of the box where she'd stored it in her bedroom closet. She knew the license plate number on his vehicle. With a few clicks and a tap, she'd take a look at his driver's license and obtain his date of birth and his Social Security number. After that, she could learn his employment history and if he'd ever been married. She'd discover other tidbits about him too, like if he had a criminal past.

But she didn't do that sort of thing anymore. Not for work. Not even to satisfy her own curiosity.

She took a sip of her beer and looked at him over the bottom of her glass. His head was bent slightly over Dixie's as she spoke, but Kate could feel him looking at her. She couldn't really see his eyes for the shadow of his hat, but she could feel his gaze touch her face and slide down her body. If she hadn't been immune to him, she might have felt her insides catch fire.

The Worsley brothers' game ended and Kate stepped forward to challenge the winner. Peirce Worsley stood five-foot-ten in his custom-made cowboy boots. Like his brothers, he had short, kinky brown hair. All three of them lived and worked at their family's ranch about twenty miles out of Gospel. Their ages ranged from thirty to twenty-five. Kate had met them the few times they'd come into the M&S. They didn't appear to be the sharpest knives in the drawer, but Kate hadn't come to the Buckhorn for intelligent conversation.

Peirce racked the pool balls while Kate tossed a coin to determine who went first. She won and positioned the cue ball near the side rail behind the foot string. She leaned over, slid the stick over the bridge of her thumb, aimed at the second ball, and shot. All fifteen balls separated, and the solid yellow rolled across the green wool and fell into a side pocket. Next she shot the three into the left corner pocket and the seven into the right. She banked the cue off the head cushion and left the solid blue next to a side pocket for a later shot. Four good shots, *and* she'd almost managed to forget Rob was in the room.

Peirce pushed up the brim of his cowboy hat and looked back across the table at her. He had light blue Helter-Skelter eyes, which should have been her first clue that the evening was going to deteriorate into madness. 'Where you from?' he asked.

'Las Vegas.'

'Are you a hustler?'

Kate stared at him and tried to remember that the brothers weren't too bright even when they were sober. If she was trying to hustle Peirce, did he really think she'd admit it to him? 'No, I'm not a hustler.'

'You play in a league or something?'

'My parents had a pool table when I was growing up,' she answered and moved to where she'd left her beer. She raised the green Bud Lite to her lips and watched as Dixie Howe leaned over the other table and gave everyone a clear view of her deep cleavage. Kate had no problem with women who put it out there. She just didn't happen to be one of them. Well, except for that one time. Kate glanced at Rob, who, like the other men, had his eyes glued on Dixie's impressive implants. He said something that made Dixie laugh, then he raised a bottle of beer to his lips.

Kate turned her attention to Peirce as he made his shot and lined up another. Kate remembered enough about the night she'd first met Rob to recall that he could be somewhat charming. She'd been fooled and taken in by it, but in her own defense, she'd been really drunk.

'If you beat Peirce, you play me next.'

She looked across her shoulder at another of the brothers. 'Which Worsley are you?' she asked.

'Tuttle.' He pointed to his left. 'This is Victor. If you beat me, you play Victor,' he said as if she didn't have a choice. 'But I doubt you'll beat me.'

'I don't think I'll be staying that long, Tuttle.'

'Are you afraid I'll win?'

Peirce missed his shot, and she set down her beer. 'No.'

'Go ahead and bet her five bucks you'll win, Tut,' Victor said, then he downed his beer.

'Wow, five whole bucks.'

Her sarcasm was lost on both men. 'If that's too rich for your blood, we could play strip pool.'

Right. She approached the end of table, and her gaze

took in the position of the balls. She had to wait for Rob to finish his shot before she could proceed further between the tables. He straightened, but he didn't move aside to let her pass.

'Excuse me,' she said as she glanced up, but the shadow of his hat hid most of his face.

He still didn't move, and she was forced to squeeze by, so close that she could see the stubble on his jaw. The rolled-up sleeve of his flannel shirt brushed her arm. She looked into his shadowy gaze as she passed. His eyes narrowed and she figured he was annoying the hell out of her on purpose. Probably because he was mad about that gay rumor thing.

'If you know what's good for you, you'll call it a night and go home.'

No probablys about it. He was mad. 'Are you threatening me?'

'I don't threaten women.'

Well, it had sounded like a threat to her. 'Just so you know, I didn't start that rumor about you.'

He looked at her for several long seconds, then said, 'Right.'

'At least I didn't mean to.' He just continued to stare, and she shrugged. 'If you're interested in hearing the truth about how it got started, maybe I'll tell you sometime.'

'I know how it got started.' He lowered his voice and said, 'Because I wouldn't have sex with you in a hotel room, you came to town and told everyone that I'm gay.'

Kate looked around to see if anyone had heard him. They hadn't, but she suspected he wouldn't have cared. 'How does it feel to be wrong?' she asked. She didn't wait for an answer and leaned over the table. She lined up a shot and tried to ignore Rob completely.

She made quick work of beating Peirce while his brothers took delight in taunting him because he'd lost to a girl. Peirce's face turned red, and he stomped off to the bar. Before she could really protest, Tuttle racked the balls, and Kate resigned herself to playing one more game.

She'd never been the sort of girl to purposely lose at anything – not to perpetrate a hustle or even to make a man feel better about himself.

Tuttle took the break and shot at the apex ball. It careened into the cushion, bounced off the two, and fell into the side pocket. Tuttle smiled like he'd meant to do it on purpose. Next, he shot the solid orange into the corner pocket. Unfortunately, the cue ball followed it in.

'Are you going to let a girl beat you?' Victor called out to his brother. 'You guys are embarrassing the family.'

'Shut up, Victor,' Tuttle grumbled as Kate placed the white ball behind the head string.

'I've been to Vegas a few times. Are you one of those topless showgirls?' Tuttle asked, then snickered like he was thirteen.

She glanced up at him then shot, knocking in the nine ball, then the fifteen. If he thought talking to her would mess up her concentration, he was wrong. She'd learned to play pool in a house filled with her loud brothers and their friends. 'Afraid not.'

'Ever work at the Chicken Ranch?' He must have thought he was real funny, because he cracked himself up.

Kate let it pass and dropped the fourteen in the side pocket, followed by the ten.

'Wanna come back to our ranch?'

The eleven and twelve dropped next. 'No thanks.'

'I could show you the horses. Lots of girls come out to ride the horses.'

Somehow, Kate doubted 'lots of girls' went anywhere near the Worsley ranch. She moved to the other side of the table and waited for Rob to take his shot. When he was through, she knocked in the fifteen, then the eight. She placed her hand on the side rail and lined up a bank shot that she'd made a million times in the past. Tonight she missed making it by a fraction.

She raised, took a step backward, and came up against something hard and unmovable. She glanced over her shoulder, past blue flannel, to Rob's chin and mouth. She looked up into his eyes beneath the brim of his hat. The room was cramped, but not *that* cramped. He was crowding her and purposely annoying her again.

'Could you move?' she asked.

'Yeah, I could.' But he didn't. Instead, his big hands grasped the tops of her arms as if he meant to move *her* away, but he didn't do that either. For half an instant a shocking urge to lean back into his chest popped into her head. To feel the warmth of him up and down her spine. To turn and press her nose into his flannel collar and take a deep breath.

Appalled by her thoughts, she told herself that it had been a long time. A long time since she'd had sex. It wasn't him. Other than the Worsleys, it could have been just about anyone. Well, not Mr Dean either.

'The Worsley boys are mean little bastards.' He leaned forward a little, and the brim of his hat brushed the side of her head. The scent of his warm skin filled her lungs. 'Not the kind of guys a girl should show her tattoo.'

She turned her head and looked up into the shadow beneath the brim of his hat. 'Gee, thanks for the warning. And I was just about to drop my pants, too.'

His lips remained in a flat line as he slid his hand up her arm and shoulder. His long, warm fingers brushed her hair from the side of her bare neck.

'What are you doing?'

'Showing the rednecks around here who want to kick my ass that I'm not gay.' His breath warmed the shell of her ear, and anyone looking at the two of them might think he was whispering naughty things to her. 'I can hold my own against one or two at a time, but a barful might be more than even I can handle.' Kate glanced about the room, but it didn't seem like the rednecks were paying Rob much attention. It occurred to her that he might be lying, but she hadn't been at the Buckhorn long enough to be certain.

She returned her gaze to the pool table as Tuttle made his shot. 'You could use Dixie. I'm sure she's more than willing to be used in that capacity. Or any.'

He slid his hand down her arm and placed his palm in the curve of her waist. 'You owe me.'

She didn't figure she owed him anything, but neither did she want him to get beat up for something she'd inadvertently done. 'Don't think for one second that I'm going to let you grope me,' she said, relieved that her voice held a conviction she didn't quite feel as strongly as she should.

'Maybe you should define grope.' His hand slid across her stomach, warming up her abdomen and stealing her breath before slowly moving back to her waist. 'Is that a grope?'

Technically, no. But she felt his touch in places where he wasn't touching her at all. 'Not unless you move your hand up.'

'How about if I go down?' His deep chuckle spread across the side of her throat. 'Do you want me to go down, Kate?'

'Don't even think about it.' Tuttle missed his next shot, and Kate stepped away. She'd had enough. Enough of Rob and enough of the Worsleys. She bent over the table and shot the eight into the corner pocket.

'My turn at her,' Victor announced and approached the end of the table.

'Guys, I'm finished.'

'You can't leave until you play Victor.'

'I'm not playing Victor,' she said as she moved to the cue rack and placed the stick inside. Her nerves were raw and she just wanted to go to bed. 'I'm going home.'

'You have to play,' Victor insisted. 'No one beats us Worsleys.'

'Especially a girl,' Tuttle added.

Uh-oh. They were drunk, she told herself. 'Maybe some other time.'

'Everyone knows that it isn't right for a woman to beat a man.'

She supposed she should let that one go, but she'd been biting her tongue all evening. She was tired of trying to be nice. 'Victor, if it takes beating a woman to make you feel better about yourself, you have some real problems that go beyond the way you play pool.'

'What does that mean?'

She really wished she didn't have to explain. 'It means that a real man isn't threatened by a woman.'

'I'll show you a real man.'

Lord, if he grabbed his crotch, she was going to throw up. She shook her head. 'Are you on crack?'

'No.'

'Fall on your head?'

'No. Got kicked by horses plenty.'

'Well, that explains it,' she said and tried to move past. He stepped in front and wouldn't let her by.

'You're not leaving till we play.'

Kate looked into Victor's mean, bloodshot blue eyes and felt her heart slam against her ribs.

'Hey, numb nuts,' Rob interrupted from behind Victor. 'She said she doesn't want to play with you boys anymore.'

Kate's gaze moved passed Tuttle to Rob who stood a few feet away. A vast sense of relief calmed her speeding heart to a steady pound.

'This isn't your business,' Tuttle said.

'I'm making it my business.'

'Figures you'd take up for her. She's mannish, but that's probably what you like about her.'

'Exactly what are you trying to say, Tuttle?'

'That you're a faggot.' He pointed with his thumb to Kate. 'And she's your dyke.'

Kate guessed that answered the question.

'That wasn't nice.' Rob sighed as he took off his hat and tossed it on the pool table. 'You owe Kate an apology.'

'Or what?'

'Or I'll make you wish you had.' He ran his fingers

through the sides of his hair. 'You might want to stand back, Kate.'

She didn't have to be told twice. She wedged herself between the racks of pool sticks.

'I'm not afraid of you,' Tuttle announced as he bobbed and wove like some sort of boxer reject. Rob stood with his hands at his sides, watching with a bemused twist of his lips. Then Tuttle finally swung, and Kate barely saw the blur of Rob's fist before it plowed into Tuttle's face. Tuttle flew back, and Kate jumped out of the way an instant before he hit the wall where she'd been standing.

Tuttle slid to the floor, his gaze unfocused and glassy-eyed. 'Son of a bitch!' Victor roared and launched himself at Rob. Hit with the weight of Victor's compact body, Rob staggered a few steps backward.

'I'm gonna kick your ass for that,' Victor warned as he swung wildly and connected with Rob's jaw. Rob's head snapped back, then he hit Victor with a one-two jab that left the shorter man dazed but still on his feet.

Peirce ran into the room and moved to Tuttle, who was muttering incoherently. Peirce waved a hand in front of his brother's face, then he grabbed a pool stick from the wall. Before he could move, Kate stepped in front of him. 'It looks like Rob's about finished with Victor. Why don't you wait your turn.'

'What are you going to do about it?'

'That depends on you.'

'Get out of my way, lesbo.'

Lesbo? Kate hadn't heard that word since grade school. The Worsley brothers obviously needed to get out more. She kept her eyes on the cue as Peirce raised it and stormed toward her, his gaze glued on Rob. Rob gave Victor one last punch, sending him to the floor. As Peirce passed, Kate stuck her foot between his big boots. Her elbow slammed into his back and he went down. On the way, he hit his head on the pool table, and he landed on the floor in a heap. He moaned and rolled onto his back, the pool cue still clutched in his hand. Within the dim light hanging overhead, he looked up, his gaze as glassy and unfocused as Tuttle's.

'Well, God damn,' he moaned just before his eyes rolled up in his head and he passed out.

Rob looked over at Kate, his green eyes alive and shining. 'Are you okay?'

She swallowed past the lump in her throat and nodded.

Outside the small pool room, someone unplugged the jukebox. Over the sound of Kate's heart pounding in her ears, she heard yelling and swearing. Through the doorway, she could see broken tables and chairs and bodies flying through the air.

'Hell, yeah,' Rob said and touched the red mark on his jaw. He grinned like he was having the time of his life.

'Did I miss something? Was that fun?'

He grabbed his hat and laughed, a sound of pure pleasure that mixed with the noise of breaking glass and the distant wail of police sirens.

He was insane. Crazy. A big old numb nuts.

7

The front of the Buckhorn was lit up like the fourth of July. Beams of red, white, and blue slid across the facade and the patrons lined up in front. The rotating lights of three police vehicles bounced off cars in the parking lot and chased the inky shadows in the dense forest beyond.

From inside the sheriff's Blazer, Rob looked out at everyone standing in front of the Buckhorn, his gaze taking in the two deputies as they checked for sobriety before letting anyone go. The backseat of the Blazer had no leg room, and a pair of cuffs cut into his wrist. He was uncomfortable as hell, and he might have stretched out a bit if not for the pain in the ass cuffed beside him.

He'd always known that Kate Hamilton spelled trouble. He just hadn't known how much trouble. Since she'd arrived in Gospel, she'd started that gay rumor that had some of the rednecks in town looking at him funny. He wasn't afraid. Just annoyed.

Then tonight she'd breezed into the Buckhorn and engaged three of the biggest idiots around. It'd been only a matter of time before things got ugly between her and the Worsleys and someone would have had to step in. That someone had been him, and now he was cooling his heels in the back of a cop car. To top it off, she didn't seem all that grateful.

He glanced across his shoulder at her dark profile. 'You're welcome,' he said.

'For what?' The lights from another squad car lit up one side of her face as she turned to look at him.

'For saving your ass.'

'I figure we're even.' She shook her head. 'Peirce would have taken your head off with that pool cue if I hadn't stepped in and saved *your* ass.'

'He would have tried,' Rob scoffed. He'd been hit in the head a few times with hockey sticks and pucks, but he'd always been wearing his helmet. He doubted the pool cue would have knocked him out, but it would have hurt like hell. 'I know you think you can do anything a man can do. That you can take care of yourself, but there's a reason why people ignore the Worsley boys. Everyone knows they don't play well with others.'

She was silent a moment, then said, 'Well, it would have been nice if *everyone* would have told me.'

'I did.' Rob scooted down in the seat as far as his long legs would allow. 'Twice.' His coat and flannel shirt fell open around him, and a chill crept across the front of his T-shirt and stomach. Nothing to do now but kick back and wait to be hauled in alongside the ingrate beside him. 'I told you to call it a night and go home.' He guessed he could have warned her about the Worsleys earlier, but he'd been busy trying to ignore her. Kate wasn't exactly his favorite person, and by the time he'd even noticed her with the Worsleys, she'd already sunk three balls. At that point, the best he could do was stand around and watch her play and wait for things to get out of hand.

Rob turned his attention to the front of the bar. Tuttle had called Kate mannish, which was just moronic. She was so blatantly female, with large breasts, slim waist, and long legs, that there was no way anyone would confuse her for a man. Sure she was tall, but Rob liked tall women. He liked long legs cinched tight around his waist, draped over his shoulders, and wrapped around his head. He liked the way a tall woman fit against him in and out of bed.

Watching her stretch her long body across the pool table had annoyed him even as it had turned him on. Then he'd touched her because he hadn't seemed able to stop himself. He'd touched the side of her throat and her hair. He'd fit his hand in the curve of her waist, and he'd slid his palm across her stomach. For a few seconds, he'd welcomed the hot punch of lust in his belly instead of fighting it.

Muttering from the other side of the seat drew his attention. 'What?' he asked.

'I'm just wondering how long it will take to bail out of jail,' she said through a sigh as she leaned her head against the window. 'I don't want my grandfather to get called about this.' One side of her hair fell forward and covered her face. 'He's old and shouldn't have to get a call from the sheriff in the middle of the night.'

'I'll bail us out.' For some reason, he was starting to feel sorry for her, and he was having a hard time remembering why he didn't like her. 'How much?'

'I don't know. It depends on the charges.'

'Well, how is it done? Is there a teller machine somewhere? Or do I write a check?'

'You can only use cash.' She straightened and looked over at him. 'Don't tell me you've never been arrested.'

'Nope.'

Even through the darkness, he could see that she found that bit of news incredulous. 'You're kidding?'

Why did she find that so hard to believe? 'No.' He scowled. He'd just offered to pay her bail and she insults him. Now he remembered why he didn't like her. 'How many times have *you* been arrested?'

'Never. I'm a private investigator. At least I used to be. I know how the system works.' She thought a moment. 'Or at least I do in Nevada.'

He turned his attention to the front of the Buckhorn once more. He no longer cared what she did. Maybe the men around town were right about her. She was a real ballbuster.

He heard her take a deep breath and let it out slow. The seat shook a little as she wiggled around, trying to get more comfortable.

'Rob?' She said his name just above a whisper.

He looked over at her. She'd turned and pulled her bent leg up on the seat. The light from outside lit up her face, and her knee almost touched the outside of his thigh. 'Yeah?'

She licked her lips and her voice got low and kind of throaty. 'Thank you.'

Hell. Just when he was trying to work up a real dislike of her, she had to ruin it by turning all nice and girly. Her change in moods was giving him whiplash. 'You're welcome.'

She leaned forward a bit and spoke into the darkness just above his left cheek. 'How's your chin?'

'Hurts like a bitch, but I'll live.'

'I'm sorry you got hit. Let me know if you need anything.'

He lowered his gaze to her mouth and wondered if she was going to offer to kiss it better for him. Not that kissing Kate was a good idea. 'Like what?' Although it would definitely keep her quiet; keep her mouth too busy to talk, too.

'An ice pack.'

An ice pack might be good, might keep him from thinking up all the ways he could keep her mouth busy. 'Why don't you tell me how the gay rumor got started?' he asked to take his mind off her head in his lap.

She leaned back. 'I think I'd only lived here a few weeks, and you weren't back in town yet. Ada came into the store one morning and started telling me about the owner of the sporting goods store not being interested in any women in town, so I said something like maybe you didn't like women. I was thinking misogynist. I really didn't know she was talking about *you*.'

Right.

She shrugged. 'I never thought you were gay. Not even after the first night we met. It never even entered my head.'

Well, that's something, he thought as he sat up and tried to get more comfortable.

'Erectile dysfunction, yes. Gay?' She shook her head. 'No.'

He stilled. 'You don't think I can get it up? I can get it up plenty!' He hadn't meant to yell, but Christ almighty, just because he hadn't been *using* his hard-ons lately didn't mean he wasn't *capable*.

'If you say so.'

God, she'd done it again in a matter of minutes. Just when he was starting to think she wasn't so bad, she pissed him off. Just when he was thinking about kissing her, she told him he had erectile dysfunction. If they hadn't been cuffed, he would have grabbed her hand and shoved it on his dick just to prove her wrong. She'd feel for herself that he functioned just fine.

The car door opened and Sheriff Dillon Taber stood in the opening. 'Come on out, you two.'

Rob didn't hesitate before sliding out of the vehicle. He wanted to be as far away from Kate as possible. 'Erectile dysfunction,' he scoffed.

'Did you say something, Sutter?' the sheriff asked.

He frowned. 'No.'

Kate moved from the Blazer and stood beside Rob within the head beams of a police cruiser. 'Peirce swears you never touched him,' Dillon informed Kate as he moved behind her to take off her cuffs. 'He says he must have tripped because there's no way a girl knocked him out.' She turned and rubbed her wrists. 'But I'm going to give you some advice which I'm sure you'll ignore,' the sheriff continued as he shoved the cuffs in a leather case hooked to his belt. 'Stay away from anyone with the last name of Worsley.' He thought a minute, then added, 'And while you're at it, go ahead and steer clear of Emmett Barnes and Hayden Dean.'

'I plan to stay clear of the bars around here,' she said as she grabbed her leather backpack off the hood of the Blazer.

'That's probably wise. How much did you have to drink tonight?'

'About half a beer.'

'Then you're free to go. Drive careful, Ms. Hamilton.'

'I will. Thanks,' she said and walked away. For one brief second, a flash of light caught in her hair. Then she was gone.

Dillon moved behind Rob and removed his cuffs. 'Several people have confirmed that Tuttle Worsley swung first,' the sheriff said as he released the cuffs from Rob's wrists. 'You're free to go.'

Rob had first met Dillon last summer when he and his son Adam had signed up for fly-fishing lesons. He'd liked the sheriff immediately and had hired Adam to help out in the store. The eleven year old had done a good job sweeping up and emptying the trash. 'What's Adam up to these days?' he asked as he rubbed his wrists.

'No good. He can't wait to knock the hell out of the trout population this summer.'

'Tell him to stop by the store and I'll put him to work again.'

'He'd like that.' Dillon pushed up the brim of his cowboy hat. 'How much have you had to drink, Rob?'

'I was on my second beer.'

The radio clipped to Dillon's shoulder squawked, and he reached up to turn it down. 'What do you know about

Stanley's granddaughter?' he asked as Kate's CRV pulled onto the road from the parking lot.

Other than the fact that he didn't like her but wanted to have sex with her? 'I know she has a way of rubbing people the wrong way.'

'I have one of those at home,' Dillon chuckled. 'Sometimes, bothersome women are the best kind.'

'I'm going to take your word for that,' Rob said as he pulled his car keys out of his coat pocket. 'Stay out of trouble, Sheriff.'

'Wish I could, but it's only March, and summer's just around the corner.' Dillon shook his head and moved toward the drunks still lined up in front of the bar.

Rob walked to his HUMMER and drove the five miles to his house. He turned up his driveway, and the motion sensors tripped the lights as he went. When he'd had the house built, he'd had the lights put in as security measures. But as he'd quickly discovered, motion-detecting lights and wildlife didn't mix. There were a lot of nights he just turned the whole system off so he could get some sleep.

He pushed a button on the garage door opener clipped to his viser, then drove the HUMMER inside. The automatic door closed behind him. He'd had the four-thousand-square-foot house built the summer before. It had four bedrooms and bathrooms and was constructed of lake rock and big wooden timbers. He loved the cathedral ceiling and huge plate-glass windows that overlooked the lake, but he didn't know what he'd been thinking, having such a big house built. Even when Amelia was old enough to visit him in Gospel, she wouldn't need so much room.

The light he'd left on over the range still burned. He

turned it off and tossed his keys on the marble counter. The carpet on the stairs muffled his footsteps as he headed upstairs in the dark. He'd spent the past weekend in Seattle with his daughter. She'd learned three new words and had started stringing them together into sentences.

Rob took off his coat and tossed it on a chair next to the oak entertainment center that held one of his big-screen televisions. Moonlight poured in through the floor-to-ceiling windows and shone across him as he shucked off his clothes. Naked, he crawled into his bed.

The cool sheets touched his skin, and he pulled the heavy wool blankets and red-and-blue plaid comforter over him. His trip to Seattle had been an improvement over the last time. He and Louisa were getting along better than they had since he'd been shot. Rob wasn't sure how he felt about it, but she'd hinted at a reconciliation.

He placed an arm behind his head and looked up at the moonlight on his ceiling. He loved Amelia, and he wanted to be with her. He still had feelings for Louisa. He just didn't know what they were or if they were deep enough. He couldn't afford to make another mistake. Both he and Louisa were older. Wiser. More settled, or at least he knew *he* was. Maybe they wouldn't mess it up this time. Maybe they could make it work.

But when he closed his eyes, it wasn't thoughts of Louisa that kept him up for several more hours. It wasn't the picture of her long blonde hair that was stuck in his head. It wasn't the memory of her voice saying 'Let me know if you need anything' that grabbed his insides and turned him hard. Or the thought of just exactly how many ways he wanted to prove to her that he was a man. A man capable of pleasing a woman. It wasn't the thought of his ex-wife who made his skin hot and the sheets suddenly too warm to bear. It wasn't the touch of Louisa's hands he craved on him.

It was Kate. It was the memory of her playing pool, spliced together with the vision of her laid out across the table like a gourmet meal. It was the hint of cleavage and flash of skin. A freeze frame of her looking up into his face as he held her back against his chest.

Alone within the darkness of his room, it was the woman who thought he was impotent that starred in his most X-rated fantasy.

Across town, Stanley Caldwell sat on the edge of his bed and looked inside the box he held in his hands. A half hour earlier he'd heard Katie return home, and he'd quietly shut his bedroom door.

In the box, he'd placed Melba's collection of Tom Jones records. A few of them were autographed. There were twenty-five of them in all. He knew because he'd just counted them.

It wasn't supposed to have been like this. He should have been the one to die first. Melba should have outlived him. It was too hard this way. Too hard for an old man like him to go on when his best friend and lover was no longer around. They'd raised children and grown old together. They'd grown fat and comfortable too. He missed her like he missed the other part of his soul. He couldn't just pack her away.

He reached inside the box and grabbed some of the albums. Then slowly he put them back. Grace Sutter had come over for a beer that night while Katie had been out playing pool. They'd laughed and talked about things they had in common. Like John Wayne movies and Tex Ritter Westerns. Glenn Miller and The Kingston Trio.

Now that Grace was gone, he felt guilty that he'd shared those memories with anyone other than his wife, Melba. Guilty that he'd boxed up her records. He'd thought he could just pack away a few of her things – nothing big – nothing like her housecoats and slippers. Just the small things that Katie had been nagging him about. He'd thought he could do it.

Stanley let go of the albums and set the box on the floor. He liked Grace. Aside from Melba, he liked her more than he'd liked any woman in a very long time. She wasn't pushy and she didn't gossip. Talking to her had been so easy, and her smile made him want to smile too.

With his foot, he pushed the box under his bed. There, he hadn't gotten rid of Melba's albums. He was just setting them somewhere else for a while. Somewhere out of sight, but not out of the house.

He turned off his light and crawled into bed. When he closed his eyes, he pictured Melba's face surrounded by her gray hair, and he relaxed. Grace Sutter was his friend. He liked her, but no one would ever take the place of his wife in his old, lonely heart.

The Monday after the Buckhorn brawl, a bad chest cold forced Kate to stay home from work. She sat on the end of her bed, flipping through television stations, feeling extremely sorry for herself. Her body ached. She was so bored that she felt like screaming, but she couldn't because her chest hurt.

Instead of giving in to her mood, she dragged out the cable Internet connection that her grandmother had installed several years ago and her grandfather continued to pay for but never used. She took her laptop computer from the closet, and within an hour she was surfing the Internet, researching really exciting stuff like integrated software for retailers. Specifically, grocery stores. Perhaps if she got the names of a few consultants, more information, or even some brochures, she could show her grandfather that his life would be so much easier if he entered the new millennium. It was crazy not to use the technology that kept track of profit and inventory at the point of sale. It was just plain obstinate to refuse to even think about it.

She bookmarked several sites and sent for information, and because she was sick and bored silly, she did a little Internet shopping to brighten her mood. She bought panties and bras at Victoria's Secret. Sweaters and jeans from Neiman Marcus and Banana Republic. She bought shoes at Nordstrom, and she splurged on a silver cuff bracelet from Tiffany. When she was finished, she was a thousand dollars poorer, but she didn't feel better. She was still sick and still bored.

She lifted her hands to close her laptop, but a little voice inside her head stopped her. *It would be so easy*, it said. She knew the license plate number on Rob Sutter's vehicle, and with a few clicks of the mouse, she could have his Social Security number and birthday. Then she could see for herself if he'd told the truth about never being arrested.

No, that would be an invasion of his privacy . . . but she could do a google search. Rob had played professional hockey. He'd been a public figure. As long as what she discovered was public knowledge, then it really wasn't an invasion of privacy.

Before she could talk herself out of it, she clicked on the Internet and typed his name into the search engine. She was shocked when it pulled up more than forty thousand hits. Most of the hits were for sports sites that showed his head shot next to a list of his statistics. In some of the photos, he had his mustache. In others he did not. In the pictures without the Fu Manchu, his jaw looked more square. More masculine, which she would not have thought possible. In all the shots of him, his green eyes looked into the camera as if he were up to absolutely no good.

On the site hockeyfights.com, there was a picture of him with some guy in a headlock. He wore a navy blue jersey and a black helmet, and the article read:

Rob Sutter may seem like a thug, but he is highly specialized and has an important role – to make the other team think twice before they do something stupid like score a goal, make a pass, or breathe the wrong way.

She clicked on sites that had photos of him skating down the ice or shooting or sitting in the penalty box with cotton shoved up his nose.

She read an article he'd written about himself in 2003 for *The Hockey News*. 'I am more than a punching bag,' it began, and he went on to list his goal and assist averages. Kate didn't know anything about hockey, but she assumed if his averages had been bad, he wouldn't have mentioned them. She read about his career highs, and she read the last *Sports Illustrated* article written about him. The glossy photograph showed him skating across the ice with a puck at the end of his hockey stick. The title read, 'Female Fan Shoots NHL Enforcer.'

Kate sat up straighter, as if she'd been pulled up by strings. If she'd been shocked by the number of Internet hits, what she read next was stunning.

According to the article, Stephanie Andrews, of Denver, Colorado, shot him three times after he'd put an end to their affair. Two bullets had struck his chest, causing life-threatening injuries, while a third had shattered his knee, effectively putting an end to his career. Kate had suspected that his knee injury had ended his career, but she never would have guessed the reality in a million years.

Kate dug a little deeper and read more about the shooting and trial. She found quite a bit written about it in the *Seattle Times* archives. Her gaze scanned the daily reports of the two-week trial, and she read that Stephanie Andrews hadn't even been Rob's girlfriend. She'd been a groupie he'd picked up in a bar, then she'd turned stalker on him.

Stephanie had pleaded temporary insanity, but in the end, the jury hadn't bought the plea, and she'd received a twenty-year sentence, with ten fixed. Kate wondered what Rob thought about that. If he thought it was fair that the woman who'd tried to kill him could get out of prison in ten years, while he had to live with his injuries the rest of his life.

Kate skimmed the last article, but a quote near the end caught her eye – '. . . Mrs Sutter has no comment.' She scrolled up a paragraph and read, 'Louisa Sutter, and the couple's child, do not reside in the family home on Mercer Island. The *Times* tried to contact her for her reaction to the verdict. Her lawyer returned our call and stated that "Mrs Sutter has no comment." '

Married. He'd been married at the time of the shooting, and he'd had a child. Still had a child. Kate pushed her hair behind her ears. She was stunned and shocked, certainly, but she was also surprised at the deep disappointment she felt. In spite of herself, she was beginning to like him. He'd stepped up and pounded on the Worsleys on her behalf. Yeah, he'd had a little too much fun doing it, but if it hadn't been for him, she was certain she'd still be at the Buckhorn playing pool. Because one thing was for sure, the Worsleys wouldn't have let her leave until she'd lost, and Kate never lost on purpose at anything.

Kate closed the laptop and placed it on the closet shelf next to a box of Tom Jones memorabilia. Rob had cheated on his wife with a hockey groupie. Kate had been cheated on before, and she hated cheaters. Still, no one deserved to get shot or lose his career over it. No one deserved to die, and there was no mistaking the fact that Stephanie Andrews had been aiming to kill Rob.

Kate climbed beneath the pink frilly covers of the twin bed. The bedding she'd brought with her from Vegas was all queen sized, so she was stuck with lace and frills and, of course, Tom.

Getting shot by a groupie he'd picked up in a bar might explain why Rob had turned her down in the Duchin Lounge. It also explained why, despite her best efforts to dislike Rob, she was attracted to him.

She reached for a Kleenex and blew her nose. For whatever reason, if there was a man within a hundred miles who would break her heart and treat her bad, Kate was drawn to him.

She flung the Kleenex at the Tom Jones waste paper basket and missed. Rob was a cheater. He had commitment issues – had 'bad bet' written all over him. He was every jerk she'd ever dated rolled into one gorgeous package. He'd smash her heart quicker than he used to smash heads.

Yeah, that might be cynical. And yeah, she was

supposed to be working on her inner cynic, but it didn't make it any less true.

Kate was attracted to Rob, but she wasn't going to do anything about it. She was through with impossible men.

She laid her head on her pillow and closed her eyes. As Kate fell asleep, she thought about her life in Gospel. Sometimes she was so bored she thought she just might go as nutty as everyone else in town. But there was something to be said about the mundane. Something comforting in things that didn't change, like the monotony of shelving groceries and ordering produce.

Kate reminded herself of that sentiment two days later when she and her grandfather were having a discussion about how to cut some of the waste out of the business. Kate thought they should stop home deliveries or, at least, charge for them. Stanley wouldn't hear of it.

She wanted to put a tip jar next to the coffee machines to help fund the coffee the locals guzzled every morning. Stanley wouldn't consider that, either. She suggested stocking gourmet cheeses and pasta. Stuffed Italian olives and jalapeño jellies. He looked at her as if she were crazy.

'No one around here eats that fancy stuff.'

'Triangle Grocery stocks it,' she told him, referring to the other store in town.

'Exactly. If they stock it, why should I?'

They finally compromised on the sticker issue. No more stickers on items that were already marked. Her grandfather finally agreed with her that it was not only a waste of money but also a waste of time.

It was a small victory for Kate, but an important one. It

proved to her that her grandfather wasn't completely unbending. He listened to her on some things. When the time came, he might be receptive to her ideas for updating the store's inventory and bookkeeping system. She might help his life get easier, after all. Things were looking up.

Or at least she thought they were until the door to the M&S opened and Rob breezed in looking slightly windblown. Over the stereo speakers, Tom belted out his version of Otis Redding's 'Try A Little Tenderness.' She hadn't seen Rob since the night of the Buckhorn brawl, and despite all she'd learned of him since, the sight of him made her want to check her posture and reach for her lip gloss.

She stood behind a bin of oranges and grapefruit, and as if he sensed her gaze on him, he looked over at her from the end of aisle two. He wore a dark green hooded sweatshirt the same color as his eyes. He had a black-and-blue bruise on his jaw, a reminder of the night he'd taken on the Worsleys on her behalf.

'How are you?' he asked, his voice a little rough, as if he hadn't been using it a lot lately.

'I'm good.'

His lips parted as if he meant to say something more. Instead, his gaze slid to the two boys buying candy bars.

It was three-thirty in the afternoon and business was slow. The only other customers in the store were Adam Taber and Wally Aberdeen, and they were arguing over who was tougher, Spiderman or Wolverine. Rob grabbed Adam around the neck and rubbed his knuckles in the kid's hair.

'Are you going to work for me this summer?' he asked.

'Yeah.' Adam laughed and wiggled out of Rob's grasp. 'Can Wally work too?'

While Rob pretended to think about it, Kate ran her gaze down his sweatshirt, over the brand name Rossignol printed on the front and down the sleeves, to his faded jeans. The seams were worn, and there was mud caked on the knees. 'If you think he can handle it,' he said.

'I can handle it,' Wally assured him.

'Good. I might have something for you two next month.' The three of them did some sort of male ritualistic high-five knuckle-smashing thing before Rob walked toward the front counter, where her grandfather stood refilling racks of cigarettes.

'How's your mother?' Stanley asked him.

'Great. I was just at her house digging up some old dead rosebushes.'

'Well, tell her I said hello.'

'Will do.' Rob leaned a hip into the counter and crossed one booted foot over the other. 'Can you get me some flaxseed?' he asked.

Flaxseed? Kate placed a few oranges in the bin, then pretended a sudden interest in apples, but her thoughts were not on produce. She was thinking about Rob and wondering if he thought much about his past. She wondered if he missed playing hockey or worried much about the day Stephanie Andrews would get out of jail. She knew she'd worry about that. She wondered if he'd learned a lesson about cheating, and she wondered if his child was a boy or a girl.

She grabbed the empty orange crate and carried it behind the counter toward the doors to the back room. On her way, she glanced at Rob out of the corners of her eyes. At the bruise on his jaw and the mustache framing his lips.

'And I need dried currants,' he told Stanley as his gaze followed Kate until she disappeared in the back room.

The door to the alley was to Kate's left, and she grabbed several more boxes before walking outside. She also wondered if Rob believed her about not starting that rumor about him. He'd never said one way or the other. The conversation had pretty much ended when she'd mentioned possible erectile dysfunction.

She tossed the boxes into the Dumpster and shut the lid. She'd been half-joking, but he'd acted so appalled that she had to wonder if she hadn't hit a raw nerve. Since the first night they'd met, she'd been telling herself that he was impotent, but if she was honest, she really hadn't believed it. Not until he'd freaked out and protested so loudly. Now she had to wonder if getting shot had damaged him mentally or physically in that department.

The sound of her grandfather's laughter reached Kate as she moved into the back room and shut the door behind her. If Rob did have a problem down below, then she felt truly bad for joking about it. She wasn't usually a mean person. Sometimes she was sort of insensitive, but she didn't purposely hurt people.

Wait. She stopped in her tracks right next to her grandfather's shiny meat grinder. She felt bad for Rob? How had that happened?

She leaned her behind against the chrome worktable and put the heel of her hand to her forehead. She didn't want to feel bad for Rob. Feeling bad could lead her further down the path of actually liking him. Liking him would lead her straight to humiliation and rejection. She was supposed to be avoiding men who'd use her and treat her bad.

Rob Sutter was the poster boy of bad.

'Katie,' her grandfather said as he walked into the back room. 'I have a delivery for you.'

'Who?'

'Hazel Avery. She's got that bad cold you had a few days ago.'

'Why didn't she call it into Crum's Pharmacy? They deliver too.' She held up a hand before he could answer. 'Forget it. I know why. You're cuter than Fred Crum.'

Stanley's cheeks turned pink, and he held out a bag containing a bottle of Nyquil and a box of Theraflu. 'Thanks,' he said.

'Is Rob still out front?'

'He left, but I think he just went across the parking lot. You can catch him if you hurry.'

Kate shoved her arms into her coat and grabbed her purse. Ever since the night of the fight at the Buckhorn, her grandfather was trying even harder to push her in Rob's direction. 'I'll catch him some other time.' She hung her purse over her shoulder and pulled her hair from the back of her coat. 'This shouldn't take long,' she said as she took the sack from her grandfather. At least she hoped it didn't take long. Last time she'd made a delivery had been to the Fernwoods over on Tamarack. They'd invited her in, then cracked open a baby book and shown her about a hundred photographs of their new grandbaby. They'd tried to feed her pie, and they'd forced her to listen to stories about their daughter, Paris, and her husband, Myron, better known to the world of professional midget wrestling as Myron the Masher. Apparently Myron was making quite a name for himself in Mexico with his latest trademark move, The Swirly.

Which, Kate figured as she walked out of the M&S and into the bright afternoon sun, was way more info than she needed to know about the Fernwoods' son-in-law. She moved down the sidewalk toward her Honda CRV and looked across the parking lot. Rob was out front of Sutter Sports, still wearing the same green sweatshirt and jeans he'd had on earlier. The only difference was that he'd put on a pair of black sunglasses with blue lenses.

Before she thought better of it, she stepped off the curb and moved across the asphalt lot. Yeah, he was the president of the 'bad relationship bet' club, but he'd also been the only man in the Buckhorn bar who'd stepped up to help her out. She wasn't sure he knew how truly grateful she was.

As she got closer, she watched him stick an ax under one arm and pull on a pair of brown leather work gloves. Then before her eyes, he turned and swung the ax at one of the four-foot evergreens growing in twin planters next to the front doors. Two swings and the tree lay on the ground at his feet.

'Hello,' she called out to him as she stepped up onto the curb.

He glanced back over his shoulder at her and straightened.

'What? Are you in desperate need of firewood?' she asked as she stopped in front of the dead tree.

'Stand back a little bit,' he said and swung at the other tree. It fell on the ground next to its twin.

'I've always hated those things,' he said as he turned toward her. He held up the ax, and the wooden handle slid through his gloved hand and stopped at the heavy steel head. 'They look like they belong at the Four Seasons, not a sporting goods store in the Idaho Sawtooths.'

'Are you going to replace them?'

'I was thinking about maybe getting some of those tall weeds.' He bit one fingertip of his gloves and pulled it off.

'You mean like pampas grass or maidenhair?'

He shoved the glove in the front pocket of his sweat-shirt. 'Yeah, probably. I have some of that stuff growing in my yard, and I like it.' He took off his sunglasses and shoved them in the pocket, too. The sun shone bright, and lines appeared in the corners of his green eyes looking back at her. He kicked one of the trees with the toe of his boot. 'Those had to die.'

'It's probably a good thing you don't sell guns.'

He smiled and, for some appalling reason, a little tingle settled in her stomach. She glanced away from his mouth to the destruction at her feet.

'No,' he said. 'No guns.'

She certainly understood why he didn't sell guns. 'Wow, I'm surprised they let you live around here.'

'I'm not anti-gun. I just don't have a need for them.'

She glanced up at the striped awning overhead. 'When are you opening?'

'April first. A week from tomorrow.'

He didn't elaborate, and an awkward silence stretched between them. She couldn't help but wonder if he was recalling the night she'd made a fool out of herself. Or the night he'd had to rescue her from the Buckhorn. She folded her arms across her chest, and Ada's bag of cold remedies swung and bumped her thigh.

'How's your jaw?' she asked as she glanced at the side of his face. 'Does it hurt?'

'No.'

'Good. If you hadn't stepped in when you did, I'm certain I'd still be at the Buckhorn playing pool.'

'The Worsleys are idiots.'

'I think you called them numb nuts.'

He chuckled. 'They're that too.'

'Well, thanks again for helping me out.'

'Don't mention it.' He tapped the ax handle against his leg as if he were impatient to get rid of her.

She took a step back. 'See ya around.'

He bent and picked up the trunk of one evergreen. 'Yeah.'

While she felt little tingles, he clearly felt nothing. It was embarrassing. She turned and started for her car. But his lack of interest wasn't exactly a news update – which was just as well. She wasn't in town to date – especially men like Rob. She was here to help her grandfather.

The following Friday she helped him out in a way that changed his life.

She'd inadvertently given her grandfather her cold, and he was forced to stay home in bed. Before Kate left for work, she spoke to Grace Sutter about bringing him into the clinic. Grace didn't believe it was necessary, but she promised to look in on him on her lunch break and after she closed up for the day.

The first thing Kate did when she got to the M&S that morning was to pull Tom Jones out of the CD player and plug in Alicia Keys. She followed Alica up with Sarah McLachlan and Dido. It was definitely kick-butt girl day.

At one o'clock that afternoon, she called a gourmet food wholesaler down in Boise and ordered olives, jalapeño jelly, and wafer-thin crackers. She thought it best to start out small, and if those items sold, her grandfather would have to agree with some of her other ideas.

At five, the Aberdeen twins came to work, and Kate changed out the tills. She counted the money, recorded the amounts in her grandfather's ledgers, and put the money in the safe until the next morning. The telephone rang just as she was about to leave the office at six. It was her grandfather, and he wanted her to do two things for him. 'Grab the books,' which she'd already done, and make one delivery on her way home.

'Rob's special order came in yesterday,' he said between coughing fits. 'Take it out to his place.'

Kate glanced down at her beige wraparound blouse that closed with three leather buckles at one side, and she brushed dust from her left breast. 'I'll call him, and he can come get it tomorrow.' She didn't want to see Rob. It had been a long, exhausting day and she just wanted to go home, get out of her black twill pants and leather boots. 'I'm sure he doesn't need whatever it is tonight.'

'Katie,' her grandfather sighed. 'The M&S has stayed in business all these years because our customers depend on us.'

She'd heard it a hundred times before, so she grabbed a pen. 'Give me the address.'

Five minutes later she was driving around the left end of Fish Hook Lake. The sun was about to set behind the sharp granite peaks, throwing jagged shadows across the landscape and into the cold bluish-green lake. Kate glanced at the directions propped up behind her gearshift and took a left up a long drive with a split-pole fence. She could barely see the roof of a house, but motion sensor lights turned on like a runway, so she figured she was headed the right way. Then the house seemed to rise up in front of her, huge and imposing within the gray darkness of the setting sun.

The house was made of lake rock and logs, and the huge windows reflected towering pine and clumps of shaded snow. 'Pa rum pum pum pum,' she whispered. It looked more like a hotel than a private home. She pulled her Honda to a stop in front of the four-car garage and grabbed Rob's grocery bag off the passenger seat. She'd never given any thought to where he might live, but even if she had, this wouldn't have been it.

She checked the address her grandfather had given her against the numbers on the house. Professional hockey must have been very good to Rob.

She got out of her car and hung her leather backpack over one shoulder. The heels of her boots echoed across the concrete and stone as she moved up the wide porch to the double front doors.

With the grocery bag hanging off one arm, she raised her hand and knocked. The light above her head wasn't on, and there didn't appear to be any lights on in the house. After several moments, Kate set the bag by the front door and opened her purse. She dug around for a piece of paper and found an old grocery list, a bank deposit receipt, and a paper gum wrapper that smelled like mint. She pulled the wrapper out along with a pen and used the door to write against.

About halfway through the note, the light above her head flipped on and one side of the doors flew open. Kate stumbled and almost did a header into Rob's chest.

'What are you doing?' he asked.

She grabbed hold of the other door to keep from falling. 'I'm delivering your groceries.' She looked up past his bare feet and jeans to an old, worn T-shirt. Blue, she believed, and stretched out of shape.

'You didn't have to do that.'

He had a white towel around his neck, and he lifted one end to dry his wet hair. The loose sleeve of his shirt slipped down the hard mounds of his muscles to the dark hair nestled in his armpit. His snake tattoo circled his thick biceps, and something warm and delicious slid into her stomach. 'My grandfather said . . .' She frowned and shoved the bag toward him. 'Never mind.'

He turned and walked into the house without taking the bag. A chandelier made of elk horns shone overhead and slid crystal prisms down his wide shoulders and back to the behind of his jeans. He looked at her over his shoulder. 'Come in and shut the door.'

'You live here alone?'

Rob tossed the towel on the back of his leather couch and finger-combed his hair. 'Yeah.' She'd caught him just out of the shower. He wouldn't have even seen her standing by the door if he hadn't walked by and noticed her through the windows at the top of the stairs.

Kate set the bag of groceries on a coffee table as she moved past him across the great room. 'Wow, I've never really seen the lake from this side,' she said as she looked out the floor-to-ceiling windows.

Rob glanced out at the patches of snow around the clear lake. In the summer, the water reflected the dense pine and took on an emerald green color. Tonight the quarter moon was just starting to rise over the jagged teeth of the Sawtooths, casting the mountains and lake in a light gray.

'Do you like it?' he asked as he ran his gaze down the back of Kate's coat and pants to the heels of those dominatrix boots of hers. No female, other than his mother, had ever been in his home. That Kate was even here felt a bit disconcerting – like watching the star from your favorite porn film step from the screen and into your living room. He'd been thinking about her so much it was embarrassing. Almost as if he were sixteen instead of thirty-six.

'It's gorgeous.' She pushed one side of her hair behind her ear. 'When I visited Gospel when I was young, my grandmother used to take me to the public beach.' She pointed to her right, toward town. She leaned forward and placed her palm against the glass, her long fingers spread out and pressed flat. Her short, shiny nails pointed toward the ceiling. 'I can see the marina over there.' She dropped her hand and looked over at him. 'Oops. Sorry.' She frowned and turned toward him. 'I got my handprint on your clean window.'

'That's okay. It'll give Mabel something to do when she cleans next week.' He folded his arms across his chest and rested his weight on one foot. His gaze took in her smooth, red hair resting against the thin column of her throat. He knew that the skin where her shoulder met her neck was as soft as it looked.

'Your house is beautiful, Rob,' she said, and it was the first time he could recall her using his name.

Of course, he'd *imagined* her using it. But in a context that would probably get his face slapped. Inviting her in had been a bad idea. Very bad. He should show her the door. Instead he heard himself say, 'Do you want to see the rest of it?'

'Sure.'

Too late now. 'You can leave your coat down here, if

you'd like.' He didn't offer to help her. He'd pretty much learned his lesson about that the last time.

She shrugged out of her coat and laid it by the grocery sack. She walked toward him, and his gaze took in her sweater, which wrapped across her breast and closed with buckles on one side. Black leather buckles. The kind that wouldn't be that hard to open. *Don't think about the buckles*.

He turned, and she followed him upstairs. The first room they entered was filled with free weights and exercise equipment. In front of a wall of mirrors sat his treadmill and Nordic Track.

'Do you really use this stuff?' She pushed up her sleeves, exposing the delicate blue veins on the insides of her wrists.

'Most every day.' First he'd noticed her neck and now her wrists. He felt like a vampire.

'I joined a gym once.' She walked in the room and ran her hand over his weights. 'The Golds on Flamingo Road. I paid a year's membership and went three months. I'm afraid I'm not dedicated to fitness.'

'Maybe you need someone to motivate you.' He watched her long fingers and hands slip across a row of chrome dumbbells. In his former life, he would have offered to motivate her.

'No, that's not my problem. I went with my friend Marilyn, and she's a Stair Master fiend. She tried to motivate me.' She shook her head. 'But once my thighs start to burn, I just have to lie down. I'm kind of a wimp when it comes to pain.'

He laughed even though he wished she hadn't

mentioned burning thighs. 'Come on.' He led her back out to the open hallway that looked down at the entrance and great room. 'That's my daughter's room,' he said and pointed to a closed door.

'How often does she visit?'

'Amelia's never visited me here. She lives in Seattle with her mother, but when the house was built, I had her room done for her.'

'How old is she?'

'Two.'

He pointed to another closed door. 'That's a bathroom, but I don't think it's ever been used.' They moved past some sort of alcove with a couch he never sat on and a big plant he never watered. 'You ever married?'

'No.'

'Ever get close?'

'A few times.' She laughed without humor. 'Or at least I thought so. They didn't, though.'

'That's a problem.' They moved to the open door of his bedroom. The place where he'd pictured her naked. Tied to his bed or on her knees in the moonlight. He wondered if he should feel like a pig for thinking about her naked so much. He wondered if it counted since she didn't know, and he never planned to do anything about it. He leaned a shoulder into the door frame and shoved his hands into the front pockets of his Levi's. As he watched her move silently through his room, he wondered if he'd ever be able to separate the Kate looking out his bedroom window from the Kate who'd wanted to have sex with him the first night they met. He doubted it. The two were so interwoven in his brain that when he looked at her, it was always there.

'Is this your little girl?' she asked as she stopped in front of his entertainment center, cluttered with pictures of his daughter.

'Yeah. That's Amelia.'

She leaned in for a closer look. 'She's cute. She looks like you.'

'My mother thinks so.'

Kate took a step back, and her gaze moved to his big-screen television. 'Hockey must pay well.'

So, she did know a thing or two about him. It was no secret. Everyone in town knew. 'It did, yes.'

'What team?'

'Ottawa Senators. New York Rangers. Florida Panthers. Detroit Red Wings. L.A. Kings, and the Seattle Chinooks.'

She looked across at him. 'Sounds like you moved around a lot.'

'Yeah.' He didn't really like to talk about the past. It brought up too many questions he didn't want to answer. Too many memories he didn't like to think about.

The carpet muffled the sound of her boots as she walked toward him and stopped about a foot away. 'Were you good?'

His gaze slid to her mouth. 'What do you think?'

She tilted her head to one side as if she were studying him. 'I think you were probably scary.'

'Do you watch hockey?'

'Just enough to know that if you were skating toward me, I'd get out of your way.' She bit her lip, and it slid through her teeth. 'And I saw you take out the Worsleys.'

He chuckled. 'Let's go downstairs,' he said before he gave in to the urge to bite her lip, too.

He pointed to two more closed doors. One bedroom was filled with his fly-tying gear. The other had boxes of his hockey stuff in it. They walked downstairs and through the house, past the dining room to the kitchen. On the granite countertops and steel gas range sat his sheets of cooling granola. He was addicted to the stuff, and he'd been making his own for several years. He'd just about perfected his honey almond crunch. When he'd played hockey, the guys had all given him a raft of shit about his granola, but they all secretly hit him up for some when no one else was around.

She stood next to the work island in the middle of the room and gazed up at the pots and pans hanging on the rack above her head. The recessed lighting cast her in a warm glow and shone in her red hair. 'Who uses all these pots and pans?'

'Me.' He lived alone and had learned a long time ago how to cook for himself. Life on the road and eating in restaurants could get real old. 'When I'm here.' He scooped up some granola and moved toward her. 'Open up,' he said as he held his fingers in front of her mouth.

She looked skeptical, as if she might argue. 'What's in it?'

'Oats, flaxseed, honey.' Or maybe she was just nervous. He liked to think he made her nervous.

'Did you know that a bee only produces one and a half teaspoons of honey during its lifetime?'

'That's fascinating. Now open up.'

Her gaze stared into his as she tilted her head back and opened her mouth. The tips of his fingers touched her lips. He dropped the granola into her mouth as if she were a bird, then he stepped back.

She chewed, then licked the corner of her mouth. 'That's pretty good stuff.'

'I'm addicted to it.' He grabbed one of the cooking sheets and sat it on the island next to her. 'Help yourself.'

'Are you sure you made it?'

'Of course. Who else?'

'I don't know, but you don't strike me as the type of guy who makes his own granola.'

It was on the tip of his tongue to ask her what she did think of him, but he supposed he already knew. She thought he drove a HUMMER to compensate for a small dick and impotence. 'That's because you don't know me.'

'That's true.' She cocked her head to one side and studied him. 'Can I ask you something?'

'Yeah, but I don't have to answer.'

'That's fair,' she said and crossed her arms beneath her breasts. 'Why do you live in such a huge house when you're not even here that much?'

'I'm here from March to September. Well, when I'm not at the store, anyway.' Which didn't answer her question. Why had he built a big house? He shoved his hip into the counter next to her. 'I guess because I've lived in big houses with pools and Jacuzzis and game rooms for most of my adult life. So, when it came time to build this one, I just went with what I was used to.'

'You have a game room, too?'

'Yeah. It's off the great room,' he said as she scooped up granola with her fingers and ate. 'Maybe we can play pool sometime.'

She brushed her hands together as she swallowed.

'Maybe, but I have to warn you, I don't lose on purpose to anyone.'

'What fun is there in that?'

'I saw you play the other night. I could beat you blindfolded and with one arm tied behind my back.'

'Trash talker,' he said through a smile. 'I'd like to see you try and kick my ass.'

'Oh, I don't know if I'd kick your ass. You're not *that* bad.' She laughed. 'I'd spank you real good, though.'

It was a hell of a deal to have the woman you fantasized about stand in front of you and talk about spanking.

She took another bite of his granola and swallowed. 'Which tends to get me in trouble with men who have fragile egos.' She looked at him through serious brown eyes and said, 'I wanted to tell you that I'm sorry about what I said in the sheriff's Blazer the other night.'

He thought a moment. 'About you thinking I must have been arrested before?'

'No. The erectile dysfunction crack.'

'Ahh . . . *that*.'

'I was kinda joking, but you didn't see the humor, so . . .' She paused, dipped her chin, and looked into his eyes. 'I'm sorry about that. It was insensitive.'

He stared at her for a few moments, then his brows shot up his forehead. 'For the love of Christ.' She really didn't think he could get it up. If she cared to glance down at his button fly, she would see that she was wrong about that.

'Sometimes I think I'm funny and I'm not, and I put my foot in my mouth.'

He grasped her shoulders and pulled her against his chest. His breath left his lungs, and he looked into her startled gaze. He lowered his mouth to hers. He wanted to teach her a lesson. To show her he was a fully functioning man. He tried to go slow. God help him he did, but it had been so long. The instant his lips touched hers, he was gone. Like a match to gasoline, it rushed across his skin and he was consumed with his burning desire for her.

He took advantage of her gasp and swept his tongue inside her warm, wet mouth. A shudder moved down his spine, and his muscles shook. While he wanted to absorb her into his flesh, to eat her up with one bite, she stood completely still within his grasp, neither protesting nor participating. He had to let her go, but just as he was about to end it, her tongue touched his, and there was no stopping him.

Her wet, warm mouth tasted so good. Like honey and sex and everything missing in his life. Her hands moved to his shoulders and her fingers squeezed his muscles through the thin cotton of his shirt. She smelled like flowers and warm woman and all the things he'd been denying himself. He soaked it all in. The taste of her mouth and the warm touch of her hands. The scent of her skin. The desire rushing across his skin spread down his back and between his legs, squeezing his testicles and burning him alive. And he wanted it. He wanted to feel it again. All of it. For the first time in a very long time, he didn't try and control it or shove it away. He let lust grab ahold of his insides even as it pounded the air around him. He shoved his fingers into the sides of her hair and cupped her face. His hands shook as he barely controlled the urge to unbuckle her sweater and fill his palms with her heavy breasts.

Her slick tongue touched his and mated, and he could feel her pulse beating beneath his thumb. Their mouths opened and closed as he fed her kisses. The woman he held in his hands was every bit as turned on as he was.

But he had to stop. He didn't know her well enough to know for certain she wouldn't turn psycho on him. He didn't think she was crazy, but she wasn't worth the risk. No woman was. There was one thing he had to do before he let her go.

He took her hand from his shoulder and slipped it down the front of his chest. The warmth of her touch heated his skin through his T-shirt. His hand pressed hard against the back of hers, flattening her palm against his hard muscles. Then he slid her hand down. Slowly down his sternum and abdomen. And it was torture. Slow torture that was so sweet he ached. He moved her hand lower across his hard belly to the waistband of his jeans.

A rough moan escaped his throat, and he pulled back just far enough to look into her face. His gaze stared into hers, watching her liquid brown eyes as he slid her hand down his button fly and pressed her palm against his erection. He locked his knees to keep from falling. He was extremely hard, and a dull throb pulled at his testicles and tugged at his gut.

'I think that should answer any further questions,' he said, his voice thick with lust.

Kate licked her lips. 'What?'

'I can get it up.' Then he did one of the most difficult things he'd done in a very long time. With his body urging him to throw her down and get medieval, he dropped her hand and stepped back. 'Anything else you want to know?'

She shook her head, and her eyes began to clear.

'No. I don't . . . I . . .' Her cheeks turned a bright red, and she pressed her fingers to her bottom lip, as if it was numb. 'I better . . . go.' She pointed toward the other room. Then she turned and walked from the kitchen. Her boot heels beat a rapid tap-tap on the hardwood floors as she went.

Anger and frustration and regret pulled him in three different directions. One told him she deserved it. The other urged him to jump her bones, while the other told him he'd been an ass and he should chase after her and apologize. He heard the door close, and he shut his eyes and pressed his palm hard against his erection.

Damn.

The sound of her SUV reached him inside the house, and he glanced out the kitchen window as she shot down his driveway, his security lights chasing after her. He was so turned on he felt like he was going to burst. Or smash something with his fists. There had to be more to his life than this. More than living out here alone in his big empty house, dreaming and fantasizing about a woman with red hair and deep brown eyes. This was no way to live.

He took a deep breath and let it out slowly. He was thirty-six. He wanted more.

The telephone rang, and he took a deep breath. He glanced at the Seattle number on the caller ID and picked up the cordless receiver on the fourth ring.

'Hey, Louisa,' he said and walked from the kitchen.

'I thought you were going to call us tonight.'

'It's early.' The hardwood was cool beneath his feet as he moved through the house, past the big stone fireplace, to the windows that looked out onto the lake. 'Where's Amelia?'

'Right here.'

'Put her on.' There was a pause, and his two-year-old daughter got on the line.

'Hello,' she said in her tiny voice that made his chest get tight. She was one of the things that he wanted a lot more of in his life.

'Hey, baby girl. What are you doing?'

'Wiggles.'

'Are you watching your Wiggles show?'

There was lots of breathing, then she said, 'Yeah.'

'Did you have dinner yet?'

'Yeah.'

'What did you eat?'

'I ate noodles.'

He smiled. Noodles were her favorite and could mean she'd had anything from spaghetti to chicken soup. Lord, he missed her, and it was times like this when, for a few brief moments, he thought of selling the store and moving back to Seattle. But ultimately he knew that he could not. He didn't belong there anymore. 'I love you.'

'Love you,' she repeated back to him.

Louisa got back on the telephone. 'Are you still planning on coming to Seattle for Easter?' she asked.

'I'll fly in the prior Wednesday, but I have to be back here the Saturday before.'

'Why? I thought we could shop for Amelia's basket and give it to her Easter morning. I thought we could spend the holiday together as a family.'

There it was. The first tentative thread. Reaching across

the distance to wrap around him. Drawing him in like always. She wanted to reconcile. He still wasn't sure that's what he wanted. He couldn't live in Seattle. She didn't want to live in Gospel. And even if she did, he wasn't even sure Louisa was 'the more' he wanted for his life.

'I have commitments here that Saturday, and it doesn't make sense to turn right around again and head back to Seattle.' The Saturday before Easter, the town was having a parade, and he'd agreed to pull the elementary school's float with his HUMMER. 'Amelia doesn't care if I'm there three days before Easter, on Easter, or three days after. It's all the same to her.'

There was a long pause, and then she said, 'Oh. That's okay, I guess.' Which meant it wasn't okay at all. 'How long did you say you were staying this time?'

'Three days.'

Another long pause. 'Short trip.'

He looked out at the lake and the lights of Gospel. 'I'm teaching some fly-tying classes that start the Monday after Easter,' he explained, although he knew she wouldn't understand. 'But I'll be there for my regular weekend.'

'Perhaps you can stay here with us this time.'

He rested his forehead against the window and closed his eyes. It would be so easy. So easy to take her up on what she offered. He knew her. He knew her mind and body. He knew how she liked to be touched, and she knew just how to touch him. He knew she wouldn't leave two hundred messages on his answering machine and travel hundreds of miles to confront him with a gun.

She was the mother of his child, and it would be easy to lose himself in her, for just one night. But there would be a price. Whether you paid in emotion or flesh, sex was never free. 'I don't think that's a good idea, Lou.'

'Why?' she asked.

Because you'll want more than I can give, he thought. Because the sex was good between us, but everything else was lousy. Because there are worse things than loneliness. 'Let's just leave it alone.' He wasn't any good at relationships. Not with her or anyone else. The scars on his body reminded him of that every day. 'I gotta go,' he said. 'I'll call you next week.'

'I love you, Rob.'

'Love you, too,' he said even though he knew it wasn't the right kind of love. Perhaps it never had been.

He pressed disconnect and straightened. A smudge on the glass caught his attention, and he raised his hand and placed it against Kate's palm print. The print was cool to the touch, unlike the woman who'd left it there.

Kate Hamilton was anything but cold. Everything about her was hot. The look in her eyes after he'd soul-kissed her. Her response to him. Her temper. The way she'd torn out of his house like she was on fire. The next time he saw Kate, he fully expected her to hit him with her white-hot anger.

He probably deserved it. He probably should apologize. Too bad he wasn't sorry.

Kate pulled her CRV into her grandfather's detached garage and cut the engine. The door squeaked as it rolled closed in the old metal track. She stared straight ahead at several boxes sitting on her grandfather's workbench.

Rob Sutter had kissed her, and she was still in shock.

Her hands fell from the steering wheel to her lap. Kiss seemed too mild a word. Consumed. He'd consumed her. Overpowered her resistance.

She touched her fingers to her bottom lip, where it was a little tender from his soul patch. She was thirty-four, and she didn't think she'd ever been kissed like that in her life. One second she'd just been standing there eating granola and talking, and in the next, his mouth had been on hers. One second the air around her had seemed normal, and in the next, it had turned thick with passion and need and lust. It had pressed in on her in hot, beating waves, and all she'd been able to do was grab onto him for dear life.

She'd held onto his big shoulders, and when he'd taken her hand and pushed it down his chest, she hadn't had a thought in her head other than the feel of hard, defined muscles and flat, corded belly. He'd scrambled her brains and sucked out her will to say no. Then he'd pressed her hand against his erection. She should have been appalled. Outraged that a man whom she hardly knew had done that. Right now, sitting in her grandfather's garage, she was outraged, but at the time, the only thought that had slid through her brain was, *I guess he can get it up*. Followed closely by, *Mmm, he's big all over*.

Kate grabbed her keys and reached for her purse. While she'd been melting all over him, he'd only kissed her to make a point. He could definitely get it up. While she'd been all light-headed and brain dead, he'd made a second point. He still didn't want her. Not only did she feel outraged, she felt rejected, too. Again. She hadn't learned her lesson the first time.

Kate walked from the garage, across the side of the yard

and into the house. There was a bowl and spoon in the sink, and Kate dropped her backpack by two empty boxes on the kitchen table. She moved through the living room and took a peek into her grandfather's room. He lay very still beneath a faded patchwork quilt her grandmother had made years ago from scraps of her children's clothes. Above the bed, the shoulders, neck, and head of an antelope her grandfather had shot back in 1979 stuck out of the wall like it was jumping through the Sheetrock. His hands were folded across his chest and he stared up at the ceiling. He looked dead.

Kate rushed to the side of his bed. 'Grandpa!'

He turned his head and looked at her though runny, bloodshot eyes. 'Did you get Rob his flaxseed?'

'Yes.' She stopped by the nightstand and pressed a hand to her beating heart. 'You scared me to death. How are you feeling?'

'Pretty good, now. Grace stopped by.'

'I know, she said she would.' She noticed the Nyquil and aspirin on the stand next to the pussycat alarm clock. Its cute little pussycat eyes winked on the half minute. 'Have you eaten dinner?'

'Grace made me soup.' He looked back up at the ceiling. 'It was pretty good. Homemade chicken noodle. You can tell a good woman by her soup.'

Kate thought it probably took a little bit more than soup. 'Do you need anything?' she asked as she shrugged out of her coat.

'Yes. I need you to do something for me.'

'What?'

'I've got some empty boxes out for you to put some of

your grandmother's things in.' A horrible cough racked his chest, then he added, 'I thought you should take anything you might want.'

This was news. Big news. Kate wondered what had happened to bring it about, but she didn't ask, in case he changed his mind. 'Okay. Anything else?'

'Turn out the light.'

She flipped the switch and moved back into the kitchen. She took the bowl and spoon from the sink and placed them in the dishwasher. As she added soap, she wondered how a nice woman like Grace could have raised a man like Rob. How a 'good woman' who made a sick old man soup could raise a man who just grabbed unsuspecting women and kissed the breath right out of them. A man who could kiss like that, get that turned on, and not try and take things further. That wasn't natural.

She started the dishwasher and glanced about the kitchen. She didn't know where to start. What was she going to do with a house full of Tom Jones stuff? Rent a shed and store it the rest of her life?

Her gaze fell on the set of Tom decorative plates held in a rack by the table, and her thoughts returned to the kiss Rob had planted on her. What kind of man grabbed a woman's hand and shoved it on his erection? She got a stack of newspapers by the back door and set them on the table. Unfortunately she knew the answer to her last question. The kind of man who wanted to prove he didn't have a problem getting it up. In the calmer part of her brain, she could even kind of, sort of, understand why he'd done it. But what she didn't understand was what kind of man got that hard and pushed a woman away? She'd never known a man that sexually turned-on who didn't think she should drop to her knees and do something about it.

Whatever his reason, it didn't matter. She should have been the one to stop things before they'd gotten to that point. She should have been the one to step back. The one in control. He should have been the one left dazed and mortified.

She told herself that at some point she would have stopped him. That before their clothes hit the ground, she would have grabbed her bag and gone home. That's what she told herself. Problem was, she wasn't all that convincing. Not even to herself.

Kate wrapped a plate in paper and set it in the box. Rob Sutter was a cheater and a bad emotional risk. He was rarely nice, and most often a jerk, which explained her inexplicable attraction to him.

He'd humiliated her twice now. Two times he'd left her embarrassed by her own behavior and stunned by his rejection. That was two times too many.

There couldn't and wouldn't be a third.

Stanley read over his poem one last time. It had taken him three days to write it, crossing out one word, substituting another, and he still wasn't sure he'd expressed himself right. The poem ended with the word *reimburse*, which was, admittedly, stupid.

He knew Grace liked poetry, and he wanted to tell her how much he appreciated her looking in on him. He wanted to tell her he thought she was a good nurse, but he hadn't been able to think up a good word to rhyme with *nurse – hearse* and *purse* just didn't do it.

He folded the poem and placed it in an envelope. He'd been out of commission with the bad chest cold for four days, and Grace had stopped by every morning before work and every night after just to check up on him. She'd taken his pulse and listened to his lungs. She talked about Rob and he talked about Katie. She always left him soup. She was a good woman.

He placed a stamp in the corner, then glanced out of the office. Katie was in front with the Frito-Lay salesman, probably getting suckered into stocking the 'Natural and Organic' products, which was a bunch of hokum as far as Stanley was concerned.

He hurriedly wrote Grace's address and stuck the envelope under a stack of outgoing mail. A pile of pamphlets sat on his desk, and he opened a drawer and dumped them inside. He knew his granddaughter wanted him to think about upgrading his cash register and book-keeping system. He wasn't interested. He was seventy-one and too old to change the way he'd been doing business for more than forty years. If his wife hadn't died, he'd be retired by now, spending his retirement fund on travel or some other type of recreation, not on some integrated accounting system.

Stanley placed a hand on top of his desk and rose to his feet. He'd come back to work to discover that Katie had rearranged a few things. Nothing big, just rearranged some of the merchandise. He wasn't quite sure why the over-the-counter medications had to be kept down below the prophylactics on aisle five. *And* she'd removed the live bait he'd kept by the milk in the reach-in cooler. For some reason, she'd put it next to the discounted meats. He knew she'd ordered some gourmet jelly and olives. He supposed he didn't mind, since it meant she was getting more involved in the store, but he didn't think gourmet items would sell in Gospel.

He placed a rubber band around the outgoing mail, and when Orville Tucker came in his mail truck, Stanley handed it over before he could change his mind. He wondered what Grace would think of his poem. He popped a few Tums and told himself it didn't matter. He'd tried his best, but Grace was a really good poet, and he was just an amateur. He cut meat for a living. What made him think he could write a poem?

He spent the rest of the day worrying about what Grace would think. By that night, he was in such agony that he wished like hell he could break into the post office on Blaine Street and steal the poem back. But the post office was one of the few businesses in town that had an alarm system. He wished he'd never sent it. He knew that if he didn't hear from Grace, it meant she probably hated it.

The next day Grace called him and told him she loved it. She said she was flattered and that the poem had spoken to her heart. Her praise spoke to Stanley's heart in a way he'd never expected. It reminded him that his heart was good for something more than pumping blood, and when she invited him and Katie to dinner at her house the next night, he accepted for both of them. Katie was always nagging him about getting out of the house more. He was sure she wouldn't mind.

'You what?'

'I accepted a dinner invitation to Grace Sutter's for the both of us.'

'When?' The last thing Kate wanted was to be stuck at a dinner table with Rob Sutter. She hadn't seen him since the night he'd kissed her. That wasn't quite right. She'd *seen* him. He worked across the parking lot, but he hadn't come in the store for five days. And every time she'd seen him, she'd gotten an odd little bubble in her chest. Kind of like nerves, but not the good kind.

'She called about half an hour ago.'

'That isn't what I meant.' Kate paused as Iona Osborn labored to the counter, her quad cane making a *ka-chink-thud* across the hardwood floors.

'How much are these?' Iona asked and set a bag of Doritos next to the cash register.

Kate pointed to the price clearly marked on the bag. 'Four nineteen.'

'It always had a sticker before.'

Kate took in Iona's blue eyes, chubby jowls, and mile-high gray hair and forced a smile in place. Iona wasn't the first person to give her grief over the sticker issue. She wondered if there was a conspiracy to drive her insane. She took a deep breath and explained yet again, 'Items clearly marked from the manufacturer don't need a sticker.'

'I like having a sticker.'

Kate held her hands palms up, then dropped them to her sides. 'But the stickers were always the same as the clearly marked price.'

'There's always been stickers on stuff.'

Kate was giving serious thought to smacking a sticker on Iona's forehead when her grandfather interceded. 'How's that hip?' he asked.

'I'm a little stoved-up. Thank you for asking.' Iona's leather purse hit the counter with a heavy thunk.

'Have you thought about getting one of those power chairs like they advertise on TV?' Stanley asked as he rang up her Doritos.

Iona shook her head and dug into her bag. 'I don't have

that kind of money, and my insurance won't pay for it.' She pulled out a wallet so full of cash and coupons that it had to be held closed with a rubber band. 'Besides, I can't sit in one of those while I work all day at the diner.' She searched all her coupons, then pulled out five one-dollar bills and laid them on the counter. 'Would be nice though, if you provided one of those chairs for seniors like they do at that ShopKo down in Boise.'

'That's certainly something to think about,' Stanley said as he took the money and made change. 'How much do one of those things cost?'

Kate glanced at her grandfather as she placed the Doritos in a plastic bag. He couldn't be serious.

'About fifteen hundred.'

'That's not too bad, then.'

He *was* serious. He wouldn't spend a dime to upgrade his bookkeeping system in order to make his life easier, but he'd blow fifteen hundred on a power chair that the kids in town would jump on and race around the store. 'I don't understand you,' she said as soon as Iona left. 'You won't make your life easier, but you'll buy a power chair for the occasional customer. That doesn't make sense to me.'

'That's because you're young and your bones don't ache when you get out of bed in the morning. You don't have trouble getting around. If you did, you might think differently.'

That was probably true, so she let it go. For now. 'When is Grace's dinner?'

'Tomorrow night.'

Now the tricky question. 'Is Rob going to be there?' Kate asked as if she didn't care one way or the other. But the reality was that if the answer was yes, she'd have to come down with cramps or something.

'Grace didn't say. I could ask her.'

'No. I was just wondering. It's not important,' she said as she grabbed the feather duster and headed toward the canned vegetables and fruits aisle. If Rob was going to be there, she'd have to suck it up and pretend he didn't bother her. That the kiss he'd given her hadn't affected her at all, which of course it hadn't. Sure, she'd felt little warm tingles, but that didn't mean anything. Lots of things gave her warm tingles. She couldn't think of any at the moment, but she would.

The jars of olives and jalapeño jelly she'd ordered had arrived the day before, and she placed them at eye level on the shelves. No one had purchased any of her gourmet items, but it had only been one day. Maybe she should take an hors d'oeuvre plate to Grace's dinner. If Grace liked the hors d'oeuvre, she might talk them up. Word of mouth was important to sales.

She wondered what Grace was serving, and if her house was as enormous as her son's.

It wasn't.

The second Kate walked into Grace Sutter's home, she could tell a woman lived there by herself. The furnishings were comfy and cozy and soft. Lots of pastel colors and white wicker. Belgian lace, cut crystal, and fresh flowers. Very unlike her grandfather's house, and completely opposite her son's. The home was filled with the smell of roast beef and baking potatoes.

Grace greeted them at the door wearing black pants

and a red sweater set. Kate felt underdressed in a jean skirt and her long-sleeve Banana Republic silk T-shirt. She handed Grace the hors d'oeuvre plate she'd made, and her gaze scanned the living room.

No Rob. She felt her shoulders relax and the tension in her back loosen. She wished she didn't care one way or the other, but for some reason he made her uptight and nervous. And again, not in a good way.

'Thank you, Kate,' Grace said as she took the plate from her. 'This was so thoughtful of you.'

Kate pointed to each section of the plate. 'Those are Italian olives, and I stuffed those mushrooms.' Grace set the plate on a coffee table. 'That's jalapeño jelly,' Kate continued, 'over cream cheese. You spread it on the wafers. It's wonderful.'

'I'm going to take your word on that jelly,' her grandfather said as he popped an olive in his mouth.

Grace picked up the Delilah cheese knife and spread some of the cream cheese and jalapeño jelly on a cracker. She took a bite and chewed thoughtfully. 'That's quite good,' she announced.

Kate smiled and looked at her grandfather.

'Thank you.'

'I still don't think it's right for people to make vegetable jelly,' Stanley maintained and refused to even try it. He'd dressed for the dinner party in his gray permanent press pants, a blue dress shirt, and a gray sweater. Which was quite dressed up for him. Kate wasn't certain, but she thought her grandfather was acting kind of nervous. He kept folding and unfolding his arms and twisting the tip of his handlebar mustache. And he was wearing so much Brut that she'd practically had to ride all the way over with her head sticking out the car window like an Irish setter.

Grace showed them her collection of Swarovski crystal, and she gave Stanley three crystal penguins on a chunk of crystal ice to hold up to the light. The two of them looked at the prism of color spilling across Stanley's old, gnarled palm, and then they looked at each other. For one brief moment their eyes held before he lowered his hand, as well as his gaze. His cheek turned a slight pink, and he cleared his throat.

Her grandfather liked Grace. More than just a friend. More than he liked the other widows in town. When had that happened?

Kate snagged a few olives, then she moved to the shelves filled with photos. What did she think about her grandfather dating Rob's mother? She'd always thought she'd be happy that he was moving on with his life. Living again. Was she? She honestly didn't know.

The photographs on the shelves were three and four deep, and in the front sat a picture of a naked baby on a white lambskin. Another was faded and yellow, of the same baby sitting on a man's lap, whom Kate assumed was Rob's father. She popped an olive in her mouth and looked at Rob in a grade school photo, his hair in a crew cut, with a mischievous glint in his green eyes. A prom picture of him in a powder blue tux and his date in silver lamé with enormous shoulder pads up to her ears. This time his hair was in some sort of spiked Duran Duran do with long bangs. But most of the photos of Rob were taken of him in different hockey jerseys.

In quite a few of the pictures, he was so young that his

hockey jersey hung over his hands. In all of them his big green eyes were bright with excitement. There were action photos of him taking a shot or skating with the puck at the end of his stick. Others with his helmet low on his forehead, this time his eyes menacing as he delivered hits to opposing players. A magazine cover of him with his arms in the air, holding a stick over his head, his smile enormous. Testosterone practically oozed from the Kodak paper, a startling contrast to the lace curtains and pink wicker sofa.

Kate reached for a more recent photograph of Rob. He held a naked baby to his chest, his lips pressed to the top of her dark head. His daughter's delicate features against his raw masculinity.

The front door opened and Kate replaced the photo. She turned as Rob walked in and shut the door behind him. He wore a long-sleeved dress shirt, white, tucked into a pair of khakis with a razor crease. He carried a bottle of wine in one hand. The last time she'd been in the same room with him, he'd kissed her and put her hand on his crotch. She felt a wary little jump in her nerves, which disturbed her since she thought she should feel a lot more angry and indignant than she actually did.

Grace moved across the room toward him. 'You're late.'

'Store closed late.' Rob gave his mother a hug. 'Hello, Stanley,' he said, then he looked over the top of his mother's head, and his green gaze met Kate's. 'Hello, Kate.'

'Hello,' she said, and she was pleased that her voice did not reflect the spike in her nerves.

'Dinner will be ready soon.' Grace took the bottle of wine and looked at it. 'I told you to get a Merlot. This is a Chardonnay.'

He shrugged. 'You know I'm a beer drinker. I don't know squat about wine. I just bought the most expensive, figuring it had to be the best.'

Grace shoved it back at him. 'Take it in the kitchen and open it. Maybe Kate can show you how to use a corkscrew.'

She could, but she didn't want to. 'Sure.' She followed Rob through the dining room, her gaze skimming down the pleat in the back of his white shirt to where it tucked into his tailored pants. The khaki fabric hugged his behind, and two brown buttons closed the back pockets. The pant legs fell in perfect, straight lines to the hem, breaking at the heels of his soft leather loafers. He might not know wine, but he did know a thing or two about expensive clothes.

He set the bottle on the white countertop and opened a drawer. 'The glasses are in the cupboard above the refrigerator,' he said and pointed with the corkscrew.

The kitchen was as feminine as the rest of the house. The walls were peach, with tulip-and-white-rose-wallpaper borders. With his wide shoulders and height, Rob looked a little out of place in the ultrafeminine surroundings. A lot like a bull in a china shop.

Kate opened the cupboard doors and reached inside to grab four glasses. An extremely good-looking, well-groomed bull who seemed perfectly at ease. 'I think my grandfather likes your mother,' she said as she set the glasses on the counter next to Rob's hip. 'I think they're becoming friends.'

'Good, my mother likes your grandfather.' He held the bottle in one big hand and twisted the corkscrew with the other. 'I can't remember her ever inviting a man over for dinner.' With little effort, he pulled the cork out with a pop and poured Chardonnay into the first glass. 'Of course, my mother and I haven't lived in the same town until recently. So she could have had lots of men in her life and just never told me.' He filled a second glass, then handed it to Kate.

'When did you leave home?' she asked and took it from him. His fingers touched hers, warm against the cool glass.

'I got drafted into the NHL when I was nineteen.' He pulled his hand away and reached for his own glass. 'Between you and me,' he said and raised it to his mouth, 'I know what a Merlot is, but I like white wine better.'

'You lied to your mother.'

'It wouldn't be the first time.' He smiled like an unrepentant sinner, and she felt herself relax a little. 'Or even the second. I guess old habits die hard.' He took a drink and watched her over his glass.

She felt the corners of her mouth tilt up despite her best effort not to smile at him. 'You should be ashamed of yourself,' she said and took a sip of her wine.

He lowered his glass. 'I'll bet you've told a whopper or two.'

'Sure.' She folded her arms beneath her breasts and swirled the wine in her glass. 'I used to tell huge lies all the time. My dad was in the military, and we moved around a lot. When you go to a new school every few years, you can make up your past. You can be anybody you want.'

'Who did you say you were?'

'Mostly head cheerleaders and class presidents. Once I said I was a prima ballerina.'

He shoved a hip into the counter and stuck his free hand in his front pocket. 'How did that work for you?'

'It didn't. No one ever believed it. I have three older brothers, and I was a tomboy. Plus, I was a complete klutz.'

'I bet you were a cute klutz.' His gaze slid from her eyes to her mouth, then moved up to the top of her head. 'I bet with that red hair, the boys loved you.'

He had to be joking. 'Believe me, no one liked my red hair. Plus, I was taller than most boys my age, I had braces and I beat most of them at basketball, I could have let them win, but I'm fairly competitive and don't like to lose.'

He chuckled. 'Yes, I know that about you.'

'Not only did I beat the boys, if I had a crush on one, I slugged him really hard. Believe me, no one ever asked me out.'

'I bet they're kicking themselves in the ass now.'

She looked into his face. Thin smile lines creased the corners of his green eyes, but he didn't look like he was joking. For some reason, that made the old unattractive gangly girl part of her heart pinch just a little. It was an uncomfortable and confusing feeling, and she raised her wine to her lips. She didn't want to feel anything for Rob. Nothing but a big empty blank. 'I wouldn't know,' she said before she took a drink.

Grace and her grandfather entered the kitchen, and Kate got busy helping Grace with the rib roast and baked potatoes. Rob dressed a salad with Italian vinaigrette and placed it in four bowls.

'What can I do to help?' her grandfather asked.

'You can place Kate's hors d'oeuvre plate on the table,' Grace answered. 'I would hate to see it go to waste.'

Five minutes later, the food was on their plates and they were all seated at a pedestal table set with white damask and bone china. Kate sat between Grace and Rob, with her grandfather across from her.

'This is all mighty fancy, Grace,' Stanley said as he picked up his linen napkin and placed it in his lap. His shoulders looked stiff, like he was afraid to breathe.

Grace smiled. 'I don't ever get to use my good stuff. It just sits in the hutch year in and year out. Let's mess it up.' She shook out her napkin.

Rob picked up his fork and speared a stuffed mushroom from the hors d'oeuvre plate in the center of the table.

'Rob,' his mother said, 'could you say the blessing, please?'

He looked up and stared at her, as if she'd just asked him to stand on his head and speak French. 'You want me to pray?' He set his fork down. 'Right now?'

Grace's smile stayed in place while she gave him a hard stare. 'Of course, dear.'

Rob bowed his head, and his brows came together to form a thick line. Kate half expected him to say something like, 'Good food, good meat, good God, let's eat.'

He didn't. 'God, please bless this food we're about to eat.' He paused a moment then added, 'So that we don't get sick or . . . choke or something. Amen.'

'Amen.' Kate pressed her lips together to keep from laughing.

'Amen.'

'Amen. Thank you, Rob.'

'You're welcome, Mother.' He grabbed his fork and ate the mushroom in two bites. He stabbed a few more and put them on his plate next to his potato, which was piled high with butter and sour cream. 'You brought these?'

'Yes.'

'They're good,' he said and reached for a dinner roll.

'Thank you.' She took a bite of her plain potato, sans everything but salt and pepper.

'How're things going for you at the store, Kate?' Grace asked.

Before she could utter a word, her grandfather answered for her, 'Katie's not a people person.'

Rob made a sound next to her like he was choking on his wine. Kate ignored him and looked across the table at her grandfather. *What?* She was a people person.

'Perhaps your talents lie elsewhere.' Grace refolded the napkin on her lap. 'Stanley told me that you used to work in Las Vegas as a private investigator.'

She'd always been good with people. Her people skills were what had made her a good private investigator. 'Yes, I was.' She turned her gaze to Rob, who was trying not to laugh. He obviously didn't think she was a people person either.

'Well, I think it's admirable that you left all that behind to help out your grandfather.'

Kate returned her attention to her grandfather. *I'm not a people person? When did that happen?* Probably about the time she'd been dumped by her last boyfriend and a psychopath had hired her to hunt down his family. 'Actually, my grandfather is helping me out. When I decided that I didn't want to do investigative work anymore, I quit my job, and he's let me move in with him until I figure out what I do want to do.'

'And I'm glad to have her,' her grandfather said with a smile, but she wasn't so sure he meant it.

She really hadn't figured anything out. She'd been in Gospel going on two months, and she was just as rudderless as the day she'd arrived. As she cut into her prime rib and took a bite, the conversation went on without her. Lately, she'd begun to feel as if the thing she was looking for was right in front of her eyes, but she couldn't see it. Maybe, if she got out of her own way, she could see the forest for the trees.

'So, it sounds like you got in some skiing before the resort closed. That's good,' Stanley said, pulling Kate's attention from her thoughts. She glanced at her grandfather, whose gaze was directed at Rob. How had the conversation turned from the M&S to skiing in Sun Valley? Kate's least favorite subject.

'Yes. The trip I took in February was great. Lots of powder. Perfect weather. Cute lodge bunnies.'

Under the table, his knee touched Kate's. She looked at him out of the corners of her eyes, but he was looking at her grandfather. 'One of them had a very interesting tattoo.'

'Robert.' Grace leaned forward and stared at her son. 'You know you have to stay away from bunnies of any kind. They're trouble.'

He laughed. 'In more ways than one,' he said, then dug into his baked potato.

Grace gave her son one last withering glance and turned her attention to Kate. 'Do you ski, Kate?'

'No. I never learned.'

'If you're here next winter, Rob can teach you.'

She seriously doubted she would be in Gospel next fall, let alone next winter. 'Oh, I don't think—'

'I'd love to,' Rob interrupted, and his thigh pressed into hers again.

Warmth from his touch seeped through her skirt and heated up the outside of her thigh. She turned her head and looked at him as he popped an olive into his mouth. 'No, really. I'd break my neck.'

He glanced at her lips and swallowed. 'I'd take good care of you, Kate. We'll start off nice and easy.' A wicked little glint shone through his eyes as he raised his gaze to hers. 'Real slow, then work up to something hard.'

Kate waited for his mother to call him 'Robert' and scold him for his obvious sexual innuendo. She didn't. 'Starting slow is so important,' Grace said instead. Then she played right into his hands. 'And good equipment.'

'Can't have a good time without good equipment.' Rob reached for his wine, but kept his gaze on Kate. 'Maybe I'll show you mine sometime.'

'Good equipment is important no matter what you do in life,' her grandfather joined in, as oblivious as Grace. 'I buy the best saws and knives money can buy. And you have to make sure your equipment is always in good working order.'

A side of Rob's mouth turned up, lifting one corner of his Fu Manchu. 'Amen.'

Kate crossed her legs and removed his touch from her knee. 'Did you know that Americans consume seventy-six billion pounds of red meat and poultry a year?' she asked, purposely changing the subject.

'Well, isn't that interesting?' Grace said.

Rob raised his wine to his lips. 'Fascinating.'

'I don't know about all that, but I do know this is the

best meal I've had in a long time,' Stanley complimented the cook.

What? Kate cooked for him all the time. She was a good cook *and* a people person.

'Thank you, Stanley. I know a very good butcher.' Grace took a bite, then spoke the words that struck terror in Kate's heart. 'I thought that after dinner, I'd read everyone my newest poems.'

'I'd love to hear them,' her grandfather said. And Kate felt like kicking him under the table. She glanced at Rob, whose fork was paused in midair. He looked like a deer in a spotlight.

'I wish I could stay,' he said at last and placed his fork on his plate. 'But I have too much work to do.'

Grace smiled. 'I understand.'

Since it had worked for Rob, Kate gave it a try. 'Yeah, I have some work to do, too.'

'Like what?' her grandfather wanted to know.

Crap! 'Like . . . making stuff.'

'What stuff?'

'Stuff . . . for the store.'

'What stuff?'

She glanced around the room, and her gaze landed on a basket of dinner rolls. 'Bread.' Her answer sounded so lame that she doubted anyone would believe it.

'Oh.' Stanley nodded. 'Your grandmother used to bake bread and sell it in the store.'

'I remember that,' Grace said through a genuine smile. 'Melba always made the best bread.'

'Well, I guess Katie and I can't stay and hear your poetry tonight.'

Grace's smile fell. 'Oh, that's too bad.'

Shame weighted Kate's shoulders, and she was just about to say she'd stay when Rob took the matter into his hands.

'I'll take Kate home,' he volunteered, and Kate didn't know which would be worse: staying for a poetry reading or riding alone in a car with Rob Sutter.

Riding alone in Rob's HUMMER was worse. The vehicle was huge, and yet he seemed to take up so much space – and not physically, although he was a big guy. It was the deep texture of his voice filling the shadows as he answered her questions about his vehicle. It was the smell of his skin and the starch in his shirt mixed with the scent of leather seats. The lights from the dash lit up the dark interior with so many digital displays that she wouldn't even guess what half of them were for. According to Rob, the HUMMER had heated seats, a Bose stereo, and a navigation system. If that wasn't enough, it also had OnStar.

'Do you know how to use that thing?' she asked and pointed to the blue navigation screen.

'Sure.' He took one hand from the wheel, pushed a few buttons, and the city display of Gospel popped up. As if a person could get lost in Gospel.

'Do you need it to find your way home?' He chuckled and glanced across the vehicle at her, one side of his face washed in blue light. 'No, but it comes in handy when I travel to places I've never been before. I used it a lot this past February when I went skiing with my buddies.' He turned his gaze back to the road, 'I've been meaning to ask you something.'

'What?'

'Do you really have a tattoo on your butt?'

Her fingers on the hors d'oeuvre plate in her lap tightened. 'You need to forget that night ever happened.'

His quiet laughter filled the space between them. 'Right.'

'I know you probably won't believe this, and it's a waste of breath, but that was the one and only time I've ever propositioned a man. I always wanted to pick up a boy toy in a bar, but I'm too inhibited. I'm sexually repressed.'

'You weren't inhibited or repressed that night.'

'I was drunk.'

He made a scoffing sound that made Kate want to hit him. 'You weren't that drunk. You had a nice buzz going, but you knew exactly what you were doing.'

True, but there was no way she was going to admit it. 'I just wanted to live out a fantasy for one night. One night, that's it. Is that so horrible?' The collar of her peacoat brushed her chin as she looked out the passenger's window at the dark silhouette of pine trees. 'All I wanted was to pick up a man and use him bad. Twist him into a sexual pretzel, then kick him out the door when I was through and never see him again. But look what happened.' She'd been turned down flat, then given a moral lecture a few weeks later. 'Why are women considered promiscuous when we take charge of our own sexuality? Why is society threatened by strong women who go after what they want? Men proposition women in bars all the time, and they're just being men when they do it.'

She turned her gaze to the front. The head beams lit up the road, and she paused a moment to think about the injustice of it all. 'Why is it different for women? We have control over our own fertility, but we still must conform to some archaic moral code. Even in the twenty-first century, women can't be as sexually aggressive as men. If we are, we're sluts. Why is it so wrong for women to admit that we think about sex like men do?'

Rant over, Kate sighed and leaned her head back against the seat. Silence filled the vehicle for several long moments, and she began to think he hadn't been listening.

He had. 'You planned to twist me into a sexual pretzel?'

'Yeah,' she said through a sigh. 'But we both know how it turned out. You ran away as fast as you could.'

'I didn't run.'

'Practically.'

He reached for the navigation system again, pushed a few buttons, fiddled with the stereo, then shut it off. He glanced over at her, and his brows were drawn together as if he were hard at work thinking about something important. He returned his attention to the road, and when he spoke, his voice was a little lower than before. 'How were you going to twist me into a sexual pretzel?'

'Forget it.'

'Will you tell me if I beg?'

'No.'

'I'll pay you.'

'No. You already think I'm a slut.'

He glanced at her then back at the road. 'I don't think you're a slut.'

'Yes, you do. You grabbed my hand and shoved it on your crotch. That pretty much says to me that you think I'm a slut.'

The lights from the dash accented the outline of his mustache and the scowl turning down the corners of his mouth. 'I shouldn't have grabbed your hand.'

'No,' she said. 'You shouldn't have.'

'I was provoked.'

Maybe.

Again he was silent for a few seconds. 'Do you really believe women can think like men when it comes to sex?'

'Yes,' she answered, although she'd never had the opportunity to try. The guy across the HUMMER had killed her only chance.

'You think women can just have a good time and that's enough?'

'Yes.' At least in theory. 'Don't you?'

'I used to, but I'm not so sure anymore.'

They entered town and drove past the big red Texaco sign. 'Why not?' she asked, although she figured she knew the answer.

'Sex can make women psycho,' he said.

'That's ridiculous.' Yep, that was pretty much the answer she'd thought he'd give. 'Sex doesn't make a person psycho. They're psychotic before the sex.'

'Yeah, but you can't tell by looking. A woman can look

perfectly normal until she shows up at your house with crazy eyes and a .22 Beretta.'

'Psycho men can look perfectly normal, too,' she said, thinking of how normal Randy Meyers had looked the day he'd walked into her office.

'Yeah, but a man is less likely to freak after a one-nighter when he doesn't get hearts and flowers and a marriage proposal.' They drove past the courthouse and Hansen's Emporium. 'But you give a woman some good sex, and she's more likely to go postal.'

Which was patently absurd. 'Are you saying that if the sex is *bad*, a woman won't go all postal?'

He glanced at her as if she'd asked the obvious. 'Why would anyone stalk a lousy lay?' He turned onto her grandfather's street. 'Do you like to flyfish?'

'What?' How had the conversation turned from psycho women to fishing?

'Fly-fishing. Do you like it?'

'Ah . . . I don't know. I've never been fly-fishing.'

He pulled the HUMMER into Stanley's driveway and parked behind Kate's Honda. 'I'll take you sometime. It'll be good for your nerves.'

'My nerves are fine,' she said and grabbed the door handle. 'Thanks for the ride.'

He reached across and grasped her arm. 'Hang on.' When she looked at him, he added, 'I'll get your door.'

'I can get it myself.'

'I know you can,' he said and was halfway out of the HUMMER. The grill lights were as big and obnoxious as the rest of the vehicle, and for a few brief moments they lit him up like he was on stage. He opened her door and took the hors d'oeuvre plate from her. His hand once again grasped her arm as he helped her out, which was ridiculous, because she was perfectly capable of getting out of a car by herself.

'We should start over.' His palm slid to her elbow then dropped to his side.

But, she did have to admit, there was a part of her that liked the old-fashioned male attention. 'Start over? You mean forget the night we met?'

'That's not going to happen.' He followed close behind as she moved up the dark sidewalk, the soles of his loafers drowned out by the sound of her boot heels. 'Maybe we can be friends.'

Wow, that's a first, she thought as she stopped beneath the porch light and took the plate from him. She usually heard those words right before she was dumped, and Rob wasn't even her boyfriend. 'Have you ever had a friend who was a girl?' she asked and hunched her shoulders as the cold night air seeped down the front of her coat.

'No. Have you ever had a guy for a friend?'

'No.' Porch light made the white of his shirt almost fluorescent, while the edges of night outlined him in black. He towered over her and managed to make her, a woman of five eleven with size ten feet, feel small. 'Do you honestly think we can be friends?'

'I have my doubts, but if my mother and your grandfather are going to be friends, we're probably going to be seeing more of each other.'

She was freezing her behind off, while the cold didn't seem to affect him. 'Probably.' Maybe the cold didn't affect him because he ate so much. She'd never seen anyone eat as much as Rob had tonight. The man should be fat, but he wasn't. The night he'd kissed her she'd felt his chest muscles and hard, flat stomach. He had to do a couple hundred sit-ups a day.

'It would be nice if you weren't always pissed off at me,' he said.

She reached into her pocket with one hand in search of her keys. 'I'm not *always* pissed off at you.' Her pocket was empty and she remembered that no one in Gospel locked the doors to their cars or houses. 'But you keep bringing up that night in Sun Valley. Obviously it doesn't hold the same pleasant memories for me that it seems to hold for you.'

He rocked back on his heels and looked down at her. 'How about I don't mention that night, and you don't walk around mad.'

She opened the door behind her. She had her doubts whether he could control himself. 'We can both try.'

'Should we shake on it?'

She held onto the plate with one hand and stuck out the other. His palm pressed into hers, calloused and so warm that her wrist tingled. She tried to pull her hand from his, but his grasp tightened.

'I guess this means I never get to hear about the sexual pretzel.'

She tried not to smile. 'No.'

'Damn.' His thumb brushed across the heel of her hand, back and forth, scattering the hot tingles in her wrist.

'Good night.' This time when she pulled her hand away, he let her go.

'Good night, Kate.'

She moved into the house and shut the door behind

her. She felt a little flushed and a frown pulled her brows even as the hot tingles settled in her stomach.

She didn't really believe she and Rob could be anything that even closely resembled friends. For some reason that defied logic but probably had a lot to do with anthropology and absolutely nothing to do with common sense, her body reacted to his. It was natural. In her DNA. Programed into females since prehistoric times, and Rob Sutter happened to be the biggest, baddest Neanderthal in the cave.

Kate set the hors d'oeuvre plate on the counter, then hung her coat by the back door. She didn't want to get a club to the head. She'd been there and done that with other men who couldn't make a commitment to one woman. There was no doubt in her mind that if she was foolish enough to get involved with Rob, he'd leave her battered like a baby seal.

She removed the plastic wrap from the tray and threw it in the garbage beneath the sink. Not only was he a bad bet, he believed sex could 'make women psycho,' which was ridiculous on so many different levels. One of which was the fact that men were much more likely to kill their coworkers, sniper cars on freeways, and wipe out their entire families. The only thing she did agree with Rob on was that you couldn't tell a psycho by looking.

Reaching into a cabinet, she pulled out a few plastic containers with snap-on lids. Almost a year later, she could still recall the absolute average-Joe looks of Randy Meyers the day he'd walked into her office at Intel Inc. She remembered the family portrait he'd brought in with him. The light blue muted background, contrasting with matching red sweaters. Doreen sat frozen in time with a pleasant smile on her lips. Her children on each side of her – Brandon with his short blond crew cut and Emily with her blonde ponytail and missing front tooth. Randy stood behind his family, his hands on his wife's shoulders while a normal smile curved his mouth.

On the surface, the perfect family. But if Kate had bothered digging, she would have found out that normalness was a carefully constructed facade. She would have discovered that Randy had exerted a systematic control over every facet in the lives of his family.

He hadn't physically abused his wife, but he'd ruled her life just the same. He hadn't isolated her from her friends and family, but he'd alienated her from them. He'd made sure he was invited and included in every aspect of Doreen's life. He hadn't allowed her to work outside the home, but he had allowed her to attend college classes. The catch was that he took them with her. He'd been his daughter's soccer coach. His son's Cub Scout leader. He was always there. Always directing. Always watching.

When Doreen left, he couldn't accept the fact that he was no longer the center of their lives. He'd driven for two days straight to find them. Then he'd perpetrated his last act of control. He'd made sure they were all together. Under the same headstone in a Tennessee graveyard.

No matter how many times Kate told herself that she wasn't responsible for what an insane freak had done to his family, she could not separate herself from her part in it. She felt the weight of their deaths in her soul, and she could not completely wash the blood from her hands.

She didn't know if she would ever get over what had happened in that small house in Tennessee, but she was going to try. She was going to get on with her life. She was going to help her grandfather get on with his, too.

She placed the olives in a container and snapped on the lid. For her grandfather's sake, she would try to be friends with Rob. If he really did have feelings for Grace, Kate didn't want to cause friction. Because despite what her grandfather thought, she was a 'people person.'

Damn it.

Kate went into work early the next morning and shifted through bread recipes her grandmother had kept in a recipe box at the M&S. Kate would have loved to bake focaccia bread, but the store didn't carry fresh cake yeast. She settled on cracked wheat bread and got busy. When her grandfather arrived to open the store at six-thirty, she was just taking the loaves out of the big ovens.

'That smells wonderful, Katie.' He hung his coat and knit cap next to the back door. He rubbed a hand over his bald head.

'You got home late last night,' she said as she sliced off a hunk for him and spread it with butter.

'Grace read me a few of her poems and then was kind enough to give me some pointers.' He took the bread from her and bit into it. She didn't know if it was the chill clinging to his cheeks, but they were definitely pink.

She moved to a cabinet and reached for bread bags on the top shelf. 'You're writing poetry now?'

'Poetry feeds the soul of mankind.'

She dropped on her heels and slowly turned toward him. The man in front of her looked like Stanley Caldwell. He stood there eating his bread, getting butter on his mustache, and he had the same white pants and shirt her grandfather always wore. Same apron he tied in place before he left the house every morning. But he didn't *sound* like her grandfather. 'Did Grace say that?'

He nodded and took his bread out into the store. A few moments later, she heard him starting the coffee machines. *He has it bad*, she thought as she shoved the bread in clear bags and closed them with twist ties. He was moving on. Starting to live again. She was glad. Really.

She got out the sticker gun and marked each loaf. Yeah, she was happy for him, but at the same time, a tiny part of her wondered when she was going to get her life together enough to move on. He was seventy-one. If he could do it, she certainly could too.

She dragged out a card table and set it at the corner of the bread aisle. She draped it with a green-and-white-striped cloth and set her ten loaves of bread on it.

Eden Hansen, owner of Hansen's Emporium, was the first to bite.

'A dollar seventy-five is a lot to pay for a loaf of bread,' she complained. 'Melba used to sell her loaves for a dollar.'

'That was several years ago,' Kate explained, purposely keeping her gaze locked with Eden's so she wouldn't get distracted by her pile of lavender hair. 'With inflation, the cost of utilities, and my labor, you're getting a bargain, Mrs Hansen.'

She pursed her purple lips. 'How do I know it tastes as good as Melba's?'

'I used my grandmother's recipe,' she said, determined to be pleasant even if it killed her.

'I don't know.'

'Wait one minute.' Kate held up a finger, then went into the back room and carved off a slice from the loaf she'd cut into earlier. She quartered it, then brought it out on a small paper plate for Eden. 'Try it.'

Eden chewed. 'Will you take a dollar fifty?'

'Sure, but only if I get to come into your store and haggle over the price of T-shirts and Cow Pie candy.'

Eden tipped back her head and laughed, or what might have been a laugh if it hadn't turned into smoker's hack.

See, she told herself and smiled. *I'm a people person.*

'Everyone says you're stiff as a dead dog in January,' she said when she quit coughing. 'But I think you're all right. I'll take your bread for a dollar seventy-five, and I'll tell my sister to get down here too.'

Stiff as a dead dog in January? That wasn't very flattering, but Kate was too happy over her first sale to let it bother her. After Eden left, she went into the back room and cut up the extra loaf of bread into bite-sized chunks. She set them on the card table, and by the end of the day, she'd sold every loaf of bread and had requests for more.

Later that night she found some wholesalers who sold the prefect ingredients for focaccia. She tracked them down on the Internet, and by the time she was through, she'd also ordered pickled asparagus and smoked cheddar.

She searched the house for her grandfather to tell him about her orders, and she found him sitting at the kitchen table working on a poem. His hand held a pencil stub over a sheet of notebook paper, and his gaze was fixed somewhere near the ceiling.

'What rhymes with *change?*' he asked.

'*Strange?*'

He looked at her, then wrote on his paper. 'Thank you. That's the perfect word.'

It certainly was the perfect word to describe his behavior lately. 'I ordered some things for the store,' she told him and expected him to raise a fuss.

'That's nice.' He was so absorbed in his poem that he didn't care.

The next morning, she made fifteen loaves of wheat bread and sold ten of them by noon. Also at noon, a delivery call came in from Sutter Sports. As always, her grandfather handed her the grocery bag he'd already filled. Kate hadn't spoken to Rob since the night they'd decided to be friends, or at least decided to give it a try.

'Why can't he walk over here and get it himself? We're just across the dang parking lot.'

'Katie, we don't complain about business.'

'We should if the business is just across the parking lot,' she grumbled as she left the M&S.

12

The sun was out, and she didn't bother throwing her coat over her lime green bebe sweater and black jeans. On her way across the parking lot she glanced in the plastic grocery bag and discovered a Paper Mate mechanical pencil, some Krazy Glue, and three granola bars. She'd never been inside the sports store, and a set of bells hanging on one side of the double doors announced her arrival.

Her first impression was of dark varnished wood and forest green wainscoting. Canoes and kayaks were suspended from the ceiling, and a row of mountain bikes were lined up in front of several aisles of fishing poles and camping equipment. She glanced around for the owner of the store, but she seemed to be the only person around.

'Kate.'

She looked up past a wall of hiking gear to the loft. Rob

stood looking down at her, his hands gripping the half wall that extended across the loft and down the stairs.

'Could you bring that up here, please?'

The sound of her shoes on the hardwood echoed off the walls. He watched her progress as she climbed up the stairs and entered the loft. An oak desk sat in the center with a flat-screen monitor and keyboard on it. Stacks of papers and folders and magazines cluttered the top of the desk.

'Finally. Lunch,' he said as he walked toward her wearing a pair of jeans and a deep beige chamois shirt with the sleeves rolled up his arms. He reached for the sack, and the sleeves slid up his forearms, the color of the shirt closely matching the deeper shades of his tattoo.

'I didn't see a snake when I was at your house,' she said as she handed him the grocery bag.

He looked into the sack, then returned his gaze to hers. 'I had to sell Chloe back to the breeder once Amelia came home from the hospital. Couldn't keep a six-pound baby in the same apartment as a python.'

'No. I guess not.' And because she was dying to know, she asked, 'How long were you married?'

He moved to the far corner of the room and, for the first time since she met him, she watched the way he walked. 'From beginning to end, a little over a year.' His long, graceful strides showed no lingering sign of injury. He moved as easily as if he'd never been hit with a .22, and his knee shattered. He set the bag on a scarred workbench crowded with feathers and thread.

'Short marriage.'

'We'd been together off and on for about four years. We never should have married, but Louisa got pregnant so we gave it a try.' He took the mechanical pencil and glue out of the bag and set them on the workbench. 'Come over here. I want to show you something.'

Kate didn't think cheating was giving a marriage much of a try, but she really didn't want to pass judgment when she didn't know anything about the relationship. Or maybe she was rationalizing his behavior because he looked incredibly hot today.

She moved across the room and stopped next to him. He was bent at the waist, inspecting something through a magnifier clamped to the front of a small vise about the size of a medium, needleless syringe. 'I just finished this elk wing caddis. Trout in the Big Wood River won't be able to resist it. Isn't it beautiful?'

She knew it was a fly. The kind you fished with, but beautiful? No. The silver Tiffany cuff she'd just gotten in the mail was beautiful. 'What's it made of?'

He reached out to adjust the gooseneck lamp and shone the light directly on it. 'The body is dubbed fur and the wings are elk hair.'

She had no idea what dubbed fur was. 'Real elk hair?'

'Yep.'

Why? 'Where do you get real elk hair?' She placed her hands on her knees and leaned in for a closer look.

'Usually I buy it, but this particular elk hair came off of Lewis Plummer's six-point buck last fall.'

She turned her head and looked at him. His face was a few inches from hers, close enough to see the different shades of green in his eyes. 'Yuck,' she said, but the word came out kind of low and lacked conviction. 'Can't you get fake hair?'

He shook his head. 'I only use organic materials.' His gaze continued to stare into hers as he asked, 'Do you want to see my yellow humpy? It's a beauty.'

His habit of inserting sexual innuendo was really juvenile. 'Gee, Rob, I don't know. Does it require you dropping your pants?'

His brows drew together, then he chuckled, a soft caress of a sound that touched her cheek. 'You have a dirty mind, Kate.' He ran his gaze over her face. 'But I happen to like that in a woman.' The shoulder of his chamois shirt brushed her shoulder as he placed a palm on his workbench and leaned past her.

Kate straightened and watched him open one of four wooden boxes about the size of a makeup case. Several levels folded out like stepladders, revealing hundreds of flies. 'It should be right here,' he said as he lightly sifted through them with his fingertips. He shut the case, then opened a drawer in the bench. 'Ahh, here it is.' He stood up straight, took Kate's hand in his, and set a brown-and-beige fuzzy fly in her palm. Coarse hair stuck out around the eye of the hook like bushing. The hair continued down the shank wrapped in yellow thread, and shot out the end like a little tail.

'Humpy is the style,' he explained as he touched the fly. The tip of his finger brushed her life line and scattered her nerves.

'This is your humpy?'

'Yeah. The dark hair is grizzly and the lighter yellow hair is yearling elk. I spent most of the winter getting this one just right.'

Okay, maybe she'd been wrong about the sexual

innuendo this time, but she didn't dwell on it because the insides of her elbows started to do the odd tingling his touch always seemed to inspire. And this time her stomach got a little light, too. She swallowed hard and told herself not to be ridiculous. This was not the man she should get all weak over. He had heartache written all over him. And yeah, she was supposed to be working on her pessimism, but that didn't mean Rob wasn't a heartbreaker.

While her sensible head fought for control of her foolish body, Rob seemed oblivious to the chaos he caused. He also seemed so pleased with the fly that she didn't have the heart to tell him that grizzly and elk hair was gross. 'Have you been tying flies long?'

'Oh yeah.' His gaze traveled up her arm to her lips, then finally her eyes. 'My dad taught me when I was a kid.' He took the yellow humpy from her and replaced it with a fly that looked like a little mouse. 'This is a muskrat. The trout in the Big Wood won't go for this, it's more for bass and pike.'

With her hand still cupped in his, she looked down at the incredibly real-looking rodent. 'Don't tell me that's a real ear?'

He chuckled. 'No. It's leather.'

Thank God. She glanced back up past the little white scar on his chin, over his nose with the slight bump she'd noticed the first night she'd seen him, and into his eyes. 'You made this too?'

'Yeah. It took me awhile to shave the hair perfect.'

She didn't know which surprised her more, that a former hockey player with big hands could tie something so intricate, or that he was interested in tying flies at all. Or perhaps it was the fact that they were actually having a real conversation. Like real adults. 'This is nice, Rob.'

'I have over a thousand.'

'Wow, that's a lot.'

His gaze dropped to her lips. 'Tying helps me take my mind off things.'

'What things?'

Without taking his eyes from her mouth, he shook his head. 'Don't ask.'

'Why?'

'It's one of those things I'd have to show you.' His gaze returned to hers and his voice lowered. 'Do you want me to show you, Kate?'

The way he said her name, all smooth and rough at the same time, as if he were making love to her, made her throat go dry. She swallowed hard, but he didn't wait for an answer. He slid his hand up her arm to her shoulder and the side of her neck. His fingers combed through her hair from underneath, and he held the back of her head in his hand. Slowly he pulled her to him, and she did not resist, sucked in by the sexual promise in his green eyes.

'I thought we were just going to be friends,' she managed before she lost her mind completely.

'We both knew that wasn't going to last long.' He lowered his mouth to hers, and she turned her face at the last moment. His lips touched her cheek, and he kissed his way to the side of her throat.

'But it was your idea.'

'I have a better one.' She felt his hot open mouth just below her ear. 'Do you wanna hear what it is?'

She placed a hand on his shoulder and shook her head.

He told her anyway. 'I think we should make out like teenagers. Just rub up against each other and see what happens next.'

Kate knew what would happen next, and a traitorous side of her wanted that too. The traitorous side that wanted to forget. Forget that she was better off not liking him. Forget that he was a bad risk and get on with kissing and rubbing and other things. A side of her that hadn't felt this good in a long time, but she was stronger than her traitorous side. 'This is a bad idea.'

He chuckled against her jaw, and a shivery warmth slid down her neck. 'There's a part of me that thinks it's a very *good* idea.'

She was afraid she knew what part he was talking about. The part of him she'd felt a few days ago.

'I want to feel you up like we're sixteen in the backseat of a car. On the outside of your clothes,' he said just above a whisper. 'Touch you all over, then slide my hands up under your shirt.' But he didn't touch her with his hands. Instead he pulled her head back and slid his open mouth to the hollow of her throat. 'Mmm, you taste good right here. Your skin is like dessert.'

Kate closed her eyes as he gently sucked her flesh into his hot, wet mouth. She liked dessert. Dessert was a good thing, and this man was very good at making her want to *be* his dessert. Very good at waking desire in every cell in her body. His every breath against her skin whispered his hunger and need, and her body responded. Her breasts tightened and her nipples got hard. She locked her knees to keep from sliding to the floor. He was very good at making her want him back, of forgetting that she had to stop him. 'You have to stop now,' she said and opened her eyes. The mouse fly fell from her free hand, and she placed her palms on his chest. She couldn't quite force herself to step from his embrace. Not yet.

'I will. Eventually.' His free hand slid around the small of her back, and he pulled her against him. Tight. He was hard against her lower abdomen, and desire pooled between her legs. He pressed his forehead to hers. 'Tell me you're not crazy.'

'What?'

'You're not crazy, are you, Kate?'

At the moment, she felt kind of crazy. Mixed up. Desire warring with common sense. 'No.'

'Stalked, harassed, or shot anyone?'

He wanted to know that she wasn't another Stephanie Andrews. A psycho who'd stalk him with a .22 after 'good sex.' The desire fogging her brain cleared enough for her to step from his embrace. 'I googled you the other night.'

His brows lowered, and he shook his head as if trying to clear his mind. 'You what me?'

'I looked you up on the Internet.'

'Ahh.' He turned away as if she'd just thrown cold water on him. 'Did you read all the juicy details of my past?'

'I don't know if I read all of them, but I understand now why you turned me down that first night in Sun Valley.'

He moved to the workbench and dumped out the grocery sack. With his broad back to her, he picked up the pencil and tore open the package. 'Getting shot tends to discourage a guy from having a one-night stand.' He pulled out the pencil and tossed the package on the desk. 'It also gets a guy divorced. Although I think that was probably doomed to fail before it even started.'

Kate walked toward him. 'Did you love her?'

'Stephanie Andrews?' He looked across his shoulder at her. 'Hell no!'

Kate had never understood how a man could love his wife yet cheat on her. 'I meant your wife.'

He nodded as he took the pencil apart. 'Yeah, I loved her. Trouble was, I didn't like her most of the time. She didn't like me either. We really only got along when we were in bed, and that wasn't all that often. Either I was on the road or we were fighting.'

Kate had never loved someone but not liked them. No, her problem was that she loved men who didn't love her enough.

'Still, I would have preferred a different end to my marriage.' He removed the spring and lead from the pencil, then set them aside. 'My career, too.'

'More dignified?'

'Dignified? Yeah, that's a good word. Getting shot takes away your dignity. You wake up in a hospital bed with tubes stuck in your stomach and . . . other places. You're weak and helpless and everything about it sucks.'

Kate imagined that to any man, being weak and helpless would be hard. But to a guy like Rob, used to hammering opponents into submission, it must have been extremely difficult.

'Then when you finally do get on your feet again, your whole life is different. No job. No wife. No nothing, except the sordid details on the Internet for everyone to read.' He pulled a sewing needle from a package and snipped off the eye. 'No love life either.'

She didn't think he was talking about the falling-in-love kind of love life. She knew firsthand, so to speak, that he was physically capable of having sex. He wasn't married, although that obviously hadn't hampered him in the past. 'How long since you've had a love life?'

He looked at her. 'Are you asking how long it's been since I've had sex?'

They both knew she was, so why deny it? 'Yeah.'

One corner of his mouth turned down in a frown. 'Never mind.'

'Six months?'

He turned away.

'One year?' She knew from interviewing a lot of people over the years that most often the answer was found in what wasn't said.

'Drop it, Kate.'

'Two years?'

He set down the needle and turned to face her. 'You seem awfully interested in my sex life.'

'You brought it up.' She shrugged. 'And I don't know if I'm "awfully interested." I'd call it a mild curiosity.'

'What exactly are you curious about?' He took a step toward her. 'How long it's been? Or how good it would be between us?' His lids lowered a fraction over his eyes. 'I gotta admit that I'm curious about that my self.'

She took a step back. 'You and I having sex together is a very bad idea.'

'You've already said that.' He took a step forward.

She stuck her hand out like a traffic cop. 'Stop. We can't have sex.'

'Sure we *can*. We're both over twenty-one and neither of us is crazy. I want you and I know you want me. You wanted me the first night we met, and I'm thinking I was an idiot not to drag you up to my room.'

There were several very good reasons that had nothing to do with age. One of which she gave. 'That's why I can't have sex with you.'

He took a determined step toward her, and her palm flattened against the front of his shirt. 'Are you still mad that I didn't drag you up to my room?'

She shook her head and her hair brushed her shoulders. 'I can't have sex with you because I know you now.'

'But you could have sex with me when you didn't know me?' He grabbed her wrist. 'That doesn't make sense.'

'Yes it does.' She looked into his eyes and tried to explain. 'That night in Sun Valley, you were supposed to be part of my fantasy. My fantasy of picking up a stranger in a bar. I was supposed to use and abuse you and kick you out.'

'You still can.'

'No. You're real now.' She tried to pull free, but he didn't let go. 'You killed all my fantasies.'

'I'll give you a new fantasy. God knows I have hundreds.' He raised her hand to his mouth. 'Do you want to hear one?' he asked against her palm, but he didn't wait for her answer. 'My favorite involves you wearing your black dominatrix boots.'

She stopped trying to pull away. He fantasized about her? No man had ever admitted that he fantasized about her. Her. Kate Hamilton and her size ten boots. She felt herself weaken. Almost give in. She should leave. Run away. Fast. And she would. But she hadn't been able to work up a good fantasy of her own for a while now. It seemed only right that he should share his. 'What else am I wearing?'

'Nothing.'

'What are you wearing?'

'A hard-on and a smile.'

She didn't know if she should laugh or pretend outrage. He looked serious except for the teasing laugh lines at the corners of his eyes. 'Where does the fantasy take place?'

'In my bed.' He placed her palm on the side of his neck and slid his hand to her waist. 'On my pool table.' He pulled her so close that her breasts touched the front of his shirt. 'My car.' The teasing lines at the corners of his eyes disappeared by the time he added, 'Right here. Anywhere I happen to be standing,' he lowered his mouth and said just above her lips.

'You star in every one of my fantasies.' He kissed her, a gentle caress of lips and tongue in stark contrast to the hard, fast beating of her heart.

Kate slipped her hand to the back of his neck and leaned into him, the weight of her breasts pressed into his chest. Her nipples tightened. She wanted this. This hot liquid pumping through her veins and pooling between her legs. Making her feel wanted and needed, her skin buzzing with sexual need. It was wrong. He was bad for her. But . . . it had been a long time since a man had wanted her anywhere he happened to be standing. A long time since she'd felt the heavy pull of desire take over and shut out the pessimist in her head.

She fed him a deep, hot kiss that had him groaning into her mouth. He tasted a little of granola, of need and sex. He cupped her breast through her sweater, and she arched against his rock-hard penis, feeling the heavy length of him pressed into her lower abdomen.

His free hand grabbed her behind, and he pulled her up onto her toes. He pushed himself against the apex of her thighs as his thumb brushed across her hard nipples. Back and forth, an unhurried rhythm in perfect time to his erection he rubbed against her crotch. A maddening, frustrated, moan escaped her throat as she threaded her fingers in the back of his hair.

The ringing of the bells on the door barely penetrated the sounds of heavy breathing in the loft.

'Mr Sutter?'

Rob straightened, and his hand dropped from her behind. He looked toward the front of the store as the sound of two young voices rose from below.

'Are you here?'

'Shit.' Rob removed his other hand from Kate's breast and looked at his watch. 'I forgot I told those two boys to come on by.' He returned his attention to Kate. His gaze filled with lust and hunger. 'Give me a few minutes, and I'll be right down,' he called out, his voice rough.

'Okay.'

'Stay here and wait for me, Kate. I won't be gone long.'

She took a deep breath, and her sanity partially returned. At least enough to allow her to take a step back. 'No.'

He reached for her, but she moved, and his hand grasped empty air. She kept on moving before he could touch her and make her change her mind. Before he could make her forget that he was just heartache number twenty-six. The latest on the long list of men that were bad for her. That wasn't her inner pessimist talking, either. It was the truth.

Just before she reached the doorway he called out, 'You can't say no forever, Kate Hamilton. Someday I'm going to make you say yes.'

She didn't dare stop. She moved down the stairs and through the store. With her hand on the front door handle, she paused and looked back over her shoulder. He stood in the loft, his hands gripping the railing.

'Someday real soon,' he said.

Rob whistled to 'Sex Type Thing' as he twisted hare's mask dubbing and tan thread into a long thin strand. He attached the bobbin to one end, then wound the dubbing around the shank of a three-inch hook clamped in a vise. Several fluffy strands of dubbing landed on the knee of his jeans, then drifted to the toe of his white sock.

As Scott Weiland sang about being a man who could give a woman something she wouldn't forget, a smile lifted the corners of Rob's mouth. Kate didn't think sex was a good idea, but she was just plain wrong. That afternoon, he'd given her fair warning that he was going to make her change her mind. He'd been serious. He was going to give her something she wouldn't forget.

He wound the thread and dubbing to the eye of the hook, then spun the bobbin and loosened the stand.

During a pause in the music, the clock on the mantel in his living room downstairs chimed ten times. He wanted Kate. She wanted him. She wasn't crazy. It was inevitable.

Both times he'd kissed her, she'd kissed him back like she was never going to stop. Earlier, she'd melted against him, so hot his hair had about caught fire. He'd touched her breast and thrust his hard-on into her, and if those boys hadn't come into the store, he would have had her naked and up against the wall before she'd known what hit her.

The bobbin swayed as he stripped the excess dubbing from the thread. He turned in his chair and selected a gold-and-black hackle feather from his assorted trays of feathers and fur. He stripped the barbs, then secured the stem to the hook shank with three tight wraps of his thread.

Other than wanting Kate on her back and in his bed, he didn't know how he felt about her. She was stubborn and competitive and had a smart mouth, but he didn't mind those qualities in a woman.

He clamped a pair of hackle pliers on the tip of the feather and wound it toward the bend in the hook. By rote, his hands passed the pliers back and forth as he wound the feather over and under the shank.

Kate was competent and believed she could damn well take care of herself. Some men didn't like that about her, but he didn't mind those qualities either. In fact, he didn't care for clinging, needy women.

At the bend in the hook, he tied down the hackle feather with wire, then wound it up the shank toward the eye. Kate was smart and beautiful and sexy. Most important, she wasn't a psycho.

The cordless telephone sitting next to his elbow rang. He glanced at the caller ID and hit the mute on his stereo. He pressed the connect button on the phone and said, 'Hey, Lou. What's up?'

'Well, I've been thinking,' his ex-wife began.

'About?'

'About our conversation the other night, and I didn't want you to think I was mad about Easter.'

He released the pliers and set them on the work-bench. 'Amelia is young enough that she won't remember, and besides, it's not your weekend anyway.'

A suddenly reasonable Louisa worried him. 'Are you dating someone?' The last time she'd been this pleasant had been the time she'd been in love with a Boeing executive. She'd wanted Rob to stay with the baby while she flew off to Cancun with her new man, which he'd been happy to do. Her relationship with the exec had ended last fall, before she'd started dropping hints of a reconciliation.

'No,' she answered. 'I'm not dating anymore.'

Rob stood and moved his head from side to side. 'Why not?'

'Because I think you and I should give our relationship another try. We're older and wiser now. We have Amelia's future to think about.'

There it was. Right out in the open now, and he could no longer ignore it. 'Why are you bringing this up now, over the phone? I'm going to be there in a few days.'

'I didn't want to hit you with it when you walked in the door. I wanted you to think about it before you got here.' She took a deep breath and let it out. 'We can make it work this time, Rob.'

He walked from the room and turned off the light behind him. 'We talked about this when I moved to Gospel. You wouldn't be happy living here, and I'm not happy living in Seattle.'

'We can work something out.'

He entered his bedroom and walked past the entertainment center to the big window. 'You'd hate it here. No Nordstrom, or jazz clubs, or dinner at The Four Seasons.' He looked out at the dark shores of Fish Hook Lake and added, 'The closest movie theater is an hour away.'

Silence stretched across the distance and he didn't think there was anything she could say to make him consider a reconciliation. They'd screwed it up too many times in the past. 'Amelia misses you.'

Except that. He closed his eyes and leaned his forehead against the cool glass. 'What's she doing?'

'She's asleep.'

He hadn't been there to put her to bed. He loved when she fell asleep in his arms and he carried her to the crib he'd converted into a little bed. Guilt ate him up inside, but he reminded himself that he would miss putting her to bed every night even if he lived full time in his loft in Seattle.

'I think we can work it out and be a family. Will you think about it?'

A family. They'd never really been a family. He loved his daughter, and at one time, he'd loved Louisa. The idea of a happy family life held a lot of appeal for him. He was often lonely, but the key word was happy. Could he and Louisa be happy together? He didn't know. 'I'll think about it,' he said.

After he pressed disconnect, he tossed the phone on a chair to his left. He scrubbed his face with his hands and looked out at the lake. The wind had picked up in the last few hours and blew black ripples across the surface.

He thought of his ex-wife, pictured her gorgeous face and killer body. At one time she'd seemed like the ideal woman. The perfect balance of natural beauty and expensive grooming. And she wanted to try and live together again. Problem was, when he was around her gorgeous face and killer body, there was no urgency to grab her up and bury his nose in her neck. There was no twist and pull of desire that made him want to run his hands all over her.

Kate made him feel those things. He wanted her like a man should want a woman. She made him feel the biting, animalistic urge to pick her up, throw her down, and get on with it. The kind of urge that a man should feel for an ex-wife he was thinking about getting back together with. But was desire, or lack of desire, a reason to reject the notion out of hand? Wasn't there more to a good relationship than sex? When he and Louisa had been married, the sex had been good but everything else had pretty much sucked. So if everything but the sex was good in a relationship, could it work?

The more Rob thought about it, the more confused he got. His temples began to pound, and the longer he let it all tumble around in his mind, the bigger his headache got until he could hardly think at all.

There was only thing he was real clear about. Until he got it all sorted out in his own mind, he'd have to resist Kate Hamilton.

He'd learned his lesson about talking reconciliation with one woman while having sex with another. He'd been there and done that, and he didn't need that kind of trouble.

13

Instead of bread, the next morning Kate made something different. It was five days before Easter, so she baked cupcakes and topped them with a thick layer of white frosting. She dyed coconut green for grass and placed tiny humming-bird candy eggs in the coconut grass. As she stuck pipe cleaners in the cupcakes to look like little handles, her thoughts turned to Rob, where they'd been stuck since yesterday.

You can't say no forever, Kate Hamilton. Someday I'm going to make you say yes, he'd said. *Someday real soon.*

His threat worried her. Not on a physical level. She didn't believe for a second that Rob would force her to do anything. She was worried about her attraction to him – worried that if he whispered her skin was like dessert, and that he fantasized about her, she'd get all weak and brain dead – again.

She knew Rob. She'd dated men just like him. She didn't want yet another bad relationship, but there was a part of her that tended to forget all of that when she was alone with him. The next time he called for a delivery, her grandfather would have to make it.

Kate placed the last tiny egg on the last cupcake and took a step back to view her work. 'Martha Stewart, wherever you are, eat your heart out.' By noon, she'd sold all five dozen and had orders for five dozen more.

At two, while Stanley sat in the back office working on a poem, Regina Cladis came in for a rump roast, a bag of baby carrots, and some red potatoes. 'Tiffer's home for a visit, and he loves my roast.'

'How long will he be staying?' Kate asked as she rang up the meat and placed it in a bag.

'Until the Monday after Easter,' she answered and dug around in her big purse.

'Perhaps you and Tiffer might enjoy a bit of jalapeño jelly.'

Regina looked up and pushed her heavy glasses up the bridge of her short nose. 'Jalapeño what?'

'Jalapeño jelly. It's very good served with cream cheese and spread over crackers. Or you can spread it on bagels.'

'No thanks. I don't eat bagels, and that jelly sounds horrible.'

'I don't understand why no one in this town will try it.' Kate sighed and rang up the carrots.

'We like our jelly made with fruit,' Regina explained. 'When I first moved here from out of town, I had a hard time fitting in, too. I was treated like an outsider, just like you.'

Kate wasn't aware that she was being treated like an outsider. 'Really?'

'Yes. Myrtle Lake and me applied for the same job at the library, and when I got it instead of her, there was a big dust up because I wasn't a local. People were all bent out of shape and wouldn't come into the library.'

'Where did you live?'

'I was born and raised in Challis.'

Challis sounded familiar. 'Where's that?'

'About forty miles north.'

Kate pointed out what she thought was the obvious. 'But that's local.'

Regina shook her head and said with an absolutely straight face, 'No. It's in the next county.'

Kate was about to ask why a city forty miles north wasn't considered local, but she stopped herself. It was best not to ask too many questions. Especially since you'd get the answers. And the answers were usually followed by a tightening of Kate's forehead and a tick in her left eye. The tightening could cause wrinkles, the tick a tumor, and Kate didn't need to borrow that kind of trouble.

'Folks did eventually warm up to me though, and they will you. Shoot, Sheriff Taber married a gal from California. If the town can get over that travesty, they'll accept Stanley's granddaughter being from Vegas. 'Course we all go to Sin City occasionally to gamble and see the shows. So that's an easier pill to swallow.'

'What's wrong with California?' Kate asked before she thought better of it.

'Filled with hippies, potheads, and vegetarians,' Regina answered with equal disdain. "Course now that Arnold is governor, he'll have that state turned around faster than you can say "I'll be back." He has a house in Sun Valley, you know.'

'Yes, I know.' Kate's forehead tightened as she hit Total. Wisely, she didn't ask any more questions.

Rob stuck a folder stuffed with invoices and price quotes under one arm and headed home for the evening. A full moon and an eighty-watt bulb lit up the small lot in back of Sutter Sports. It was a quarter past eleven, and he'd spent the five hours since closing putting together a special rental package for a Boy Scout group planning a camping trip the first week in June. He was leaving in the morning for Seattle, and he wanted the packages finished before he left so he could devote his full attention to his daughter.

He still hadn't figured out what he was going to say to Louisa about a reconciliation. He'd pushed it to the back of his brain, concentrating instead on getting his work done. His work was done now, but he still didn't want to think about it. Maybe it was best to wait and see how he felt once he was in Seattle.

He locked the store behind him and jumped into his HUMMER. The store had been open for the season less than a week, and the rental side of the business was already keeping him extremely busy.

As he drove around the side of the building, he noticed that a light was on deep inside the M&S. More than just the light Stanley always left burning in the corner near the produce. Rob pulled around the back of the grocery store and shut off the vehicle. He got out of the HUMMER and pounded three times on the solid wood door.

He rocked back on his heels and wondered what he was doing. It was late, and he still had a ton to do before he left in the morning.

A few moments passed before Kate called out from behind the closed door. 'Who is it?'

'Rob. What are you doing here so late?'

The dead bolt clicked, and she stuck her head out. The light from inside lit her from behind, shifting through her beautiful red hair and surrounding her in a soft glow. Suddenly he knew why he'd come. 'I'm working,' she answered. 'What are you doing out here so late?'

No matter how hard he tried or what was going on in his life, he couldn't seem to stay away from her. She drew him in like a ship to a bright shiny beacon. 'I'm just leaving work.' The scent of warm cake escaped the building, and he didn't know which made him more hungry – the sight of Kate or the smell of cake. 'Are you baking something?'

'Yes.' She opened the door wider and stood before him in a white T-shirt with a pair of red dice on her breasts and the words Feeling Lucky? over the top in black. A brown belt was threaded through the loops of a pair of tight jeans. 'I'm baking seven dozen cupcakes for tomorrow.'

Without a doubt, Kate was definitely better than cake. She didn't invite him in, but she didn't protest when he moved past her into the back of the store. He walked by a meat slicer and grinder toward the bakery tucked in the corner of the large room. A few dozen white cupcakes sat on a stainless steel table a few feet from the duo commercial ovens. He told himself that he wouldn't stay long.

Instead of the usual Tom Jones pouring through the speakers, a female voice sang about not missing someone once she got to Jackson. Rob didn't recognize the song, but he really wasn't into chick music. Especially the folksy angsty stuff that was always about the same three issues: love, broken hearts, asshole men.

'I hear you're pulling the elementary school's float in the Easter parade this Saturday,' she said as she shut and locked the door behind her. 'How'd you get roped into that one?'

Rob turned and watched her walk to him. He purposely kept his gaze off those dice on her breasts and on the relative safety of her hair. It hung loose about her shoulders and shimmered deep red and gold beneath the long tubes of fluorescent lighting. Just yesterday he'd held her hair in his hands while he'd kissed her throat, and he knew her hair was as soft as it looked. 'The principal asked me.'

She opened a cabinet and stretched to reach something on the top shelf. Rob's gaze ran down her long body to her feet in a pair of Tasmanian Devil slippers. 'You're easy,' she said and pulled down a box of Ziploc freezer bags.

'Where're your shoes?'

She looked down, then back up. 'At home. These are more comfy.' She set the box next to an industrial mixer. 'I think my grandfather is getting serious about your mother.'

He knew his mother liked Stanley, but she'd never mentioned that she cared for him more than as a friend. 'What makes you think it's getting serious?'

Her pink lips turned up at the corners. 'He writes

poetry now, and they've started critiquing each other's poems.'

'When do they do this?'

She stuck her hands in two Tom Jones oven mitts. 'Every night after he gets off work.'

'Every night?' His mother hadn't said a thing. He leaned his butt into the stainless counter and folded his arms across his green dress shirt with his store name and fish logo on the breast pocket. 'How long has this been going on?'

'Since we had dinner at her house last week.' She took out two cupcake trays and set them on the counter next to him. 'He's been getting home late each night.'

Rob watched her bend at the waist and take out two more trays from the second oven. 'How late?'

'Ten. Which is late for him. He's usually in bed right after the nine-thirty news on Fox. Sometimes he doesn't even wait until the sports report is over.'

'Mom really hasn't said anything, but I'm glad she has someone to share her interest in poetry.' Someone who didn't happen to be him.

Kate dumped the cupcakes on the counter and began to set them upright.

He told himself to leave. That if he stayed, he'd touch her. If he touched her he was a goner, but he just couldn't force himself out the door. Not yet. 'Do you need help?' he asked.

She looked up at him out of the corners of her brown eyes and smiled. 'Are you volunteering to help me bake?'

Except for granola, which he made because he was

addicted to the stuff, Rob wasn't into baking. He'd leave in a minute. 'Sure.'

'That's sweet of you, but you're in luck. These are the last.' She handed him the box of freezer bags. 'If you want to help, you can put six cupcakes in each. Not the hot ones, though. They get too mushy if you don't wait until they cool.'

'How many did you make again?' he asked as he pulled out a plastic bag.

'I have pre orders for five dozen, and I made two dozen extra to sell in the store.' She moved a few feet away and placed a large mixing bowl in a sink of soapy water.

Her domestic side surprised Rob, but again, he didn't know why he should be surprised. He really didn't know all there was to know about Kate. What did surprise him was that he wanted to know more. He glanced over at her as he unzipped the bag and shoved a few cupcakes inside. 'You think you're going to sell all twenty-four?'

'Yeah, I know I am.' She looked at him. 'I've figured out the key to selling anything to the people in this town.'

He closed the bag and started on another. 'What's the key?'

'Giving away samples,' she answered, then turned her attention to washing the dishes. 'They'll buy as long as they get a free sample.' She shook her head, and the ends of her blunt red hair brushed her back. 'I used to think my grand-father wasted money on giving away free coffee, but I've come to learn that he lures people into the store with free coffee. Once they're in here, chatting and drinking, they buy other things.' She set the soapy bowl in the empty side of the sink. 'I'm going to give samples of smoked cheddar next.'

He finished with the third bag and started on the last. 'You going to trick them into buying it?'

She laughed, and the soft, feminine sound from her lips seemed to slip between his ribs and take up space in his chest. 'I'm going to change their way of thinking without them even knowing it.' She looked over at him again, her brown eyes lit up and shining. 'Soon, I'm going to have them all eating seared tuna and wasabi mashed potatoes.'

'Right.' Tonight she reminded him of the girl he'd met in the Duchin Lounge several months ago. Relaxed and warm.

'You don't think I can?' she asked, an edge of steely determination in her voice.

He wondered if he should warn the town that they better get used to Japanese horseradish. 'I think you have your work cut out for you.'

'That's true.' She reached for two cupcake pans and stuck them in the water. 'But I love a challenge. I figure all I have to do is join the Mountain Momma Crafters, then I'm in.'

Rob set the last bag next to the cooling cupcakes, then he shoved a hip into the counter and listened to her while she chatted about turning Gospel into the gourmet eating capital of the Northwest. He watched her hands as she ran the wet washcloth over the pans. At the ends of her long fingers, her short nails were painted a light pink. She set the pan in the empty sink and turned on the water.

'I'll start them out slow,' she continued as she opened a cabinet and stood on her tiptoes. 'Get them hooked on focaccia bread then introduce them to flavored olive oils.'

Rob pushed away from the counter and moved up close behind her. He lifted the bowl from her hands and placed it on the shelf. She looked up at him over her shoulder. Her hair brushed the front of his shirt, but he felt it in his groin. His hands grasped the edge of the bowl to keep from lowering them to her stomach and pulling her back against his chest. Her gaze stared into his, and it would be so easy to lower his mouth to hers.

'Thank you,' she said and ducked beneath his arm before he could give in to his urge to kiss her. She moved to the cupcakes sitting on the counter and tested the temperature with her fingers.

He lowered his arms. 'Are you going to give me one of those?'

'What?' She turned around and looked at him. 'You want a cupcake?'

He nodded. 'Why do you think I'm here?'

'My witty conversation?'

'That too.'

'You're a bad liar,' she said through a laugh. The warm pleasure of it settled in his chest and reminded him that he'd been lonely for a long time. Starved for soft laughter and feminine conversation. Starved for more than just sex. 'I don't have any frosting.'

'I don't care.'

'Wait.' She held up one finger, then disappeared into the walk-in refrigerator. She came back out shaking a can of whipped cream, and Rob couldn't help but notice that her breasts did interesting things to those dice on her shirt. 'I used this in my cocoa this morning.' She picked up a cupcake and squirted it with whipped cream. 'The nice thing about working in a grocery store is that you never run out of anything.' She handed it to him. 'The downside is that you can get fat.'

'You're not fat.' Rob pulled off the paper and took a big bite.

'Not yet.' She tipped her head back and shot whipped cream straight into her mouth. It was the most erotic thing he'd seen in a long time, which told him just how long it had been.

He took another bite, and he recalled the few occasions when he'd had the privilege of eating a whipped cream bikini. He wouldn't object to eating one off of Kate sometime. He finished off his cupcake in four more bites, then held out his hand. 'Give me some of that.' Instead of handing him the can, she placed a hand on his shoulder. She rose onto the balls of her feet, and her breast brushed his arm.

'Open up.'

He didn't trust her. Not for a second. He stared into her gaze a few inches from his and slowly opened his mouth.

She shot cream between his lips and across his cheek.

'Oops, sorry.' She dropped onto her heels.

Rob swallowed. 'You did that on purpose.'

'No, I swear it was an accident.' She shook her head and tried to look contrite, but she ruined it when she burst out laughing.

He wiped his finger across his cheek, then licked it clean. 'Accident my ass.' He held out his hand. 'Give it to me.'

She shook her head and held the can behind her back.

'You don't think I can get that out of your hands?'

'No.'

Of course she didn't. She was stubborn and competitive, and the thought of wrestling with her turned him on more than a whipped cream bikini. 'You wanna bet?'

'What do I get if I win?'

'You won't.'

Her eyes narrowed. 'Don't be so sure about that.'

He humored her. 'What do you want?'

'You have to tell everyone how much you love jalapeño jelly.'

Jalapeño jelly? What the hell?

'What do you want if you win?' she asked.

He smiled. A deliberate, carnal curve of his lips. He knew exactly what he wanted. 'I get to lick whipped cream off your nipples.' Whipped cream wasn't sex. It was dessert.

Her mouth fell open and her eyes got huge. Then the corners of her mouth curved up, and she spun on her heels and ran through the back room and out into the store. Rob followed close behind and nearly tripped on a Tasmanian Devil slipper in the doorway. His gaze scanned the dark store, and he caught a flash of white T-shirt just as she dashed between aisles three and four.

'Your white shirt is giving you away.' He stepped into the aisle. She stood at the end, a barely discernible outline in the darkness. If it hadn't been for her shirt and the white can in her hand, he might not have noticed her at all. 'Maybe you should take it off right now.'

She laughed, a low, throaty caress within the variegated shadows. 'Yeah, right.'

He walked toward her, and she took a few steps backward. 'It'll save me the trouble of taking it off of you.'

'I don't want to save you trouble.' She moved behind a bin of fruit. The weak light in the corner of the produce slashed across her mouth and shoulder and lit up the dice on her T-shirt. He watched her lips move when she added, 'I want to cause you as much trouble as possible.'

'Oh, you do.' His hands grasped the edge of the bin, and he thought of picking up an orange and nailing her with it. Stunning her for a few fortuitous seconds while he made his move. 'You've caused me all kinds of trouble since the night we met.' He picked up an orange, but instead of beaning her with it, he pitched it at a cardboard Keebler Elf display and knocked over bags of cookies.

'What was that?' she asked and turned her attention toward the sound. Then before she knew what hit her, Rob was on her, wrapping his arms around her waist, just beneath her breasts and slamming her back into his chest. 'Rob!' she shrieked and laughed at the same time. He grabbed the can and tossed it on a pile of fruit. 'No fair. You cheated.'

'Fuck fair.' He breathed in deeply the scent of her hair and said into the top of her head, 'I never play fair. Fair is for whiners and weenies.' He slid one hand to her belly and bunched her T-shirt in his fist. The sound of his breathing and hers filled his ears. Standing within the dark corner of the store with Kate in his arms, the rest of the world and its problems faded. 'I've pictured you here,' he said as he slid his other hand up and filled his palm with her soft breast. 'In one of my fantasies. You let me eat strawberries off you.' Through her shirt, he felt her hard nipple against his palm.

His lungs squeezed, and the pit of his belly got tight. His dick got so hard that he had to lock his knees. 'Then you rode me like a rodeo queen.'

She turned her head and looked up at him. 'Where?'

'Checkout counter.'

'Perverted.' Her lips softly kissed his jaw. 'That's where I bag groceries for little old women. I like it.'

'Then we had sex a second time in the back on the table where your grandfather cuts meat.'

'Am I on top again?' She kissed beneath his chin.

'No. I'm driving that time.'

'Stainless steel is chilly.'

'Not when we're on it.' He lowered his head, and the instant his lips touched hers, the raw, naked edge of desire sliced right through to the primal place in his being that screamed for him to go for it and fuck everything else. To rip off her clothes and touch her everywhere at once. To throw her down and crawl on top.

She inhaled, sucking his breath from him, and he was lost. Lust thumped through his body and grasped his testicles in a fiery squeeze. Her mouth opened and she kissed him. A sweet, liquid warmth that tasted like whipped cream and sex. Their slick tongues touched, and he gave in to the overwhelming urge to touch her everywhere at once. He slid his palms over her breasts, her belly and thighs. He slipped his hand between her legs, feeling her on the outside of her clothes. The heat of her body warmed the seam of her jeans, and he pressed his finger tight against her. He pushed his erection into her behind and felt the deep, primal response that he'd resisted for far too long. It rose up and urged him to devour her. To eat her up and rip out the throat of anyone who tried to stop him.

He bunched her T-shirt in his fists and broke the kiss to pull it over her head. The shirt fell from his fingers and she stood before him wearing a white satin bra that pushed her breasts together. It had been so long since he'd seen breasts that he was afraid to move. Afraid it would all fade away – like a fantasy.

Kate pulled back just far enough to look into his face. Her heart pounded in her chest and she fought for breath. The light from the corner lit up the little scar on Rob's chin. She didn't need to see his eyes clearly to know they burned with desire. She didn't need to feel the long hard length of his erection pressed against her to know the depth of his need for her. It surrounded them both in hot waves. Pressing in and taking over. Making her ache for his touch. She'd never felt anything like the weight of it. It was like Rob himself. Big. Forceful. Dominating. And this was one of those times when she didn't mind being dominated by something stronger than herself.

She ran her hands up his chest, and she felt a shudder deep within him. She pressed her open mouth to the hollow of his throat just below his Adam's apple. He moaned and she tasted the warm muskiness of him on her tongue. She unbuttoned his shirt and pulled it from the waistband of his pants. Once she had it open, she touched his hard chest and ran her fingers through the hair she found there. The thick, coarse hair of a man on testosterone overload.

The small lightbulb lit up slices of her and pieces of him. Disjointed. Fragments and shadows, and none of it seemed quite real.

In the dark, he stared at her. So intense she could feel his hot gaze, and she raised her hands to cover herself.

He grabbed her wrists and stopped her. 'No. Don't. Let me see you.' He finally touched her, running his fingers along one edge of her bra, between her cleavage, and up the other side. He unhooked the center, and the cups parted. He pushed the straps down her arms, then his big, masculine hands covered her. His warm palms pressed against her tight nipples and the ache between her legs constricted into a painful knot that only he could satisfy.

'Kate,' he said, his voice a low gravel. 'You're better than anything I could dream up.'

In that instant she knew there was no turning back. She leaned forward and kissed his neck. His hands slid to her back and he pressed her breasts against his hot, naked chest. He grabbed her waist and lifted her to sit in the produce bin behind her. Oranges toppled and landed on the floor, and he reached for the can of whipped cream. Light from the weak corner bulb shone on her breasts as he covered each of her nipples with perfect white triangles. He was a little too practiced, and she wondered how many times he'd done this before, then his hot mouth was on her and she didn't care. Her hands grasped the oranges beside her and she arched her back. He sucked and licked her clean, then he reached for the can and started all over again.

Before she lost all reason and gave up caring along with everything else, Kate said, 'I don't have a condom. Do you?'

He lifted his head and looked at her. 'Shit.' Then he said

a few more swear words she didn't quite catch. 'Wait. This is a store. Where's the damn condom aisle?'

'Five.'

He grabbed her waist and set her on her feet on the floor. Then he took her hand in his and pulled her along behind him. Several boxes of condoms hit the floor and suddenly everything turned hotter, more intense. A blur. A rush. A throbbing urgency. She tore at his clothes, and he pushed her pants and panties down her legs. She stepped out of them and reached for him. In the dark aisle, he was naked, and she took his penis in her hand, huge and hot, his pulse pounding against her palm.

He groaned long, as if he were in pain, and then he sank to the floor, taking her with him. He kissed her and touched her and somehow she ended up on her hands and knees. He knelt behind her and slid his hand across her bare behind and between her legs. He parted her and touched her. She bit her lip to keep from moaning and rested her forehead on her forearm. 'You're wet.' The hot head of his penis replaced his fingers, touching her where she craved it most.

'Kate,' he said over the tearing of the condom wrapper and snap of latex. 'I want you more than I want anything.' Then he shoved into her, huge and thick. A dark, primal groan was ripped from his chest as he pushed deeper, the head of his penis pressed against her cervix, stretching and filling her.

She'd known he was big, and she cried out. He wrapped his right arm around her waist. 'I'm sorry, Kate.' His body covered hers and he supported himself on his left elbow and forearm. He spoke close to her ear, his breathing fast and hot through her hair. 'I would never hurt you.

Never.' His grasp tightened and his arm trembled. 'Do you want me to stop?'

A moan slipped past her lips. A moan that would have embarrassed her in the light of day. She pressed her behind against his groin. 'No,' she answered in a voice that sounded desperate even to her own ears. 'Make love to me, Rob,' she said into the darkness, where nothing mattered and nothing was quite real. 'Please, don't stop.'

She felt his hot mouth on her shoulder and the sharp edges of his teeth. He pulled out and plunged even deeper. 'You're good, Kate. So good.' He started slow, pumping his hips in a smooth rhythm. 'More?'

'Yes.'

And he gave her more, hitting just the right place deep inside her.

'Kate,' he whispered into her ear. 'I'm going to fuck you hard now.'

'Yes.'

He raised, and his hands gripped her waist. If he hadn't been holding on to her, the first deep plunge would have knocked her flat. He drove into her faster harder deeper. Stroking her g-spot with the thick head of his penis and hard shaft. Over and over until she felt the first hard tug of orgasm. It started deep inside and radiated outward. She cried out again, this time at the intense pleasure that swept across her flesh, from the soles of her bare feet to the top of her head. Her ears rang and her body shook as her vaginal walls convulsed around him. She heard his deep groan, followed by a string of curse words she couldn't hear clearly. Something about Mary and Jesus and holy shit.

Then it was over and all that was left was the sound of harsh breathing and the realization that she was naked with her behind in the air.

The mountain was out when Rob's flight landed at SEA-TAC. He rented a Lexus and called Louisa on his cell to let her know he was on his way to pick up Amelia. He tuned in a radio station and headed for Interstate 5.

He slid his Maui Jims on the bridge of his nose and adjusted the sun visor. The polarized lenses cut the glare of the morning sun, and Rob merged onto the interstate, only to get stuck in stop-and-go traffic headed into Seattle. He hadn't slept a whole lot the night before, and he'd downed a boatload of coffee on the flight. His brain was fuzzy, but he could recall with absolute clarity how the light in the grocery store had cut across Kate's naked breasts. Her breasts were firm and white with small pink nipples balanced perfectly in the center, like tight raspberries. He remembered how hard they'd been against his palms and tongue, and they'd tasted so good covered in whipped cream that he'd gone back for a second helping.

He recalled every detail of the night before. The touch of her soft skin beneath his hands and his struggle for control. He'd wanted to go slow, draw out the pleasure, while at the same time, he'd fought a battle within himself to just throw her down and get on with it.

In the end, he'd lost the fight. He'd grabbed her up, pushed her to the floor, and gone for it. He'd come so hard that he'd thought he was going to black out, but even as he'd felt every ripple and pulse of her orgasm, he'd known she deserved more from him. More than a quick one on the floor.

Rob flipped on his blinker and eased the Lexus in between a delivery van and a silver Camry. Pushing Kate to the floor hadn't been one of his better moves, but it might have been forgivable if he hadn't followed it by a bigger mistake. One that had kept him up last night feeding himself his own lunch. One that he wished he didn't recall with the same clarity with which he recalled everything else about the previous evening.

Without saying much more than a mumbled 'I'll be right back,' he'd gathered up his clothes and made his way to the bathroom. He'd dressed, and as he'd stood in front of the toilet, watching the condom swirl around and get sucked down the bowl, he'd freaked. Not because of the usual past issues, like what lie he was going to tell or how to get out of the room without a scene. No, he'd freaked because there had been a point in the evening when he hadn't given a damn about anything but getting Kate naked. It wasn't that he'd forgotten his past mistakes or the trouble it had caused. It was more that Kate made him not care. While he'd been with her, eating whipped cream from her breasts and thrusting deep inside where she was slick and tight around his cock, he hadn't given a damn. He'd wanted Kate, and nothing else had mattered. But after the fever had passed, his disregard for the consequences had freaked him out and he'd run like hell. But not before he'd kissed her on the forehead and committed the most spectacular fuck-up of the night.

He'd looked into her brown eyes and told her 'thanks' like she'd just passed him the salt. Then he'd bolted out the back door.

Rob glanced at his watch and turned off the freeway at the Denny exit. It was ten o'clock in Gospel. If he called the M&S, he could catch Kate and try to explain or apologize or something. He reached for the cell phone hooked to his belt but returned his hand to the wheel. He'd deal with that problem when he got home – in person. Hell, maybe he hadn't even messed up. Maybe she wasn't all that upset. Maybe he'd imagined the look on her face when he'd told her thanks and kissed her head.

Right now, he had another problem to face. One that was very real.

He found a parking spot a few blocks from Louisa's condo, and by the time he knocked on her door, he'd pushed Kate to the back of his head. A problem he would deal with later.

Louisa's blonde hair was pulled back in a ponytail, and she was dressed as if she were about to go out for a jog in tight black spandex. She was fit and toned and could probably crack a walnut on her ass. She hugged him and kissed his jaw, and he felt nothing. No stirring interest in the pit of his stomach. No desire to turn his face and kiss her lips. No pinch in his chest or tug at his heart. Nothing.

He found Amelia sitting in her highchair in the kitchen eating dry Cheerios on her tray. She held up her arms for him and said through a bright smile, 'Daddy's here.'

At the sight of his child his heart lifted in his chest. 'Hey, baby girl.' He nibbled a Cheerio stuck on her finger, and then he nibbled her neck. She laughed and shrieked and pulled his hair. 'Ready to go?'

'What are you two doing today?' Louisa asked from the doorway.

'I'm not sure.' He took Amelia from the chair. 'Maybe we'll go see if the guys are in town,' he said, referring to his old Chinook teammates. 'Maybe we'll go skate, or if the sun stays out, get a kite and go to the park.'

'I thought we could all go to the zoo tomorrow. She really likes the pygmy marmosets.'

Rob looked over the top of Amelia's dark head at his former wife. He didn't love her and knew he would never love her again. He would have to tell her, but not now. Not while he held his daughter in his arms. 'Sounds good.'

Louisa smiled. 'I'll pick you and Amelia up around noon tomorrow then.'

Before he left town he knew she'd want to talk about getting back together, and he wasn't looking forward to the conversation. Maybe he'd invite her over to his loft in a few days, after he figured out exactly what he wanted to say. While Amelia napped, he'd make her see that a reconciliation wouldn't work. He'd figure out some way of telling her that he didn't love her without making her angry or hurting her feelings. Hell, he wasn't convinced she still loved him. More than likely, she was just falling back into the same old pattern of their past.

The next day Louisa showed up at the loft right on time. The weather held as they walked about the Woodland zoo, looking at water buffalo and tomato frogs. When Amelia fell asleep in her stroller at the coastal desert exhibit, she brought up the subject of getting back together. 'Have you given any more thought to what we talked about on the phone the other night?'

He really didn't want to talk about it in public.

'I don't think this is the place to talk about it.'

'I do.' She looked up at him and shoved her hair behind her ears, revealing the three carat diamond earrings he'd given her the day she'd given birth to Amelia. 'The answer is easy, Rob. Either you've thought about it or you haven't. Either you want to be a family with me and Amelia or you don't.'

It was so typical of Louisa to push until she irritated him. Leaving him no choice, he said, 'Yeah, I've thought about it. Amelia is the most important thing in my life. I love her and I would do anything for her.' He could tell Louisa a kind lie, but the problem was, he didn't know any kind lies. 'The thing is, I don't love you the way a man should love a woman he is thinking about living with. If we got back together, it would end as badly as it did last time.'

Her brows drew together and he saw the hurt in her eyes before she turned to look at the penguins diving off rocks into the water. She started to cry, and he felt like an asshole. People walking by looked at him like he was an asshole, too, but he hadn't known what else to say. And now she was crying right in front of him and everyone else in the coastal desert exhibit. 'I'm sorry.'

'I guess I'd rather you told me the truth.' She brushed her fingertips beneath her eyes, and her shoulders shook. Rob didn't know if he should hold her or stand back. He never knew what to do with a crying woman. Guilt churned in his stomach, and he tightened his grasp on the stroller's handle.

'Could you get me a tissue?' she asked between sobs.

'Where are they?'

She waved a hand toward the stroller. 'Baby bag.'

Rob squatted down and rummaged through the huge pink bag in the bottom of the stroller. He found a box of Kleenex and handed Louisa a few.

'Thank you.' She wiped her eyes and her nose, but she kept her head down and wouldn't look at him. 'Are you in love with someone else?'

Rob thought of Kate. He thought of her laughter and soft red hair. Of the way she made him feel, like he wanted to grab her and roll around with her. 'No, I'm not in love with anyone else.' It was the truth. He wasn't in love with Kate, but he liked a lot of things about her.

Somehow they got through the rest of the zoo with only a few more breakdowns. One in the tropical rainforest building, the other by the kangaroos. Louisa didn't mention a reconciliation again until he dropped Amelia off on his way to the airport for his return flight to Idaho.

'Since neither of us are in love with anyone else,' she said, 'maybe we can be friends. We'll start there and see where it goes.' She stuck out her hand. 'Friends?'

He took Louisa's hand as Amelia started to cry and cling to his neck. 'Don't go, Daddy,' she wailed.

'We can be friends, Lou. That'd be great,' he said over Amelia's crying. He didn't add that he wasn't interested in seeing where it went. Right now, one crying female was enough, and he didn't think he could handle another scene like the one at the zoo. He kissed his daughter's cheek and pried her arms from his neck. He handed her over to Louisa, and she gave a bloodcurdling scream as if he'd just cut off her little arm or something.

'Go, Rob,' Louisa said above the racket. 'She's tired. She'll be fine.'

With his heart throbbing painfully in his chest, he walked from the condo, hearing Amelia's pitiful wailing halfway to the elevator.

'Christ,' he muttered and swallowed hard. He was Rob Sutter. For over a decade, he'd been one of the most feared players in the NFL. He'd been shot and lived to talk about it. He took a deep breath and punched a button for the elevator. If he didn't get a grip, he was going to start crying like a little girl.

Barely an hour after Rob returned home from Seattle, he hooked up the elementary school float and pulled it behind his HUMMER in the Easter parade. He looked for Kate as he passed the M&S, and he saw her standing with a cowboy from the Rocking T ranch. His name was Buddy something. Through the HUMMER windows, her gaze met his. Then her eyes got the squinty look he recognized, and she turned away. No smile. No wave. He got his answer. Yep, she was mad as hell.

After the parade, he went to Sutter Sports and tried to catch up on his work. He had over a thousand e-mails to read or delete. Of those thousand, about thirty were business related, and he had to respond. Forty boxes of inventory had arrived while he'd been away and needed to be processed. By eight that night, he'd gotten through half of what he needed to get done.

He was wiped out, but there was one more thing he had to do that couldn't wait. He reached for the telephone on his desk and dialed Stanley Caldwell's home number. No one picked up. Kate wasn't home, but he figured he knew where he could find her.

He stood and unbuttoned the cuffs of his black-and-green flannel shirt. He rolled up the sleeves and headed for the grange.

The trip took him about five minutes, and he could hear the thump of heavy bass and the twang of steel guitar as he pulled into the dirt parking lot. The door to the grange vibrated as he opened it and stepped inside.

Except for the bright lights shining on the stage and the bar at the other end, the inside was pitched in darkness. Rob ordered a beer from the bar then found a spot in front of a wall where it wasn't quite so dark. He wasn't sure, but it looked like tinfoil Easter eggs were hanging from the ceiling beams. Someone in a white bunny costume hopped around and handed out something from a basket. Rob placed a foot on the wall behind him. While his gaze scanned the crowd, searching for a certain redhead, a man with a head like a cue ball squeezed beside him.

'Hi,' he said over the music. Rob glanced at him, at the words LIZA MINNELLI written in silvery glitter on the front of his sweatshirt. 'I'm Tiffer Cladis. My mother may have mentioned me to you.'

'Yeah, and I'm not gay.' He returned his gaze to the crowd and spotted his mother and Stanley out on the dance floor.

'That's a shame. I've never been with a hockey player.'

Rob raised his Budweiser to his lips. 'That makes two of us.'

'You're into women exclusively?'

'Yep, just women.' Rob took a drink and spotted Kate over the bottom of the bottle. One of the Aberdeen twins had her out on the dance floor, two-stepping to some band's crappy rendition of Garth Brook's 'Low Places.' She had on a white shirt and some kind of pleated skirt. Red and really short. From halfway across the room, he watched her weave in and out of the crowd of dancers. He got a flash of leg, and desire curled in his stomach. 'I'm into women in skirts,' he said as he lowered the bottle.

'I could wear a skirt.' Tiffer raised his beer. 'I like to wear skirts.'

Rob chuckled. 'But you'd still have a dick and a five o'clock shadow.'

'That's true.'

Rob imagined Tiffer hadn't had an easy life. Especially living in a small town in Idaho. 'Your mom tells me you're a female impersonator.'

'Yeah. I do a very good Barbra.'

'Is there a lot of demand for that in Boise?' The music ended and he watched Kate move from the dance floor to a small group of people that included the sheriff's wife. The light from the stage lit up the bottom half of her, and Rob could see that her skirt looked like a little kilt.

'No. That's why I work in an antique shop with my lover.'

Rob had heard that Scottish men went commando beneath their kilts, and he wondered if Kate was keeping up with tradition. His gaze lowered down her long legs to those boots that kept him up at night. Literally. She placed the toe of one boot behind the heel of the other. She rocked her heel from side to side, enticing him. 'Don't you think your lover might object to you propositioning other men?'

'No. He's married and has three children. He blends better than I do. Even when I try. Like tonight.'

Rob looked at Tiffer's Liza sweatshirt and figured Tiffer might as well have had a neon sign with an arrow pointing at his head. If he really wanted to 'blend,' he should man-up. Scuff his white sneakers, chug his beer, and leave Liza at home.

'I date other people, too.'

Rob returned his gaze to Kate. 'Do you find anyone to date in Boise?'

'Actually, the gay population in Boise is bigger than you might think. There are several gay bars right in the heart of the city.'

As Tiffer rattled on about the dating scene in Boise, Rob watched Kate. He'd come here to talk to her about the other night, but that wasn't all he wanted. Kate gave him something that had been missing in his life. Something that made her occupy his thoughts and order granola bars just to see her face. Something more than sex, although he wanted more of that too. And when he was through getting more, he was sure he'd want more of the same.

He took a drink of his beer and watched her laugh at

something Shelly Aberdeen was saying. What he should have done was call her while he'd been in Seattle, but each time he'd reached for a phone, he'd stopped himself. The conversation he wanted to have with her should happen in person, and to be completely honest, he hadn't known what to say. He still didn't. 'I'm sorry I pushed you to the floor and climbed on top of you,' might be a good start, but not if she'd enjoyed herself as much as he'd enjoyed himself. Or as much as he'd thought she'd enjoyed herself. If he apologized, she might think he thought the sex had been bad, when it had really smoked. She was already mad at him, and if he . . . 'Christ,' he muttered – he was starting to think like a girl.

'Who do you keep staring at?'

He turned his attention to Tiffer. 'Come on, I'll introduce you.' He definitely should apologize for running out like he had. He'd start with that and see where it got him.

He moved through the crowd with Tiffer on his heels. They passed the Worsley brothers, who gave him evil glares until they spotted Tiffer. Then they put their heads together and pointed. It didn't take a genius to know what they were saying. Rob hoped they didn't make the mistake of saying it to his face. His mother and Stanley were in the crowded grange somewhere, and he didn't want his mother to see him mop the floor with the numb-nutted Worsleys.

Hope Taber looked up first and saw him. 'Hey, Rob,' she said and moved to include him and Tiffer in their circle. 'How's Adam working out at the sporting goods store?' she asked as the band tuned up for another song.

'Real good. He and Wally both.' He stood next to Kate

within an oblong pool of blue light that spilled from the dance floor. The sleeve of his flannel shirt brushed her arm. 'Have you ladies met Regina's son, Tiffer?'

'Of course,' Shelly said and reached for Tiffer's hand. 'Your mother told me you were coming home for Easter. She's been excited for weeks.'

'It's good to be back for a visit,' he said, but he didn't sound very convincing. He glanced across Rob at Kate and looked her up and down. 'Love the naughty highlander look.'

'Thank you.' She subjected Tiffer to the same up and down scrutiny. 'Love your Liza sweatshirt.'

The band struck up Tim McGraw's 'Real Good Man,' and Rob leaned closer to Kate. 'I need to talk to you.'

'Talk.'

'On the dance floor.'

She pasted on a phony smile and turned to look at him. Her voice was a tad too cheerful when she said, 'Whatever you have to say to me, you can say it right here.'

He wasn't buying the cheery crap for a second. He leaned in and spoke next to her ear. 'Are you sure about that? 'Cause I was going to comment on how much I enjoyed eating whipped cream off your nipples.'

Her mouth fell open, then snapped shut. 'You wouldn't say that.'

'Yeah, I would. Especially since the Worsley brothers are gearing up to tell everyone that Tiffer here is my boyfriend. Call it a preemptive strike just to prove I'm into girls.' Her hair smelled like it had the other night. Kind of like spring flowers. 'If you don't believe I'll do it, we could always bet again. I like betting with you.'

'You don't play fair.' She folded her arms across her chest. 'You cheat.'

'Guilty.' He leaned back and looked into her face. 'Shall we?' He didn't wait for her answer before taking her elbow. 'Excuse us.' He set his beer on a nearby table and moved with her to the middle of the dance floor. He placed his palm in the middle of her back and folded her hand in his. They both took a step forward at the same time, and her chest collided with his. Not that he minded. 'Honey, I'm going to lead this one.' They started again. She let him lead, but dancing with her was like holding on to a wooden cutout. 'Relax,' he said next to her temple.

'I am.'

'No. You're moving like you have a stick up your butt.'

'Charming.' His hand slipped a little lower to the waist of her wool skirt. 'Say what you have to say, but make it quick,' she said.

'Are you wearing panties under that skirt?'

'Is that what you want to know?'

Well, it was *one* of the things he wanted to know. 'Not if you don't want to tell me.' He moved with her closer to the stage, and the bright lights slid through the deep reds of her hair. The music was too loud, so he waited until they moved away from the stage and into the deeper shadows of the dance floor. 'I think I need to apologize, but I'm not sure exactly what I should apologize for.' He pulled back and looked at her for some clue as to how to proceed. Women could twist things until a guy didn't know which end was up. He spun her around and brought her so close to his chest that her breasts brushed the front of his shirt.

'Are you waiting for me to tell you what you should apologize for?'

That might help. He shook his head. 'No.' But he was absolutely not going to admit that she'd scared the shit out of him. 'I know you're mad about the other night.' He looked down into her face, and she lowered her gaze to his shoulder. 'I know that I had a great time, but I'm just not sure you did. You said you wanted me to make love to you, and I got kind of carried away. I'm afraid I might have been too rough and hurt you.'

Her brows drew together. 'You didn't hurt me.'

'Oh, that's good.' She wasn't mad about doing it on the floor. He was relieved and pulled her closer to his chest. Again he wondered if she was wearing panties under that kilt, but he knew better than to ask. 'I'm sorry I ran out like I did.'

She pushed away and put a few inches between them. 'You're only saying you're sorry because you think I'm going to have sex with you again.'

That wasn't the only reason. Although he'd been kind of hoping she'd be open to more than dancing in the grange. He'd been thinking along the lines of a mattress tango. 'I was sorry about it the night I walked out of the grocery store.'

'If that's true, you wouldn't have waited so long to talk to me about it. No, now that we've had sex, you think I should just have sex with you whenever you feel like it.'

He might have taken a few punches to the head during his former career, but he wasn't idiot enough to confess that sex whenever he felt like it sounded like a damn good idea.

'I've been out of town. True, I could have called, but I wanted to talk to you face-to-face.'

The music stopped, and she pulled out of his embrace. 'And now you have.'

He grasped her arm to make sure she didn't run away. 'Come home with me.'

'Why?'

Why? He thought the answer was obvious. 'So we can talk.' Among other things. Like checking out what she was wearing under that skirt.

'And end up in your bed.'

'I'd love to have you naked in my bed.'

'Then afterward you can kiss me on the head and tell me thanks, as if I just bagged your groceries? I don't think so.'

'Not one of my finer moves.' He cleared his throat and scratched the side of his neck. 'I'll make it up to you.'

'No.'

'Excuse me,' Tiffer said as he joined them. 'I'm hoping the tart in the tartan will dance with me.'

Rob stepped back, expecting all hell to break loose. Instead she tossed her red hair and laughed.

'I'd love to dance with you,' she said and took Tiffer's arm. They moved onto the dance floor, leaving a stunned Rob to watch from the sidelines.

He'd bet his left eyeball that if he'd called her a tart, she wouldn't have laughed about it. She would have gotten that squinty look in her eyes and called him a few choice names. Then she would have puckered up and given him a cold shoulder. Or in her case, *colder* shoulder.

He turned away and moved through the crowd toward

the bar. Maybe he was wasting his time on Kate. She was uptight and mad most of the time. Sure he liked her, but at the moment he couldn't recall why.

'Hey there, Rob,' Rose Lake called out. He stopped and watched her approach. Her blonde hair was like a shiny beacon in the dim lights of the grange. A genuine smile curved her mouth. Imagine that. An attractive woman who was actually glad to see him.

Kate was beautiful and sexy and smart, but she was not the only woman in town.

15

Easter Sunday, Stanley Caldwell stayed home from church, which he never did unless he was ill. He had a few important things to do, and he wanted to do them in private.

Kate slept in her room with the door closed, and he figured that when she woke up, she'd feel the effects of partying late with Tiffer Cladis. Watching her dance all night with a female impersonator instead of Rob had been a big disappointment. She'd never get married if she danced with men who were more interested in sharing makeup tips than making out. Which is what the two had been discussing when he and Grace had approached them during a break in the music. While Kate had spent her evening with Tiffer talking about eyeliner and cover sticks, Rob had stood within a circle of young women. They'd flattered and flirted with him, something Stanley wished Kate would do. Rob had eventually left with Rose.

Stanley slipped on his Minnetonka slippers that Melba had bought him for Christmas the same year she'd died. There was a lot of comfort in knowing a woman most of your life and of her knowing you. He'd loved Melba with all of his heart. He knew it sounded clichéd. The sort of thing people just said without giving it a whole lot of thought, but he had. He'd loved her. He'd loved his wife, but she was gone. The day he'd put her in the ground, he'd thought he should just die too. He'd thought he should just hurry up and follow her into the grave because he hadn't wanted to live without her. He hadn't known *how* to live without her.

Lately, though, he'd been thinking that following her into the grave was maybe not the best plan. Apparently, he was too healthy, and it was taking too long.

He opened the closet he'd shared with his wife for nearly fifty years. Her housecoat was in the same place where she'd left it. Her slacks and blouses and her Tom Jones leather jacket were in there too. Stanley reached for their hangers and laid the clothing on his bed. He went back three more times, and when he was through, there was quite a pile.

Last time he'd asked Katie to pack up a few of Melba's things, but it was his job. She would have wanted it that way, and maybe he was ready. Melba lived in his heart, not in her clothes hanging in the closet and not in her collection of Tom Jones memorabilia. No matter what happened to him or how much longer he lived, he would never forget her. He would never stop loving her.

But maybe, just maybe, he didn't have to live the rest of his life alone, waiting to die. Maybe it was time to move forward. Time to live his life again. Maybe there was room in his old heart for two women.

Grace Sutter wasn't at all like Melba. Melba had loved to have fun, and she'd had a wicked sense of humor and a loud laugh. Grace was a bit more refined. She liked to write poetry and watch birds out her kitchen window. Both women were wonderful in different ways.

Stanley went to the garage and brought in some boxes he'd carted home from the store. The part of his heart that had loved his wife for fifty years broke all over again as he put her things into the boxes. He opened her drawers and emptied them into the cardboard cartons. He paused to touch the pink nightie she'd worn when she'd wanted some time alone with him in the bedroom.

He loved her. Still. He always would. He picked up the packing tape and closed the box flaps. His eyes watered, and a tear ran down his wrinkled cheek. 'Good-bye, Melba. I'm giving your things away, but I will not forget you. You were my wife, my lover, and my friend. You were my life for a long time, but you're gone. When you left, I was so lonely, but not so much now. I have Katie and Grace.' He moved to his dresser and took a handkerchief out of his drawer. He wiped his face and blew his nose, a loud honking sound that filled the room. 'You always liked Grace. Now I do too.' He more than liked Grace. He loved her. He stuffed the handkerchief in his pocket. 'You don't have to worry about Ada Dover or Iona Osborn getting their hooks in me.' Sometimes at night, when the two of them had lain awake in bed talking about what would happen if one of them died before the other, Melba had made him promise that out of all the women in town, he wouldn't let either Ada or Iona reel him in. It had been an easy promise to keep.

One by one, he carried the boxes outside and placed them in the back of his '85 Ford pickup truck. As long as Melba's clothes still hung in the closet, and her unfinished craft projects sat on the shelf, he didn't feel right pursuing another woman.

He filled up the back of his truck with boxes, and the next morning he left Katie in charge of the M&S and headed to Boise and the Salvation Army. He unloaded Melba's things, then headed toward home again. He knew there were closer charity drop boxes, but the thought of running across someone else wearing Melba's Tom Jones jacket would have been too difficult to bear.

When he returned to Gospel, he went to Grace's and watched the sun set over the pines in the backyard. She made him a sandwich, and he told her what he'd done that day. She gave him one of her soft smiles and placed her hand on his. 'I will always miss Melba,' she said. 'You two were lucky to have found each other. My husband passed away twenty-five years ago. I have never thought of replacing him in my heart, but I've come to learn that there is room in the human heart for more than one love.'

Then he kissed her. For the first time in more than fifty years, he kissed a woman who wasn't Melba. For a few seconds, it felt awkward. For both of them. Then it felt right, and damn if his heart didn't start beating like he was forty again. He broke the kiss and told her of his deep affection and love for her.

She looked him right in the eye and said, 'It's about time. I've loved you for almost a year now.'

He'd had no idea. None, and all he seemed capable of doing was standing there marveling that someone like Grace could love someone like him. He was almost ten years older than her, and every one of those years showed. She didn't look a day over fifty-five.

She wrapped her arms around his neck. 'Stay the night,' she whispered.

'Grace, I respect you and—'

'Stop,' she interrupted. 'Of course you respect me. That's one of the things I love about you, Stanley Caldwell. You're a good and decent man, but even good and decent men have needs that can only be met in bed. Good and decent women do, too.'

God almighty. His insides started shaking so hard that he felt like he was going to shake himself apart. He wanted to have sex with Grace. He was pretty sure his equipment was still capable, but there was a part of him that was terrified. 'Things are different today. A person has to have that safe sex.'

'I don't think we have to worry about that. I haven't had sex since I voted for the first George Bush and you were married to the same woman for almost five decades.' She looked at him, and the crow's-feet at the corners of her eyes deepened. 'In case you're worried, I can't get pregnant.'

'God almighty.'

At half past midnight, Kate picked up the telephone and punched seven numbers. Worry knotted her stomach, and she feared she might get sick. She half hoped he wouldn't pick up. The night he'd run out of the M&S had humiliated her, and she really didn't want to speak to him ever again. That night, he'd made her feel so good, and then he'd turned around and made her feel so bad.

The phone rang five times before it was answered. 'This had better be good.' His voice was sleepy, sexy as hell, and very cranky.

'Rob, it's Kate. I hate to wake you, but have you seen my grandfather today?'

'Kate?' He cleared his throat, and she could almost see him sit up in bed. 'No, I haven't seen Stanley. He's not at home, I take it.'

The knot in her stomach tightened. 'No, he left for Boise this morning and I haven't seen or heard from him since. Have you talked to your mother today?'

'Yeah. I saw her around noon. Why?'

'I called her house two hours ago to ask her if she'd seen Stanley, and no one answered. I called back fifteen minutes later, and still no answer.'

'No one picked up at my mom's?' The sound of dresser drawers opening and slamming filled the background. 'Did you dial the right number?' She repeated the number she'd called. 'Shit.'

'I don't know what to do. I'm afraid my grandfather is in a ditch somewhere. I guess I'll call the sheriff.'

'Hold off on calling just yet.' Kate heard a soft thump and muffled curses, then a clearer, 'Sorry, I dropped the phone while I buttoned my fly. I'll pick you up on the way to my mother's.'

'Do you think they're together?'

'Since both of them are missing, yeah, I do.'

Kate hung up the phone and reached for her coat. She

wished there'd been someone she could have called besides Rob. Before she could stop it, a memory of the other night flashed across her brain, and a mortifying moan escaped her lips. She couldn't believe she'd done that particular sexual position. It was hard for a girl to keep her dignity with her bum in the air, but for some reason keeping her dignity hadn't entered her head that night. Then while she'd been basking in afterglow, he'd been in the bathroom plotting his escape. The second the condom had come off, he'd been out the door as fast as his boots could carry him.

At the grange party, he'd apologized. Maybe he was sorry, but Kate figured he was mostly sorry that she wasn't going to have sex with him again. Yeah, she knew that sounded cynical. So sue her. She wasn't going to ever let him hurt her again.

She watched for Rob out the window. A crescent moon provided little light over the wilderness area, and her thoughts turned from the other night to the crisis at hand. If her grandfather was stranded somewhere, he wouldn't be able to see more than a foot in front of him.

Within fifteen minutes Rob pulled his HUMMER into the driveway. Kate shoved her arms into the sleeves of her coat and was at the passenger door before he could put the vehicle into park.

'After I hung up from talking to you, I phoned my mother,' he said as she jumped inside and shut the door. 'No one answered.' He looked behind him as he backed out. The blue lights of the dash shone on the side of his face and filtered through his hair, unkempt, unruly, and unbelievably hot.

That she even noticed in this time of crisis was incredibly annoying. And especially since she thought he was a big old jerk. 'Does your mother ever unplug her phone?' she asked.

The HUMMER stopped in the middle of the street. He looked across at her as he shoved the vehicle into drive. 'No. At least she never has before.' He gave her a reassuring smile that did little to reassure her. 'They probably decided to go off and write poems in the moonlight somewhere and lost track of the time.'

'Do you honestly believe that?'

He turned his attention to the road as he stepped on the gas. 'Honestly? No, but I figured you might believe it and not worry so much.'

She was absolutely not going to let him charm her. 'Aren't you worried?'

'If I wasn't concerned, I wouldn't be driving around at,' he paused and read the digital clock within the navigation system, 'at twelve fifty-two. I'd only been asleep about half an hour when you called.'

She turned and looked out her passenger window as they passed the Texaco and the courthouse. She wondered what had kept Rob up so late. The unwanted memory of him leaving the grange with Rose forced its way into her head. Yesterday, she'd seen him outside his store chatting it up with Dixie Howe. The woman had given him a hug before she'd left, and Kate wondered if he'd been up till midnight with one or the other. Given his past, probably both.

'I went to church with my mother Sunday, and afterward she did finally mention that she had feelings for

Stanley. I'm sure that wherever they are, they're okay.'

Kate wasn't convinced. She turned her head and looked at him. 'You went to church?'

'Sure.' He glanced at her. 'It was Easter Sunday.'

'And lightning didn't strike?'

'Ha-ha. You're a regular laugh riot.' He returned his attention to the road. 'I noticed you weren't there.'

She tried not to put any significance in his last sentence. So, he'd noticed she hadn't been in church. Of course he'd noticed. It was a small congregation. 'I'd done a little too much sinning the night before with Tiffer Cladis?'

'Couldn't have been the good kind of sinning, since he's gay.'

No, she'd reserved that kind of sinning for the man across the HUMMER, and look how that had turned out. Which should probably tell her that she should give up sin altogether. 'I ended up at his mother's, tossing back hairy sluts all night and listening to Tiffer's Stephen Sondheim collection. Regina had to take me home around three.'

'What's in a hairy slut?'

'Rum, Triple Sec, pineapple juice. It's Tiffer's favorite drink.'

'I could have guessed that.' Rob pulled the vehicle into Grace's driveway. There were no lights on and no sign of Stanley's truck. Old oak trees and pine all but blocked the weak light of the moon.

'He's not here,' she said.

Rob turned off the HUMMER, and the two of them walked toward the side of the garage. 'I can't see a thing,' Kate complained. Rob stopped, and she ran into his back.

'Sorry.' He took her hand and shoved the tips of her fingers down the back of his jeans.

'What are you doing?' she yelped and pulled her hand free. 'You pervert.'

'I'm giving you something to hang on to.'

'Your butt?'

'No. My belt.' He took her hand again and held it instead of shoving her fingers down the back of his pants again. 'Get your mind out of the gutter, Kate. I'm not perverted enough to stick your hand down my pants.' He pulled her along a few steps before he added, 'Not while your grandfather's missing, and not unless you ask real nice.'

The press of his warm palm against hers heated up more than her hand. She felt it in her chest and stomach. 'Don't worry. I'm not going to ask.'

'You might.'

'You wanna bet? No. Forget I asked that.'

His soft laughter was drowned out by the squeak of the garage door as he opened it. He flipped on the light and looked inside. 'His truck's parked next to her Blazer,' he said and turned to face Kate. The garage light lit him up from behind, kind of like a saint.

She pulled her hand free and stuck it in her coat pocket. Rob Sutter was no saint. He was too good at sinning. 'Do you think they're in the house?'

'Yes.'

'What can they be doing? The lights are out.'

He rocked back on his heels, and the light from the garage poured over the shoulders of his dark blue coat and lit up the side of his face. He raised a brow.

It took her several seconds to understand the significance of his cocked eyebrow. 'Gross! He's seventy. He'll have a heart attack.'

'My mom's a nurse, she'll thump him back to life.'

Kate sucked in a breath. 'Aren't you even a little freaked out about them doing' – she pointed to the back door – 'that, in there?'

'First of all, my mind isn't going to go down that path. And second, I'm glad my mother's found someone.'

'Well, I'm glad too. That my grandfather has found someone, I mean.' But was she? 'Do you have a key, or should we knock?'

'Neither.'

'What? Neither?'

Rob turned off the light and shut the garage door. 'I'm not going to bust in on my mother.' He took Kate's hand and headed back to the HUMMER. 'I doubt you would have appreciated Stanley busting in on us the other night while we were doing the wild thing in the condom aisle.'

'I don't want to talk about that. It was a mistake. It shouldn't have happened.' Especially since she was fairly certain he was seeing other women now.

'I'm getting really tired of what we can and can't talk about. We can't talk about the night we met. We can't talk about the first night I kissed you. We can't talk about the night we had sex. That's bullshit, Kate.' They stopped by the passenger side of the HUMMER, and Kate reached for the door handle. 'Some mistakes were made the other night. I'll give you that.' He planted his hand on the window and kept the door closed. 'Maybe it shouldn't have happened *the way* it did, but it was going to happen. And you know what? I'm really not sorry about the way it happened. I had a hell of a good time. Sooner or later, we were going to have sex. It was inevitable.'

'I don't know if it was inevitable, but what I do know is that each time you make me feel good, you turn around and make me feel like shit.'

'Maybe you're looking for something to get pissed off about.'

Was she? No.

He opened the door. 'I said I was sorry for kissing you on the head and saying thanks. Don't you think it's time to get over it?'

Over it? She crawled into the car and looked at his inky black outline. 'It's only been a week.'

'A week's a long time to walk around mad,' he said and shut the door.

On the drive home, neither spoke. Kate stared out her window and wondered if Rob was right. Did she look for reasons to be angry? No, she didn't think so.

Rob pulled the HUMMER into Stanley's driveway and walked her to the door. 'Thanks for coming over here and helping me look for my grandfather,' she said as she stood on the top step and turned to face him.

'Any time.' The light on the house shone down on him, and she saw his face clearly for the first time that evening. A lock of brown hair fell across his forehead and touched his brow. She looked into his green eyes looking back at her. Then his gaze lowered to her mouth. 'Good night, Kate.'

'Good night.'

He brushed his fingers across her jaw, and she thought

he might kiss her. Instead he turned and walked down the sidewalk. As she watched him move away from the light of the house, she felt an irritating little tug of disappointment.

He walked in front of the HUMMER and looked back at her. He raised his hand in an abbreviated wave, and she got that feeling again. The dangerous one that said maybe he wasn't such a bad guy. He'd apologized twice now for running out on her the other night with nothing more than a hasty thanks. He'd gotten out of bed in the middle of the night to help her search for Stanley.

Kate watched him pull out of the driveway before she walked into the house. Even if he wasn't such a bad guy, he wasn't the guy for her. She was tired of relationships that ended in a broken heart. And Rob Sutter was a smooth-talking heartbreak, just waiting to happen.

She hung her coat by the back door and had just finished putting on her pink-and-white-striped flannel pajamas and brushing her teeth when she heard her grandfather's truck. She moved to the dark doorway of the kitchen and waited. Her grandfather entered as quietly as possible, then he turned and slowly closed the back door.

Kate flipped on the light, and her grandfather spun around on the heels of his wingtips. He froze like a kid sneaking home after curfew.

'I didn't think you'd still be up,' he said as color rose up his neck to his cheeks.

She folded her arms beneath her breasts. 'I was worried you'd been wrecked in a ditch.'

'I was with Grace.'

She didn't bother mentioning that she already knew

where he'd been. 'You could have called. The last time I talked to you was this morning when you left for Boise.'

'I'm sorry you were worried, Katie.' He took off his coat and hung it by the back door. 'I've asked Grace to marry me.'

Kate dropped her hands to her sides. 'What?'

'I've asked Grace to marry me. She said yes.'

'But . . .' Kate stared at him, sure she'd misunderstood. Married? People didn't get married after one night in the sack. That was afterglow. Not lasting love. 'But Granddad . . . just because you have sex with someone doesn't mean you have to get married. It's the twenty-first century, for God's sake. Don't be so old-fashioned.'

He slowly turned and looked at her. 'I may be old-fashioned to you, but I am an honorable man. I would never disrespect a woman. I would hope that a woman I cared about would expect me to be honorable. That's what's wrong with your generation, Katherine. You reduce sex to fornication.'

Katherine? She moved toward him. 'I'm sorry. It just seems sudden.'

'My feelings for Grace started the night I heard her poetry at the grange and have gotten deeper ever since.'

'Don't you think you should date for a while first?' She'd never had a marriage proposal, and she'd dated men for as long as three years.

'Katie, I'm in my seventies. I don't exactly have a lot of time to mess around with dating.' He patted her on the shoulder as he moved past. 'When two people are in love, why wait?'

Kate could think of a lot of reasons. She kept them to

herself. If Grace made her grandfather happy, then what kind of granddaughter would she be if she rained on his parade? She just hoped he knew what he was doing. 'And you are positive this is what you want? And you're not just feeling – you know – afterglow?'

'This is what I want. I want a woman who is worth more to me than' – he paused and his cheeks turned pink again – 'afterglow.' He shook his head. 'You are worth more than that too, Katie. You are worth everything a man can give you.'

Now it was her turn to get red-faced. 'I know.' But knowing it in her head and not getting 'afterglow' until she got a marriage proposal were two different things. That pony was already before the cart. Or was it that the pony was already out of the gate? Or was it that the pony was giving the milk for free? She wasn't sure.

There were a few things she did know for sure, though. There was no way the pony was going back in the gate. Not when the pony was thirty-four and really liked pulling the milk cart. But her grandfather was right. She deserved more than relationships that went nowhere. Which left her in the same quandary she'd been in the day she'd arrived in Gospel.

'What kind of bread you selling today?'

'Focaccia.'

Ada Dover scrunched up her nose and leaned in for a closer look. Her hair was perfectly sculpted, and the scent of Emeraude engulfed her like a toxic cloud. 'It's weird.'

'It's very good.'

'Still looks weird.'

'It has fresh thyme and scallions, Nicoise olives and Parmesan cheese. Would you like to try a sample?'

'I think I better.'

Kate bit the inside of her lip to keep from laughing as she cut a piece of bread and handed it to Ada. Ada's brows lowered as she chewed. 'Yep, I better have a loaf of that,' she said.

'Would you like some jalapeño jelly to go with your bread?'

'No. Same as yesterday when you asked.'

Kate moved from the bread aisle and walked behind the counter. 'I'm going to keep asking until you say yes.'

'Well, don't get your heart too set on it. I've liked your bread and some of that fancy cheese, but I just don't see myself warming up to jelly made with jalapeños.' Ada set her purse on the counter and pulled out her wallet. 'How's your granddad?'

You've wasted your Emeraude, Kate thought as she rang up the bread. *He's off the market.* 'He's at home today taking it easy.'

'Is somethin' wrong with him? His joints acting up? He should get some glucosamine. That'll heal him huckety-buck.'

'No. He's just taking the morning off.' *To recover from his wild night.* 'He said he'd be in around noon.'

Ada handed Kate a five, and Kate handed her back her change. 'Are you coming to the poetry reading tomorrow night?'

'Oh, I don't know.' Kate's mind raced to think up an excuse. 'I think I'll be too busy getting bread ready for the next day,' was the best she could do.

'Too bad. You'll miss my new and revised poem about Snickers.'

Kate smiled. 'Yeah, that is too bad.'

Ada put her change away and picked up her bread. 'Well, I'll tell ya what. I'll bring over a copy tomorrow afternoon, special for you, so you can read and enjoy it.'

'Really?' Kate forced her smile to stay in place. 'That would be great.'

After Ada left, Kate restocked the 'ethnic food' aisle,

which consisted of refried beans, salsa, and canned chilies. At noon, Stanley arrived, as he'd said he would. His smile curved up the corners of his mustache, and he hummed what sounded like the *William Tell Overture* all day. Not 'What's New Pussy Cat' or 'Delilah,' but classical music like Grace listened to.

He had it bad.

At three, Rob called with a delivery for across the parking lot. Kate didn't balk at his laziness this time since she figured he probably wanted to talk over the latest news with her.

As Kate left the grocery store; dull gray clouds hung over the wilderness area, threatening rain. A strong breeze played with the ties that closed her cuffs and secured the front of her cream-colored blouse. She wore a peach flared skirt and cream pumps with ankle straps. Wind whipped her hair as she glanced in the bag and smiled. Four granola bars and a bottle of passion fruit juice. Some people were so predictable.

Inside Sutter Sports, a man and his son looked at a row of mountain bikes while a woman leaned her elbows on the checkout counter. She'd squeezed herself into a tight pair of Wranglers, and her behind was pointed at Kate. Rob stood on the other side of the counter, chatting and tapping a pen on the cash register. He wore a dark green polo with the store's fish logo on the breast pocket, and when he looked up, a smile curved his lips.

'Babe,' he said, 'I'm so glad you finally got here.'

Babe? Either he was really, really hungry, or he was talking to someone else. Kate glanced over her shoulder as she walked toward him. There was no one behind her, and she turned back as Rob came out from behind the counter and moved to her. She was about to ask him if he'd been eating paint chips when he stunned her even more. He wrapped her in a big hug that lifted the heels of her shoes off the floor. The scent of his sandalwood soap filled her lungs and her stomach got a little light, like she'd swallowed some air.

'Pretend to be my girlfriend,' he said next to her ear.

Kate glanced behind him as Dixie Howe straightened and turned around. She'd somehow managed to squeeze her breasts into a little midriff top that was more suited for the beach than an overcast day in April. More suited for someone half her age, too.

'What's it worth?'

'I'll give you ten bucks.'

'Forget it.'

'I'll tell everyone I know that your jalapeño jelly is great and to scoot on over to the M&S and pick up a jar before it's all gone.'

She smiled and leaned back far enough to look into those eyes of his surrounded by thick, dark lashes. She placed her free hand on the side of his smooth face and planted a loud kiss on his mouth. His soul patch scratched her chin, and she pulled back and smiled. 'Is it me you're glad to see or my granola bars?'

He laughed and set her back on her heels. 'Both.' One of his hands slid down her spine and rested on the curve of her behind. She gave him a hard look, and he gave her a heart-stopping grin in return. 'I'm sure you've met Dixie,' he said and turned to face the other woman. He did not, however, remove his hand.

'Yes,' Kate answered. 'Dixie comes into the M&S. How are you?'

'I'm good.' Dixie looked Kate over and shrugged, as if she didn't see the attraction. 'Well, I'm going to head out, Rob. If you change your mind, you let me know.'

'See ya.'

'Change your mind about what?' Kate asked in a hushed voice as soon as the front doors shut behind Dixie.

He glanced at the man and his son looking at bikes, then slid his hand from her behind to her waist. Once again he pulled her close. His Fu Manchu tickled her temple when he spoke close to her ear. 'Her version of the sexual pretzel.'

'And you're not interested?'

'No. She's . . . too available to everyone in town.'

'And she has those scary fake boobs.'

There was a long, silent pause before he said, 'Yeah, that, too.' He dropped his hand and took the grocery bag from her. 'Passion fruit. I thought I told Stanley kiwi.' He shrugged. 'Want some?'

'No. It's too sweet. I have to be in the right mood for passion fruit.'

'That's the difference between men and women. Women have to be in the right mood. Men are always in the mood for a little passion fruit.'

'Women need a reason. Men just need a place?'

He popped the top. 'You know it, babe.'

'Dixie's gone. You can stop calling me babe.'

He just gave her another grin and turned toward the man and his son. 'That Heckler is a nice bike,' he said and moved toward them. He took a drink of his passion fruit. 'Lightweight and can take a lot of punishment.'

'A thousand dollars is a little steep,' the father said with a shake of his head.

'How much do you want to spend?'

'I can't afford anything more than three hundred.'

'I just got in a Mongoose for two-fifty-nine.' Rob pointed toward the back with his bottle. 'I'll show it to you.' The three of them moved past the helmets, and he looked at Kate across his shoulder. 'Can you stick around? I need to talk to you.'

Since she was curious and wanted to know what he thought of his mother's impending wedding, she decided she could 'stick around' for a few minutes. 'Sure.' While she waited, she cruised the store, looking at everything from one-man tents to fly-tying equipment. In one aisle, she pulled on some fingerless gloves and looked at Road Dog headbands and bandanas. She took off the gloves and moved to the checkout counter, where she tried on Oakley sunglasses.

As she tried on her third pair, Rob walked from the back room beside the little boy and his dad. 'I can have that ready for you tomorrow,' he said. By the front door, the two men shook hands, and Kate turned her attention to a small mirror on the sunglasses case. She turned her head from one side to the other and couldn't determine if she looked good or like a bug.

'Do you want to learn to fly-fish?' Rob asked as he moved across the wooden floor toward her.

She glanced over at him through a pair of blue-and-red iridium lenses, and the hundred-and-fifty-dollar price tag hung from the bridge of the sunglasses and jabbed her nose. His mother was marrying her grandfather, and that's what he wanted to talk about? 'Today?' She took off the Oakleys and put them back in the case. Surely he'd heard the news by now. If he hadn't, it wasn't her place to tell him. It was his mother's.

'Sunday.' He set his empty bottle next to her. 'Both stores will be closed on Sunday. I'll bet you look hot in hip waders.'

She lifted a brow. 'Hot?'

He chose a pair of tortoise-framed Brinkos from the case, and the tips of his fingers brushed the sides of her face as he slowly placed them on the bridge of her nose. 'Sexy.'

Kate looked at him through gold lenses, and her voice took on that embarrassing breathy quality that his nearness sometimes brought on. 'I'd look ridiculous.'

'Will you go with me?'

She shook her head. 'If I want fish, I'll just walk to the meat cooler at the M&S.'

'It's catch and release.' He took the glasses from her face and looked away long enough to place them back in the case. 'I'll pick you up at six.'

'In the evening?'

'In the morning.'

'That's my only day to sleep in.'

'I'll make it worth your while.' He slid another pair of glasses on her face and brushed the backs of his fingers across her cheek and down the side of her neck. His touch was like magic, sending his incredible sexual energy dancing across her skin.

She looked at him through the dark lenses, and her breath got stuck in her chest somewhere around her heart. 'How?'

'I'll let you use my second favorite rod.'

'Why can't I use your favorite rod?'

He laughed and set the sunglasses on top of the cash register. His dark head dipped, blotting out everything but him. 'Anytime, babe,' he whispered just above her lips.

Her hands grasped the front of his shirt. 'Rob, I think—'

'Don't think.' He pressed one of her hands over his heart, and she felt the strong beat against her palm. 'Just feel. Feel what you do to me. Feel what happens when I'm around you.' His mouth covered hers and blotted out everything but the warm male scent of his body filling her lungs, the slick tangle and slide of their tongues, and the taste of him. He tasted good, like passion fruit and lust.

He tilted his head to one side and turned up the heat. The kiss turned hotter, wetter, and he peeled her fingers from his shirt and slid her hands up and around his neck.

He gently sucked her tongue into his mouth, and she swayed against him. He pressed a hand to the small of her back and brought her breasts in contact with his solid chest. Her nipples tightened as desire pulled like a knot in her stomach, a visceral reaction to the taste of his mouth, the touch of his hands, and the heavy bulge brushing against her lower belly. Her body remembered his and wanted more of the pleasure he could give.

His kiss was like the hot buttered rum she'd drunk the first night they'd met. It tasted very good in her mouth and spread fire throughout her body, heating up the pit of her stomach and making her light-headed. The kiss turned urgent, needy, like he wanted to suck the air from her lungs. He was so good at making her body react to his, and making her forget exactly why she should avoid any sort of relationship. She tore her mouth from his. 'I can't do this,' she said as she took deep breaths. 'I came here to talk about Stanley and your mother. We shouldn't do this again.'

'Sure we should.'

No they shouldn't. He was bad for her. He'd crush her heart and she didn't think she could take another heartbreak. She turned her face away. 'I think we should just be friends.'

'I can't be just your friend now.' He touched her chin and brought her gaze back to his. 'The other night when I came to the M&S, I didn't plan on making love to you. I didn't even know why I was knocking on the door until you answered. Then I saw you standing there and I knew.' He pressed his forehead to hers. 'I'm drawn to you, Kate. I used to think it was just sex. That I just wanted to get you naked, but it's more than that now. I like talking to you and being with you. I look for you in a crowd or the second I walk into the grocery store, and most of the time I don't even know I'm doing it.' He brushed his nose back and forth against hers. 'After I made love to you the first time, I should have taken you home and made love to you in my bed. All night long.' He paused and his voice got lower, rougher when he spoke again. 'That's what I wanted to do then. And what I want to do now.' He pulled his head back. 'I think about you when you're not around, and the really pathetic part is, I'm not sure you even like me very much.'

'I like you,' she whispered and ran her fingers through the back of his fine hair. He seemed to know just what to say to wear down her resistance. 'Even when I try really hard not to like you.'

He grasped her waist, picked her up, and sat her back down on the counter. 'Just think of all the fun we could have if you didn't try so hard.' He stepped between her legs and pushed his hands beneath her skirt. He slid his palms up the tops of her thighs. The warmth of his touch spread to her crotch.

She grabbed his wrists, and with her last shred of sanity said, 'We can't do this here. I have to go back to work.'

He kissed the side of her neck. 'What are you wearing?'

She tilted her head to one side. Okay, one more minute. 'A skirt.'

'No.' His fingers brushed the edge of her panties. 'Here. It feels like lace.'

'It is.'

'What color?'

What color? At the moment she couldn't recall. 'White.' Maybe?

He groaned deep in his throat and pulled back far enough to look into her face. 'Show me.'

'Right now?'

'Yes.'

'Someone might come in.'

'No one's coming in.'

'The last time I was here, two little boys walked in.'

He moved his hands up the outsides of her thighs and pressed his thumbs into the lace covering her crotch. 'Your panties are wet.'

'I have to go help Stanley,' she said on an intake of breath. 'The store gets busy around five.'

He smiled. 'We have over an hour then.'

'Someone could walk in here,' she protested once again, but she didn't remove his hand.

He slid a thumb beneath her underwear and touched her there. 'Do you care?'

Did she? He stroked her slick flesh and she couldn't remember the question. Oh yeah. 'Someone could walk in.'

'Pull up your skirt so I can chew off your panties.'

Could she let a man she'd only had sex with once in a dark store chew off her underwear? Right now? She looked into his heavy eyes, filled with lust and the promise of great sex. She slid her hands down his shoulder and arms and pulled her skirt above her waist.

He smiled and lowered his gaze down the front of her shirt to her thighs. 'I've wanted to do this for a long time now.' He kissed her mouth and the side of her neck, then he knelt in front of her. He raised his gaze to hers, and his smile was filled with the promise of dark, delicious sin. 'Put your feet on my shoulders,' he said as he pulled her bottom to the edge of the counter.

Kate planted her hands behind her as he kissed the inside of her knee and worked his way down. He didn't waste time on foreplay. He just got busy. He pulled her panties aside, then he drew her to his mouth. The immediate, hot suction of his warm mouth stole her breath, and her head fell back.

He kissed between her thighs the way he kissed her mouth, with overwhelming passion, drawing mindless sounds of pleasure from her throat and from his. She closed her eyes as desire pulsed and beat just below her skin, out of control and curling her toes inside her shoes.

He caressed her with his tongue, pressing into her slick flesh and drawing her into his mouth for a luscious kiss that nearly sent her over the edge. Repeatedly, he coaxed her to the point of orgasm only to back off and nibble on the inside of her thigh and touch her with his fingers. Each time he took her higher, farther, until a deep, shattering orgasm took her apart. It started in the pit of her abdomen and worked its way outward, rushing across her skin like liquid fire. Her fingers and the backs of her knees tingled, and she heard herself call out his name. It seemed to go on forever and then he was above her, kissing her and touching her breasts through her clothes.

Like always, desire surrounded him, hot and vital. Kate felt the relentless force of it as she wrapped her arms around his neck. She kissed his throat and he reached for his wallet. He removed a condom from inside and she took it from him. He unbuttoned his pants and pushed them and his white briefs down his thighs.

Kate took his thick penis in her hand and rolled the thin latex over the head and down the long shaft to the base. Rob looked at her, fire and need and greed burning in his eyes as she positioned him. His mouth lowered to hers and his tongue thrust into her mouth as he entered her body, plunging so fully, so deep, that if she hadn't been so ready, he would have hurt her.

She wrapped her legs around his waist as he drove into her, again and again, hard and deep. She clung to him, welcoming each thrust of his pumping hips and feeling each stroke push her toward orgasm once more.

Rob tore his mouth from hers and crushed her against his chest. His fingers tangled in her hair as he plunged into her one last time. He held her that way, tight against his chest, until their breathing returned to normal. 'That was . . .' He spoke into the top of her head. '. . . I'm not quite sure, but I believe that was the best . . . I don't think I've ever come like that.' He lowered his hands and rubbed the tops of her bare thighs. 'Thank you, Kate.'

She pulled back and looked into his face. 'You're welcome, but you did all the work.'

'Yeah.' A crooked smile twisted his lips. 'But it's the kind of work I don't mind doing.' He pulled out of her and reached for his briefs. He zipped up his pants, then helped her off the counter. Her underwear was twisted to one side, and she moved quickly to the bathroom at the rear of the store and slipped inside.

She took care of business, then turned on the water to wash her hands. She looked into the mirror above the sink and at the reflection staring back at her. Her hair was messed up, her cheeks were flushed, and her bottom lips looked chapped from Rob's soul patch. She looked like a woman who'd just had sex.

The water ran over her hands as she stared at herself. She'd just had sex on the front counter and anyone in town could have walked in. 'Oh my God,' she whispered. Her face got hot and her ears started to buzz. She couldn't believe she'd just done that.

'Kate.' Rob rapped on the door. 'If you're finished, I need to get in there.'

She turned off the water and dried her hands. She opened the door but couldn't quite look into his face. She slid past him, and he grabbed her arm.

'Stay right here.' He let go of her and unzipped his

pants. He pushed down his briefs, and she turned her back to him.

'Geez, close the door. Isn't that kind of personal?'

'Honey, we just moved beyond personal.' He dropped the condom in the toilet and flushed. She heard him zip his pants, then turn on the faucets. 'It doesn't get much more personal than me going down on you on my checkout counter,' he said as he dried his hands with paper towels.

'I can't believe I just did that.' She put her palms on her cheeks. 'Someone could have walked in the door and seen . . . you . . . your face . . .'

He turned her around and threw the paper towel away. 'The door was locked.'

'What?'

He grasped her wrists and looked into her face. 'No one could get in. I locked the door when I let out the guy looking at mountain bikes.' He gave her a quick kiss, then took her hand in his and led her from the back room. 'Two fantasies down. Nine hundred and ninety-eight to go.'

'You locked the door?'

'Yep. Couldn't have anyone walking in on us.'

Her feet slowed. 'You were that sure I'd have sex with you?'

'Hell no.' He turned and looked at her. 'Where you're concerned, I never know what to expect. I just like to be prepared. I'm like a Boy Scout.'

She laughed, and they continued toward the door.

'Come home with me.'

'I have to work until six.'

'I'll pick you up afterward. We can have some dinner and then you can show me your tattoo.' He raised her hand

and kissed the back of her knuckles. 'I'll just drive across the parking lot at six.'

'No, I'll drive out to your house.' She wanted her car, just in case there was a problem. Not that she was going to look for one. She was going to be optimistic if it killed her.

He slid his lips to the inside of her wrist, then dropped her hand. 'If you're not at my house by six-thirty,' he said as he unlocked the big double doors, 'I'm going to come looking for you.'

'Are you afraid I won't show?'

'I told you I never know what to expect out of you.'

'I'll be there,' she said as she walked away. She moved to the curb and glanced back to see if he was watching her.

He was.

He stood with his arms folded across his chest, his weight resting on one leg, and his head tilted to one side.

Rob Sutter was a heartbreak just waiting to happen, but not unless a girl was foolish enough to fall in love with him. His past proved he was bad at relationships, but if a girl didn't want that from him, it wasn't an issue.

Kate moved between two parked cars next to a light pole. If all a girl wanted or expected was a real good time, remorseless lust, then Rob Sutter was definitely her guy.

Two fantasies down. Nine hundred and ninety-eight to go, he'd said. If all a girl wanted was a fantasy man, Rob Sutter would be perfect in that capacity.

Nine hundred and ninety-seven to go.

Kate lay in a tangle of sheets and legs, Rob's moist mouth in the small of her back and his hands on her behind.

'Your tattoo turns me on.'

A lot of things turned him on. Her walking in his front door had had him jumping on her like a duck on a bug. At least they'd made it to his bed this time.

She turned, and his mouth found her navel. Her stomach growled, although at the moment she wasn't sure if she was more hungry for him or for food.

He rose and sat back on his heels. 'Want something to eat?'

Golden sunlight from the window spread across Rob's bed, filtering through dark, fine hair covering the thick definition of his chest muscles and flat ridges of his stomach. A dark, happy trail circled his navel, leading straight down his lower belly to his pubic hair and his erection. A long, angry scar ran from his sternum to his navel, marring the perfection of his body.

'What did you have in mind?'

'Ham sandwiches.' He got up from the bed and moved to his dresser. He pulled on a pair of gym shorts and tossed her a big T-shirt with a hockey logo on the front. As they made their way to the kitchen they stepped over her panties and his briefs in the middle of the bedroom, her bra and his shirt on the stairs, and her dress by the front door.

The kitchen light shone off the pots and pans and the stainless steel appliances. Rob opened the refrigerator and looked inside. 'Did your grandfather mention that he asked my mother to marry him?'

'Yes.' Her gaze took in the gold scales etched in black on his shoulder and down the left side of his smooth back. The tattoo dipped beneath the waistband of his shorts and appeared again wrapping around his right thigh. Earlier, she'd run her fingertips across the tattoo. Rob had shivered and the snake had seemed to come alive and move across his skin. Two small scars marked his back about a hand's width apart. 'My grandfather told me when he got home last night. When did you hear the news?'

'This morning.' He set a jar of mayonnaise, a head of lettuce, a package of ham, and two wheat beers on the work island. 'That's what I wanted to talk to you about earlier when you brought over the granola bars.' He moved to the pantry and grabbed a loaf of bread. 'But I got sidetracked. Remember?'

Yes, she remembered. 'What do you think of their plans?' Kate asked and grabbed a bottle opener that was stuck on the refrigerator. She popped the tops and handed him a bottle.

'I told her she didn't have to get married just because she slept with Stanley.' He raised the beer. 'And she reminded me that the most serious problems in my life were caused by sex outside of marriage.' He took a long drink, then sucked a drop from the corner of his lips. 'I think if I'd been nine, she would have smacked me.'

Kate laughed. 'I said about the same thing to my grandfather, and his reaction was pretty much like your mother's. He actually used the word *fornication* as if it was a *bad* thing.'

Rob's laughter joined Kate's, and he set down the bottle and took eight slices of bread from the bag. As Rob spread mayonnaise on the bread, Kate tore lettuce and watched him out of the corners of her eyes. She liked the way his tattoo moved when he flexed his arms. In fact, there was a lot to like about him. His broad, hairy chest and flat abs were high on her list.

'If Stanley makes her happy, then I'm happy. It'll be a little weird at first.' Rob piled ham on the bread, then cut the sandwiches with the knife. 'Will this make me your uncle or your cousin?'

She hadn't thought of that. 'Let's just say neither.'

He put the sandwiches on a plate and looked down into her face. 'You know what they say?'

She gazed up past his mustache and nose and into his eyes. 'What?'

'Incest is best.' He lightly took her chin between his fingers and kissed her mouth. 'Of course, I don't know that firsthand.'

'I'm glad you cleared that up.'

Together they moved to the dining room to sit at the long, formal table. In between bites of sandwich and potato chips, he told her it was the first time he'd eaten in the room. He talked about his daughter and the plans he had for them when she was old enough to visit during the summer months.

'Why do you live in Gospel?' she asked as she pushed her plate aside after one sandwich.

'My mother lives here.'

'But your daughter lives in Seattle. It sounds like you miss her.'

'I miss her a lot.' He took a bite, then washed it down with beer. 'At first I moved here to recuperate because my mom's a nurse. She helped me with my physical therapy, but mostly I couldn't stand to live in Seattle and not play hockey. It reminds me of everything I used to have and everything I lost.' He placed the bottle on the table, and his green eyes stared into hers. 'I used to think I moved here because my mother's here. The truth is I came here because I needed a change.' He reached for a chip and munched on it. 'I ended up staying because I like it here.' He washed the chip down with his beer. 'Don't you want another sandwich?'

'One's my limit.'

'Now it's my turn to ask you a question.'

She took a drink from her beer, then set it back down. 'What?'

'Why do you live in Gospel?'

'My grandfather needs me,' was the easy answer.

He scratched the scar running down his bare chest and

leaned his chair back on two legs. 'Not buying it. Your grandmother's been dead for more than two years.'

She looked over at him, her relaxed, sexy fantasy man. What did it matter what she told him? It wasn't as if she should hold back for fear of killing the relationship. She pushed her hair behind her ears and told him about Randy Meyers. How she'd found his family for him and what he'd done with the information she'd given him. She told him how Randy had looked and seemed so normal.

'You can't always tell a crazy person by looking,' she said.

Rob nodded. 'Stephanie Andrews didn't look crazy until she shot me. The scariest thing about crazy people is that they can look so normal.'

He was right.

'Did you see Kathy Bates in *Misery*?' he asked as the legs of his chair hit the floor. 'She was scary as hell.' He reached for another sandwich and took a bite.

'Yes she was, Mr Man.'

He laughed and swallowed. 'So you quit your job and moved to Gospel because a psycho nut killed his family?'

That was one reason. 'I quit because I could no longer tell myself that the people I tracked down were lowlifes and deserved to be found and that I was somehow better.'

'You came here for a change just like me,' he said as if it was fact.

'Maybe.'

'Do you think you'll ever go back?'

'To detective work?' She shook her head.

'To Vegas?'

She thought a moment. Vegas had chewed her to pieces and spit her out, but sometimes she really missed the bright lights of the big city that truly never slept. 'Maybe. I've spent a lot of my life there. That's where I graduated my last year of high school, and I went to ULV. That's where I used to party like a rock star and later got my PI license. It always felt like home to me. Maybe it will again.'

Rob polished off his sandwich and hers, then he took her back upstairs. They had sex against the granite wall of his shower, taking care of fantasy number nine hundred and ninety-six. Afterward, he dried her off and they watched the ten o'clock news. He fell into an exhausted sleep during the weather report.

Kate removed his arm from her waist and gathered her shoes and underwear. She looked at him one last time, asleep within the tangle of sheets and the sliver of moonlight pouring across the bed. She walked downstairs and pulled her dress over her head. She stepped into her shoes and shoved her panties and bra into her little black bag.

Then she left, quietly shutting the door behind her, because that's what you did with a fantasy man. You left before you did something stupid like spend the night. Before you could fool yourself into thinking that what you had was real.

Rob walked into the M&S the next morning, and his gaze instantly sought Kate. She stood behind the counter ringing up items from a blue plastic basket for Regina

Cladis. She looked good. Good like something he wanted to toss over his shoulder and carry home. The older woman said something and Kate laughed, a warm, amused sound that seeped between his rib bones and lodged in his chest.

'Morning, Rob,' Stanley called out to him from his position at the coffee machine.

'Hello, Stanley.'

'Hey, Rob,' Dillon Taber said from behind his coffee mug.

'Hey, Sheriff. How's it goin'?' Rob asked as he walked through the store to the counter.

'Can't complain.'

Kate looked up at him. The corners of her mouth curved just a little, as if she was trying *very* hard not to smile. She wore a white shirt that closed with laces across her breasts and had some sort of black thing beneath it. The shirt wasn't real tight, and it didn't show off anything fun, but it still managed to be sexy as all hell.

'You should try the jalapeño jelly,' he told Regina as he moved behind her in line. 'It's really good.'

'That's what Kate says.' Regina turned and squinted at him through her thick glasses. 'But I'm going to pass.'

'Okay, but yesterday I saw Iona fighting with Ada over a jar.'

Her magnified eyes narrowed. 'Why would they fight over the same jar?'

He hadn't thought of that. 'Who knows what drives some women to drop their gloves.'

'Huh?'

'Here's your change, Regina,' Kate said through a smile that she could no longer contain.

As soon as the older woman grabbed her bag and walked away, Rob took her place at the counter. 'We need to talk about somethin', babe.'

Her smile flattened. 'You're calling me babe again.'

'I know.' He placed his hands on the counter and leaned closer. 'Do you want to talk here, or somewhere more private?'

She glanced around the store, then her brown eyes met his. 'My grandfather's office.'

'Lead the way.' He moved behind the counter, and his gaze slid down the back of her white shirt to the waistband of her black pants. He'd finally seen her tattoo. It was blue and gold and covered one cheek on her nice, smooth butt. He liked it. He liked all of Kate. Except for one thing.

'Why did you leave last night without telling me?' he asked as soon as they were alone.

She leaned back against the closed door, her dark red hair falling to her shoulders. 'You were asleep and I didn't want to wake you.'

'Why the hell did you leave at all?' When he'd woken and found her gone, he'd been angry, and not just because he'd wanted another shower with her.

'I couldn't stay. Not after the lecture I got about fornication from my grandfather.'

In the past, he'd used women and they'd used him. He didn't want that with Kate. He'd had a bad marriage. He didn't want that either. He wanted something in between. Something he'd never had before. A woman in his life that he actually liked out of bed. He took a step toward her and combed his fingers through the side of her hair as he looked down into her eyes. Eyes that had just the night before gazed back at him, shimmering with the same aching desire he'd felt for her. 'If you won't stay the night, at least tell me you're leaving. Even if I'm asleep. That way I won't wander around looking for you, thinking maybe you got lost in my house.'

She bit her bottom lip. 'You did that?'

'Well . . . yeah.' Maybe he shouldn't have admitted that. Before he could confess anything else potentially embarrassing, he kissed her. He meant to give her a quick peck, but he stayed a fraction too long, and the want and need that had not been sated the night before settled low in the belly and twisted into a hard knot. Her lips parted and her tongue touched his, slick and warm and tasting of cocoa and whipped cream and Kate.

When he came up for air, his hands were beneath her shirt on her breasts. Her nipples were hard against his palms and her fingers were wrapped around his wrists. Through the door, he heard Stanley moving around in the storage room.

'Rob, we can't do this here,' she said in a shaky voice just above a whisper.

'Are you sure?'

'Yes. This is my grandfather's office. He's right outside the door.'

She was right. This time. 'Sorry,' he said as he slid his hands to her waist. 'I got sidetracked again.'

She licked her lips, moist from his kiss. 'That seems to happen to you quite often.'

Only with her. She made it hard to breathe. Made him lose his mind. Maybe because he felt safe and comfortable with her enough to lose his mind. Knowing that he made her lose her mind as well was a huge turn-on. He squeezed her waist and forced his hands from her. 'Come over tonight.'

Her eyes were a little dazed, and she blinked a few times as if she were trying to clear her head.

'We'll have dinner,' he added. 'Shoot pool. Six-thirty?'

She nodded and tucked her shirt back into her pants.

'If you don't show up,' he warned for the second time in less than twenty-four hours, 'I'll come looking for you.'

'I'll be there.' She took a deep breath and opened the door. 'I'm going to kick your butt at pool.'

'Right,' he scoffed, but a few hours later, she'd won four out of six games. Probably because he got distracted by the way she looked leaning over his pool table.

He grilled steaks, and they ate in his dining room again. Then he took her to bed, where he scored big.

Over the next week, they knocked out a few more fantasies, including a quicky in the alley behind Rocky's and – Rob's personal favorite – a hummer in the HUMMER.

She brought over a picnic basket, and they ate in bed while watching the Chinook's Avalanche game on the big-screen television in his bedroom.

She knelt in the center of his blue plaid quilt wearing a T-shirt from his old Red Wings days. It covered her from shoulders to her upper thighs, and he wondered why she bothered with the shirt at all. He'd just spent a pleasant hour getting up close and personal with the parts she covered.

'Ouch.' She winced as the camera zoomed in for a

close-up of Chinook goalie Luc Martineau thumping Teemu Selanne in the back with his stick. When that didn't seem to faze the Finn, Luc hooked his skates and took him down.

'Yeah,' Rob said through a laugh.

She spread Brie on a slice of baguette and handed it to him. 'That wasn't very nice.' She picked green grapes from the stem and handed those over too. 'That number sixty-eight is kinda cute?'

'Selanne?' He popped a grape in his mouth and frowned. *Cute?* Something that felt a little like jealousy jabbed his chest. Only he didn't think it was jealousy because he wasn't a jealous guy. 'Selanne hits like a girl, and his accent is so thick, you wouldn't be able to understand him.'

'Who cares about talking,' she said and glanced at him out of the corners of her eyes.

He grabbed her wrist and pulled her onto his bare chest. 'No more staring at Selanne.'

She rose above him and straddled his hips. 'Too bad I never saw any hockey games when you played.'

'I have a lot of old game tapes.' He slid his hands up under the T-shirt to her waist. 'Maybe someday I'll show them to you.' But not today. The tapes were packed up in a box, where they'd been since he'd been forced to resign. He had more important things to do today.

And the next day, too. For the first time in his life, Rob began inventing reasons to see a woman. He checked up on her in the morning while she baked bread, and he convinced her that she needed to drive out several nights a week to help him perfect his granola. He told her that he had to find just the right balance so it didn't taste like cardboard and vitamins. He said he wanted to hire someone to make it for him so he could sell it to campers and backpackers in his store. He knew that would appeal to her entrepreneurial spirit.

It was pretty much a lie and he wasn't the least bit sorry.

On the first Sunday in May, he picked her up at six in the morning and they headed to a little spot he knew on the Big Wood River where the trout couldn't resist a chamois nymph this time of year.

'These are *not* cute,' Kate said as she stepped into the neoprene waders he'd given her. Rob helped her pull the straps over the shoulders of her sweatshirt and put on the fishing vest he'd rigged for her. She shoved a ski cap he'd given her over her hair, and she watched him tie a creamy beige fly to the end of her leader.

'We're using that for bait?' she asked as she leaned in for a closer look.

'No, babe. This is a lure. Not bait.' And just as she was about to remind him not to call her babe, he dropped a kiss on her mouth, then waded into the river. She followed close behind him, hanging on to the back of his vest as he tested the slick rocks before committing his weight. The icy current pushed at the backs of their knees as he showed her how to hold her rod. He stood behind her, his arms alongside hers as he taught her the basic cast just like his father had taught him.

'Keep the tip between one and eleven o'clock,' he told her, and when she'd mastered the basic cast, he showed her how to add line. 'Now we'll strip about twelve feet.' He pulled the line from the reel to float on the current in front of them. He showed her how much line to let out at each back and forward cast. 'The idea is to have the fly barely touch the water before bringing it back up.'

Her nymph got hooked in the thickets behind them, and rather than waste time retrieving it, Rob reached into his vest, pulled out his scissors, and snipped the line.

'Sorry I lost your fly,' she said as he plucked another from his vest.

'Don't be sorry. I lose them all the time. It's part of the sport, and I've got thousands.' He took his place behind her once more and slid his hand around her waist as she stripped line and started casting. 'No, you're snapping your wrist. Smooth strokes.' He lowered his mouth to her ear. 'You know about smooth strokes, don't ya, babe?'

'You're not going to distract me,' she said as she worked, keeping the tip of the pole between one and eleven. 'And don't call me babe.'

'Why not?'

'Because you've probably had a lot of "babes" in your life.'

He thought a moment. 'No. Only you.'

The third Sunday they went fishing together, she caught her first fish. An eleven-inch rainbow that took off downstream and gave her a fight. The bright morning sun shot sparks off the water swirling about her long legs encased in dark green waders. Her laughter mixed with the rush and ripple of the river as she fought to land her trout.

While he removed the hook for her, he watched her admire the brilliant colors of the rainbow. She slid her fingers down its slick body. 'It's beautiful, Rob.'

Her bright eyes glanced up into his, and her cheeks were a shiny pink from the crisp morning air. He'd never known a woman like Kate. One who wore Tiffany bracelets and lace underwear while she stood in a freezing river fishing beside him.

She took the fish from his hands and carefully lowered it into the water. The fish flipped its tail and splashed her waders. Then it darted beneath the surface, and she rinsed her hands in the freezing water. She looked up at him with pure pleasure and said, 'That was awesome.' He felt a pinch in his chest. A confusing little compression near his right ventricle. It wasn't as if he'd never seen pleasure on her face. He'd seen it a lot because he put it there.

He stripped ten more feet of line, brought the tip of his pole up and cast his fly near the head of a pool. The nymph started to drag, so he rolled the rod tip upstream and mended the line.

He glanced at Kate out of the corners of his eyes as she checked the condition of her fly. No pinch or tug this time. Nothing to get confused about. He rolled his head and relaxed. There was nothing he had to try and figure out.

The next Sunday was Mother's Day and they didn't fish. He and Kate ate dinner with his mother and Stanley. Over mint-crusted lamb chops and red potatoes, they listened to the wedding plans. The date was set for the second Saturday in June. Stanley and Grace were getting married in the park by the lake, and both planned to read poems to each other. They asked Rob and Kate to stand up with them.

'Sure,' Kate said as the corner of her lips twitched.

'How long are the poems?' Rob asked.

'Oh,' his mother answered, 'fifteen or twenty minutes.'

He groaned inwardly and Kate cleared her throat behind her cloth napkin.

When the meal was over and everyone had pushed their plates away, Kate offered to help his mother clear the table.

'No, you stay out here and keep your grandfather company,' Grace insisted. 'Rob will help me.'

Rob was leaving for Seattle in the morning, and he figured his mother wanted to talk in private about his trip.

'What's going on between you and Kate?' she asked instead.

'What?' He looked at her and set the plates in the sink. He hadn't seen that one coming, but he wasn't all that surprised.

'Don't play games.' She placed a serving dish on the counter, then reached into a cabinet and pulled out a can of decaffeinated coffee. 'I see the way you look at her.'

'How do I look at her?'

'Like she's special to you.'

He opened a drawer and took out several plastic bowls with lids. 'I like her.'

'You look at her like you more than like her.'

He spooned red potatoes into a bowl and didn't comment.

'You weren't fooling me. I know you were playing footsies with her under the table.'

Actually, his feet hadn't been that close to her, but his hand had been on her thigh most of the evening. Nothing sexual, just touching her. He shrugged. 'So, I like her a lot.'

'You're thirty-six.' She filled the carafe with water then said, 'In three weeks you'll be thirty-seven.'

'And next year I'll be thirty-eight. What's your point?' he asked even though he knew.

'Just that Kate's a nice girl. Maybe someone you could get serious about.' She paused, and he didn't have to wait long for the rest. 'Maybe marry.'

'Maybe not. I've done that, and I sucked at it.'

'You got married because Louisa was pregnant.'

'Doesn't mean that I didn't love her.' He looked at his mother and asked, 'Where's the pie?' Subject closed.

There was nothing that could mess up a good thing like talk of marriage. Thank God Kate wasn't pushing him in that direction. She never asked where he was going or when she would see him again. She didn't get jealous when he talked to other women or paranoid when he had to work late and couldn't see her. She didn't get all girly and want to talk about their 'relationship.'

As far as he was concerned, that made their relationship just about perfect.

Rob's trip to Seattle turned into the trip from hell. Since his last visit, Amelia had decided to take up permanent residency in terrible-twos town, and she regularly threw fits like she was possessed. The first hint that she'd turned to the dark side happened the day he took her to play with his former teammate's little girl, Taylor Lee. They'd only been at Bruce Fish's about half an hour when Amelia strong-armed Henry the Octopus from Taylor Lee, then whacked her in the head with it.

The fit at Fishy's was tame in comparison to the

spectacular fit she threw his last night in town when he took her to the Old Spaghetti Factory. She was perfectly fine during dinner – well, as fine as a two year old could be – but on the way out, he told her she couldn't have the Lifesavers she knew he had in his pocket. She threw herself on the ground and beat her heels on the floor, and all he could do was watch, for fear that if he picked her up, she'd nail him in the nuts with her little pink boots.

His sweet baby girl had turned into a demon child, and to top it off, Louisa had clearly lost her mind, too. Just as he was leaving for his return trip, she mentioned that she and Amelia should come and stay with him in Gospel. Not permanently, just on the weekends.

During the summer months, business kept him from seeing as much of Amelia as he'd have liked, and he wasn't opposed to seeing more of her. But he didn't want Louisa staying with him. If she brought the subject up again, he'd give her the names of local real estate agents.

By the time his plane landed in Boise around noon, he was exhausted and not looking forward to the long drive to Gospel. An hour from town, he called Kate on his cell phone. She arrived fifteen minutes after he got home, and seeing her standing on his porch was like looking at sunshine.

The second the door shut behind her, she pushed him up against the hard wood. A surprised *oomph* left his chest, and she grabbed his wrists and pinned them above his head. The gold Rolex he'd been given when he'd signed with the Seattle Chinooks slammed into the door and dug into his skin. He didn't mind. 'What are you planning?' he asked.

'An assault.'

She kissed his neck, and the touch of her wet mouth sent shivers down his spine, working out the tension he'd felt for days. 'Are you going to hurt me?'

'Yeah, but I don't think you'll complain.'

He closed his eyes. 'Does this mean you missed me?'

'No,' she said, but her actions attested to the lie. 'I was too busy to miss you.' She let go of one of his wrists and slid her hand down his chest. 'Mmm,' she murmured as she softly sucked his throat. She unbuttoned his shirt and pulled it from the waistband of his pants. Then she cupped his crotch and gave him a gentle squeeze. 'Does this mean you missed me?'

'God yes,' he said through a tortured breath.

She laughed and kissed her way down his chest and scar. She knelt in front of him and pressed her face into his belly as she unbuttoned his pants. She looked up at him and took him into her hand. Then she kissed the head of his hard dick, and he spread his feet to keep from falling. She sucked him into her hot, wet mouth and she stayed with him through his climax.

When it was over, she pulled his underwear and pants back up. 'I think I'm in love,' he said, totally relaxed.

She reached for his fly and buttoned it. 'No, you're not. That's just your afterglow talking.'

She was probably right, but there was a little part of him that wished she wouldn't have dismissed what he'd said so quickly, as if he couldn't possibly mean it. He didn't know why it should bother him, but it did. He liked her a lot. Liked having her around. He loved how she made him feel. He loved having sex with her, but that wasn't love. Love didn't feel this relaxed. This good.

His life here in Gospel was turning out to be just about perfect. Why would he want to mess it up with love?

18

Kate pulled her CRV to a stop at the only traffic light in town. On the passenger seat next to her sat a little Tiffany box with an Egg Sucking Bugger inside. For the past week, she'd worked on tying the fly for Rob's birthday. It wasn't near as good as anything he could tie. She'd worked hard on it, though, and she wondered if he'd appreciate the effort.

She shifted in her seat, trying to find a more comfortable position. The rhinestone thong she'd ordered from Frederick's of Hollywood was uncomfortable as hell and cut into her hips, not to mention other places. It was made of hundreds of clear glass stones, all strung together to form a shiny triangle. The matching bra itched her nipples, and the center clasp dug into her left breast. She looked like an escaped showgirl from the Rio. She didn't have to wonder if he'd appreciate her underwear.

The light turned green and she took off from the

intersection. She reached for the sunglasses clipped to her visor and slid them on her face. It was seven in the evening and the June sun was starting its descent. She'd never just shown up at his house unexpected before. She didn't think he'd mind.

He'd mentioned his birthday in passing a few weeks ago, but she'd avoided the subject so she could surprise him. She had plans for him that he wasn't likely to forget anytime soon.

She hadn't seen Rob all day, but it wasn't the first time. He'd gotten so busy lately that he'd hired two people to work for him in addition to the little boys he paid to clean camping gear. She figured he'd probably been at the marina.

The thin rhinestone halter dug into her shoulder, and she ran a finger beneath the collar of her wrap dress and adjusted the strap. Since the night Rob had returned from Seattle, she'd noticed a subtle change in him. His touch seemed more personal. More possessive, as if he was trying to pull her closer. He'd made her a fishing vest and given her some of his most prized flies. The day he'd given her a book on how to become an entrepreneurial genius had been the day she'd no longer been able to keep him at arm's length. She hadn't been able to tell herself that he was just her fantasy man. She'd looked up into his smiling face, and she'd done the one thing she'd told herself never to do.

She'd tried to keep her emotions at a safe distance, but her heart hadn't gone along with the plan. She'd fallen in love with Rob. Truly, madly, full tilt in love. The kind of love that snatched your breath away, and it scared the hell out of her.

She turned up his long drive and pulled to a stop in

front of his garage. She grabbed the Tiffany box off the passenger seat and shut the car door behind her. The heels of her silver sling backs tapped on concrete as she made her way across the driveway. The rhinestone string of her thong pulled, and she walked very carefully up the steps to his front door. She rang the bell and had to keep her hands purposely at her side. She didn't want to get caught picking at her backside when Rob answered the door.

The door swung open, but it wasn't Rob. A short blonde in a red tube dress stood in the threshold. She had blue eyes and perfect skin, not a mole or blemish or enlarged pore to be seen on her beautiful face. An alarm bell rang in Kate's head.

'Yes?'

Kate looked beyond the blonde inside the house. 'Is Rob around?'

'Yes. He's around,' she answered, but she didn't move. 'Maybe I can help you?' There was a slight edge of hostility to her smooth voice.

'No. I don't think you can.' Kate hadn't a clue who the woman was, but she was acting like she owned the place. 'Who are you?'

'I'm Louisa.'

Ah. The ex. 'Yes. Rob has mentioned you.' He didn't, however, mention that Louisa was gorgeous. The kind of gorgeous usually found on the arm of a very rich man. He also didn't mention that she was going to be in Gospel for his birthday. The alarm bell ringing in Kate's brain got a bit louder, but she ignored it. Rob had divorced this perfect woman, and as Kate recalled, he'd said he'd loved her but never liked her. 'I'm Kate Hamilton.'

'Hmm.' She tilted her head to one side, exposing one earlobe decorated with a few shining carats. 'Interesting that Rob's never mentioned you.'

Whoa. Kate hadn't been mistaken about the hostility. And as much as she hated to admit it, Louisa's barb nicked her somewhere in the area of her heart. 'Why would he mention me to his ex-wife?' But why *hadn't* he mentioned her?

'Because Rob and I have been talking about a reconciliation. I think if you were an important part of his life, he would have mentioned you.'

Okay, she felt a little more than an alarm bell in her head and a nick that time. But she told herself that Louisa was lying. She had to be. Rob wouldn't do that to her. She opened her mouth to respond, but Rob moved into the foyer from the kitchen. He wore a white tank and blue swim trunks and carried a little girl in a pink bikini and flip-flops. The little girl had her arm around Rob's neck, and Kate recognized her from her pictures scattered around Rob's house. When he looked beyond Louisa and saw Kate, his footsteps slowed. 'Kate.'

'Happy birthday.' She held out the Tiffany box, loving him so much that her nicked heart swelled beneath her rhinestone bra. She was going to remain optimistic or die trying.

'Thank you.' He set his daughter on her feet, then took the box. 'Come in.'

Optimism was one thing. Sitting around with Rob and his bitchy ex while rhinestones rode Kate's crack was another. 'No. I didn't know you had company. I should have called.'

'That would have been nice,' Louisa said.

Rob looked at his ex and frowned. 'You don't have to call first. Stay for dinner. I'm just about to fire up the barbeque.'

If he was planning to reconcile, would he invite her to dinner? asked her newfound optimism. 'No, thanks.' But optimism only went so far. It didn't mean she was suddenly blind. 'Louisa was just telling me that the two of you are planning to get married again.'

'That's not true,' he said, and Kate felt the pain in her chest recede. A deep furrow appeared between Rob's brows, and he patted his daughter on the head. 'Go get your baby. She's on the couch.' When Amelia took off, he turned his attention to his former wife. 'Let it go.'

Louisa looked up at him. Even her profile was perfect. 'You told me you'd think about it.'

'I did and the answer is still no.'

'You really need to think harder about whether you want to throw away a chance at being a family again.'

'Louisa, for God's sake!' he exploded. 'Why do you always have to keep pushing at the same thing until I get pissed off? I'm not remarrying you. I'm not marrying anyone. Ever. Once was enough.'

It took several long seconds for his words seeped into Kate's brain. When they did, she felt the direct hit, and she took a step back. *Oh God*. The pain shot up and slapped her. It was happening again. Déjà vu. Different guy. Different naughty underwear. Same heartbreak.

'Sorry to interrupt your birthday.' She turned in a blur of pain and confusion and walked away before she did something really embarrassing like burst into tears in front of that raving hag Louisa.

Rob caught up with her at the bottom of the step. 'Kate. I swear I'm not getting back with Louisa. You don't have to leave.'

'Yes. I do.' She kept walking. She needed to get in her car. If she could just get into her car.

'I didn't even know she and the baby were coming until she called me from the airport in Sun Valley this morning.'

'It doesn't matter.' She reached for the door handle.

He put his hands on her shoulders and turned her to face him. 'I'll call you tomorrow.'

The backs of her eyes stung and she felt as if she were about to implode. She recognized the symptoms. She was going to fall apart, but not yet. Not until she was alone. 'No. Don't call. I can't do this anymore. I thought I could, but I can't.'

His brows wrinkled. 'Can't do what?'

'I can't tell myself that the fantasy is enough. It's a lie.' Her voice wavered, and she looked down at her feet. 'No matter how many times I told myself that you'd hurt me, I've fallen in love with you.'

After several heartbeats, he said, 'I care about you.'

She'd told him she loved him, and he'd said he cared about her. She guessed it was better than a 'thank you.' She looked up at him and blinked back tears.

'You care about me?'

'More than any other woman.'

It wasn't enough. Not this time. 'For how long? What's going to happen in a year from now? Two years from now? Five years from now? How much of my life do I give up for you? How many lies do I tell myself? How much longer until you decide we should date other people or just be friends or you've found someone else?'

'I don't know! For as long as it lasts.'

She took a breath and let it out slowly. 'That's not enough.'

'What the hell is?'

'A man who will promise to love me forever.'

He squeezed her arms. 'Christ, are you talking about a wedding ring?' He shook his head. 'That's crazy.'

Crazy. Anger mixed with heartbreak. 'Let go of me.'

His eyes narrowed and he dropped his hands. He stepped away from the car, and she yanked the door open and climbed inside before she started to cry in front of him. She shoved her key in the ignition and drove away. She glanced in her rearview mirror one last time and caught a glimpse of him walking up the steps before her vision blurred and she turned her attention to the road.

What was the matter with her? She'd told herself to stay away from Rob. She'd come to Gospel to try and figure out what was wrong with her, not to fall in love, heart and soul, with a man who could never fully commit to loving her as much as she loved him.

She pulled onto the highway. No, there was a difference now. The difference was that she was no longer willing to settle for less than she deserved. She loved Rob. More than she could remember loving any other man, but her grandfather was right. She was worth everything a man could give her. His heart. His soul. His promise to love her forever.

*

Rob took Louisa and Amelia to the airport the next morning. It had cost him a lot of money to get them on another chartered flight out, but he was afraid he was going to kill his ex-wife. And he really didn't want to do that. He didn't want to spend the rest of his life in jail and have Amelia raised by relatives.

But as angry as he was with Louisa, it didn't come close to what he was feeling for Kate. What the hell was wrong with her? Why had she messed everything up with talk of wanting more from him, wanting marriage? He'd thought she was different, but she wasn't.

He should have known better than to get involved with her. He'd learned the hard way that sex was never free. There was always a price. Kate's price was a wedding ring. He'd been forced into one bad marriage. He wouldn't be coerced into a second.

It was just never going to happen. She could just sit over in her store and bake bread and grow into an old maid for all he cared. He'd liked Kate. He'd told her the truth when he'd said he cared about her. He did care about her, but he was going to try and forget her.

No way was he going to let her make him crazy.

When he pulled the HUMMER to a stop at the back of Sutter Sports, Adam Taber was waiting for him. Rob opened the doors for business, and Adam followed him inside.

'Mr Sutter,' he said. 'Wally can't make it today 'cause he got the chicken pox.'

'That's okay. I don't have that much for you to do.' Rob looked back at Adam over his shoulder and did a double take at the bag in the boy's hand. 'What is that?' he asked and pointed to what looked a lot like granola.

'Granola.'

'Where'd you get it?'

'At the M&S. The lady over there is making it.'

'Kate? The lady with the red hair?'

'Yep. She gave it to me free 'cause she wants me to tell people it's really good. Then they come buy it.'

She'd stolen his granola idea! 'Adam,' he said. 'You're in charge of the store until Rose gets to work. I'll be back in a few minutes.' He hit the front door with the heel of his hand and shoved his sunglasses on his face, so angry he didn't care that he'd left an eleven year old to run his store. He couldn't recall a time when he'd been so enraged. Yes, he could – last night, when Kate had told him she loved him, then, practically in the same breath, said it was over. His anger burned a hole in his stomach, and he clenched his teeth.

'Hi, Rob. Haven't seen you for a few days,' Stanley said as Rob entered the M&S.

'Hello, Stanley.' Rob took a breath and forced his jaw to unlock. He didn't want to take out his anger on his soon-to-be stepfather.

'Your mother should be here in a minute to talk about flowers at the wedding. It's coming right up, you know.'

'Yeah, I know. Is Kate around?' he asked and thought he'd managed to sound damn pleasant.

Stanley paused a moment then said, 'She's in the back bagging up some granola she made this morning. It's been selling like crazy.'

Rob thought his head just might explode. He moved around the counter to the back room.

Kate's back was to him as she took a pan from one of the

ovens. She set it on the counter and looked up. She didn't even try and look guilty. 'What are you doing here?'

He stopped in front of her and put his hands on his hips. 'You stole my granola idea.'

'Don't be absurd.'

'You knew I was working on perfecting the recipe and you stole it.' Never mind that he'd mostly used it as a ruse to get her out to his house so he could get her naked.

She took a spatula and stirred the granola around. Taunting him. 'It wasn't a secret recipe like Colonel Sanders's seven herbs and spices.'

'You knew I was working on it to sell in my store.'

She shrugged. 'You snooze. You lose.'

'What?' He wanted to grab her and shake her and press her so tight into his chest that he just absorbed her into his body.

She took a bite and chewed thoughtfully. 'Mmm. Want a bite?'

God, she had balls. He loved that about her, and he wanted his life to go back the way it had been before she'd decided he needed to make a permanent commitment. 'Have you given up your crazy idea to get married?'

'To you? Yes.' She folded her arms beneath her breasts and said, 'Harvey Middleton's son, Brice, asked me out.'

It had been less than twenty-four hours since she'd told him she loved him and she already had a date? 'You can't go out with him.'

'Why?'

Because I said so probably wasn't a good answer. 'Because he's losing his hair.'

She looked at him as if he'd lost his mind. More than

likely because he felt like he'd lost it. 'Go out with him. It's none of my business,' he said and turned away. He moved from the back room to the front of the store. If Brice Middleton put his hands on Kate, Rob was going to put him in a head lock and feed him his lunch.

Grace looked up from a conversation she was having with Stanley. She smiled. 'How are you feeling, Robert?'

'Compared to what?' he snapped.

So much for not letting Kate make him crazy.

A slight breeze rippled across Fish Hook Lake, and the warm afternoon rays reflected like tiny mirrors on the waves. The hem of Grace Sutter's cream chiffon dress fluttered about her knees as she read the last line of her poem to her groom and those gathered at Sockeye Park.

The bride and groom stood beneath a lattice arbor entwined with wildflowers on a small grassy point. A preacher from the nondenominational church in town presided over the ceremony. Kate stood behind her grandfather and watched his hands shake as he pulled his poem from his pocket. He unfolded it and began:

'My life was filled with black and gray,
all my sorrow running into the next day.'

Kate lowered her gaze to her pink toenails and listened as her grandfather spoke of his lonely life before Grace. She concentrated on her favorite Fendi sandals. The beige straps wrapped her feet in soft leather, and a gold sleeve hung from the heel and made a little sound when she walked. Her favorite shoes usually boosted her spirits and made her feel like a diva.

Today, nothing was making her feel better. She slid her gaze across the six-foot patch of grass that separated her toes from Rob's black leather shoes. The cuffs of his charcoal trousers broke over the laces, and razor-sharp creases ran up each leg to the bottom of his suit jacket. In one hand at his side, he held his mother's small bouquet of white roses pointed at the ground. Kate didn't allow her gaze to roam any further, but she didn't have to to know exactly how good he looked.

Rob and Grace had arrived at the park shortly after Kate and Stanley. Watching him walk his mother up the aisle, Kate's chest had gotten tight and her breathing a little shallow. He'd cut his hair short, shaved off his soul patch, and trimmed the Fu Manchu framing his lips. In his gray suit and short hair, he was GQ handsome, but you would still never mistake him for a male model. He had too much testosterone just beneath the surface to allow anyone to gel his hair or spritz him down with water.

She hadn't spoken to Rob since the day he'd barged into the M&S, raging about his granola. That had been a week ago, and her heart had yet to begin healing. In fact, it seemed to break just a little more every time she saw him. In the past, with each heartache, she'd been able to tell herself that she was fine. She was okay. This time she wasn't so fine. She was definitely not okay.

Stanley finished his poem, then Kate handed him the

simple gold wedding band from the purse hanging on her shoulder. She smiled at her grandfather and Grace as they promised to love each other until their deaths. She felt the pull of Rob's gaze on her face, and she looked at him. She couldn't seem to help it.

His green eyes looked back at her from across the short distance, and she was reminded of the day she'd first seen him standing in the M&S, his face void of expression. He was a lot better at pretending he didn't care than she was. Or maybe he wasn't pretending at all.

The sound of the preacher pronouncing Stanley and Grace husband and wife pulled Kate's attention back to the ceremony. She pushed up the corners of her mouth a little more and looked out at the guests seated on chairs borrowed from the grange. Her mother and father sat in the front row beside her brother Ted and her great-aunt Edna. Kate's other two brothers were stationed overseas and hadn't been able to make it.

Applause broke out when Stanley and Grace Caldwell kissed, then the guests stood and moved toward the couple. Kate took a step back, and her heels sunk into the grass. The town's widow posse was the first to step up and congratulate Grace. Some of them even managed to look sincere.

Kate's mother and father hugged Grace and welcomed her and Rob to the family. Kate was pretty sure they meant it, too. Anyone just looking at Stanley could tell that Grace made his life better.

Rob was Stanley's stepson now. Even if Kate managed to avoid him all year, she'd have to see him at Thanksgiving and Christmas. How was she ever going to get over her feelings if she had to see him across the parking lot all the time or talk to him over a turkey and ham dinner?

She needed a vacation. Some distance. Perhaps when her grandfather and Grace got back from their honeymoon, Kate would drive to Vegas and catch up with her friends.

Maybe she should move. Her grandfather was happy now. He didn't need her, and there was a whole big world outside of Gospel city limits. A world without Rob Sutter – except on holidays.

From a few feet away, Kate recognized Rob's deep laughter, and she looked over at him. Rose Lake had her hand on his shoulder and had raised on her toes to say something into his ear. Kate turned her attention to the preacher and thanked him. She chatted with the Aberdeens, and all the while she managed to keep her smile in place and pretend she wasn't dying inside.

Yeah, she should move, she decided. But she really didn't want to. Not right now. She'd just started to fit in. She'd joined the Mountain Momma Crafters and would attend her first meeting the following night. She'd volunteered to bring refreshments and planned to introduce them to the wonders of gourmet food and jalapeño jelly. Gospel was just starting to feel like home, which was scary if she thought about it too hard.

Kate excused herself and wandered over to the covered pavilion, where the caterers Grace had hired from Sun Valley were setting up. She helped them set out mints and nuts and looked up as she heard the unmistakable sound of Iona Osborn's quad cane.

Iona wore a red dress with so much blue rickrack on

the ruffles that she looked like she was about to break into a square dance. 'Hi, Iona.'

'Hello, Kate.' She stopped and looked over the three-tier white-and-blue wedding cake. 'Did you make the cake?'

'No. I haven't graduated past cupcakes.'

'You did a good job with those.' Kate was about to thank her when she asked, 'When is it your turn to get married?'

Kate thought the obvious answer to the question was, When I get asked. She didn't bother stating the obvious, though. 'I just haven't found the right person yet,' she answered. But she had. Or at least she thought she had. She glanced over Iona's ten-gallon pile of hair at Rob. He stood talking to her brother, pointing out at the lake toward town. The two shook hands, then Ted made his way toward Kate beneath the pavilion.

'How many times have you been asked when you're getting married?' he asked as he reached for a glass of punch.

'About ten. How about you?'

'Five.' He drained the small glass. 'You win.'

This was one competition she didn't want to win. She was feeling a little testy, and her face hurt from smiling. Her head was pounding, too.

Great-aunt Edna grabbed a piece of cake and moved to stand by Kate and Ted. Edna's skin looked as tough as an old army boot, and Kate wasn't sure if that was due to her pack-a-day habit or the toxic effects of her bologna pie. 'Are you next?' Edna asked as she reached for a little cup of nuts.

Kate didn't have to ask her what she meant. 'No.'

'Well, dear, if your grandfather can find someone at his age, there's hope for you.'

Kate tilted her head to the side. 'Did you know that Harvard researchers have concluded that Coca-Cola is not an effective spermicide?'

'Huh?' Edna stared, her mouth slightly agape.

Kate patted her great-aunt on her bony shoulder. 'So not enough if you ever find yourself without a condom.'

Ted laughed and put his arm around Kate. 'What do you say we cut out of here and find a bar?'

It was early enough that the Buckhorn wouldn't be filled up with knuckleheads. 'Wanna play a game of pool?'

He smiled. 'I'm not going to let you win.'

They moved from beneath the pavilion. 'You never let me win.'

'Kate.' She didn't have to turn to know who'd called her name. Even after everything, the sound of his voice still poured over her like warm rum. She took a deep breath and turned to watch Rob walk toward her.

He stopped a few feet from her and looked into her eyes. 'Do you mind if I steal your sister for a few minutes, Ted?'

'No, I don't mind. Kate?'

She handed her keys to her brother. 'Wait for me at my car.'

Rob waited until Ted had walked away before he said, 'Why are you leaving so soon?'

Because you don't love me and it's too hard to stay. 'Ted and I are going to go play pool and catch up on what's been happening since Christmas.'

He'd unbuttoned his jacket, and he shoved his hands in

the front pockets of his pants. 'Are you planning to tell him about us?'

She shook her head. 'There's nothing to tell.'

'There could be.'

It was so tempting, even now, to believe that. But it was an illusion. A fantasy. 'I knew when I got involved with you that I would end up hurt. I should never have told myself that I could handle it. I couldn't and I can't. It's over, Rob.'

He rocked back on his heels and rubbed one hand across his chin and mouth. 'The thing is, I think I might be in love with you.'

Might? She waited for him to elaborate, but he didn't. He looked at her as if he expected something from her. It was just too painful, and she turned to walk away before she could give in to the tears stinging the backs of her eyes.

His grasp on her arm stopped her. 'I tell you that I think I love you and you walk away?'

'Either you love someone or you don't. *Thinking* you *might* be in love is not the same as *being* in love. It's not enough.'

His gaze narrowed. 'And a piece of paper and ring are going to ensure that I do love you enough?'

'No, but they're the first step to spending your life with the person you love.'

He held up his hands. 'Have you seen the divorce rate lately?' he asked incredulously as he lowered his arms. 'You can bet every damn one of those couples thought they'd spend the rest of their lives loving each other.'

'Keep your voice down. You're at your mother's wedding, for God's sake.' She folded her arms across her chest, across her heart. 'I happen to think your mother and my grandfather will be happy and stay married to each other.'

'Yeah, but they're still only one out of sixty. Since you love statistics so much, I think you'd know that one.'

Actually, it was 50 percent. 'I don't care about statistics. I care about me. Finally. I care enough about me to never settle for less than I deserve.'

'You think you deserve marriage?' he asked, but he had lowered his voice. 'Babe, no one deserves that slice of hell on earth.'

'I still want it. I want to try with someone who loves me enough to try with me. I want to grow old looking at the same face every morning. I want to grow old looking at the same face every night at the dinner table. I want to be one of those old couples you see still holding hands and laughing after fifty years of marriage. That's what I want. I want to be someone's forever.'

'So that's it. I either marry you or you walk out of my life? Just like that? That easy?'

No, it wasn't easy. Breaking up with Rob Sutter was breaking her heart, but it would be so much worse if she let it go on.

'Marriage is just a piece of paper,' he scoffed.

'If you believe that, no wonder your marriage to Louisa ended in disaster.'

Rob watched Kate walk away, and he felt his jaws clinch. He'd just told her he might be in love with her, and she'd thrown it right back in his face.

He turned, and his gaze landed on Dillon Taber and his wife, Hope, standing a few feet away under the shade of a tree. Dillon turned his face toward his wife and pressed his forehead to Hope's temple. He said something that made her kiss him. A quick peck that had the sheriff sliding his hand down his wife's back to the curve of her behind. A familiar touch between two people who knew each other intimately.

That's what Kate wanted, and if Rob were honest with himself, that's what he wanted too. But at what price? A piece of paper and a gold ring? Those things didn't make people stay in love.

Rob reached into his pocket and pulled out his keys. He found his mother and Stanley and told them good-bye. He didn't feel like talking to anyone. He had too much on his mind.

He went home and fell into his usual routine of tying flies to take his mind off his troubles with Kate. It didn't work, and after he closed the store the next day, he grabbed his fishing rod and headed to the Big Wood.

The early evening sun turned the clouds orange and vibrant purple. He pulled his waders and vest over his T-shirt and headed into the river. The solace and comfort he usually found in the steady rhythm of stripping and casting his fly eluded him. The peace of mind he always found out in the open with nothing but the sound of the river and occasional dove evaded his grasp.

He thought about what Kate had said yesterday at the wedding. She thought marriage meant that people would love each other forever and never be lonely. He loved Kate. He didn't just think he did. He knew it down to the bottom of his soul, but there were worse things than being lonely.

He cast his nymph downstream on the edge of a deep

pool. The fly drifted a few feet, and within seconds he felt the nibble and tug at the end of his line. He pulled the rod tip up and reeled in the excess. His rod bowed in half, and he knew he had a big fish on his hook. It shook and rebelled, then it took off downriver and gave him one hell of a fight.

Fifteen minutes after it began, the fight was over and a sixteen-inch rainbow flipped its tail against Rob's waders. He lifted the big fish from the water and admired the colors.

'Isn't she a beauty,' he said before he realized he was alone. He was so used to Kate being by his side that he'd spoken out loud. In just a short period of time, she'd become an intrinsic part of his life.

Gently he removed the hook and turned the fish loose. The current pushed against his legs as he moved through the river toward the shore. He leaned his rod against the HUMMER and unlocked the back. Just because Kate wasn't around didn't mean he had to be alone. Not like before. Just because he didn't have Kate didn't mean he couldn't have a woman in his life.

He shrugged out of his vest, but he couldn't shrug away the loneliness that settled on his shoulders. Problem was that he couldn't see himself with anyone but Kate. And that was a big problem, because she wanted more than he could give her. He'd made a lousy husband to Louisa and they'd made each other miserable.

Rob stepped out of the waders and shoved all his gear in the back of the HUMMER. He loved Kate. The kind of love that tied him up in knots. He'd married Louisa. Had had a baby with her, but he'd never loved her like that.

On the drive home, Rob took a hard look at his life. He was a guy who learned from his mistakes. But maybe he hadn't learned from his mistakes so much as he'd just avoided living his life. Then he'd met Kate, with her beautiful face and smart mouth, and she'd made him want more.

Kate wanted more too. She wanted to grow old with someone, but was that what Rob wanted? It wasn't a hard question to answer. He wanted Kate. He wanted to take her hand without thought, just because it was there to take. He wanted to press his mouth to her ear and say something that would make her laugh. He wanted to slide his hand down Kate's back to the curve of her behind. A familiar touch between two people who knew each other intimately.

He wanted to watch her try to outfish him, all the while knowing she was wearing a lace thong. He wanted her to be his friend and lover, and he wanted it for the rest of his life.

He took a left and headed for the M&S, but Kate wasn't baking bread for the next day. One of the Aberdeen twins told him that she'd mentioned something about the Mountain Momma Crafters.

He wouldn't be surprised if she was planning to force-feed them jalapeño jelly. He drove to the grange, and his heart pounded as he moved up the steps. Even before he opened the door, he could hear the voices of dozens of women. He paused with his hand on the door, manned up, and slipped into the grange. His gaze landed on Mrs Fernwood, who stood between two long tables. She had a piece of paper in her hand.

'Fold the left side of your triangle in half,' she said.

The door closed with a loud bang, and heads swivelled to look at him. He only had interest in the redhead at the end of the furthest table. She looked up, her gaze wary as he moved toward her.

'Hello, Rob,' Regina called out. 'Have you come to make an origami cicada?'

He'd rather get puck shot than make a damn origami cicada. With dozens of pairs of eyes staring holes in him, he walked across the grange until he stood before Kate. 'I need to talk to you.'

'Now?'

'Yes.' When she only scowled at him, he added, 'Don't make me throw you over my shoulder.'

Iona Osborn heard him and started to giggle.

Kate set down her folded paper and stood. 'I'll be right back,' she told the group. He took her soft hand and led her back outside.

As soon as the door shut behind them, she pulled her hand from his. 'Has something happened to Grace and my grandfather?'

The setting sun washed the wilderness area in shadows and brushed silver light across her pale cheeks. They stood on the steps of the grange, and he'd bet that if he opened the door, twenty old ladies would come spilling out.

'No.' He looked at her, the woman he wanted to spend the rest of his life loving. 'It's not about that.'

Her nose wrinkled. 'You smell like fish.'

'I know. I just caught a sixteen-inch beauty. You would have loved it.'

'Is that what you came to tell me?'

'No, but while I was fishing, I realized how much I've missed you and that my life is shit without you.'

'Rob, I don't—'

'You're right,' he interrupted before he lost his nerve. 'You deserve more. You deserve someone who loves you enough.'

Pain clouded her eyes and she looked away. He placed his hand on the side of her face and brought her gaze back to his. 'I love you, Kate. I don't just *think* I *might* love you. I've never loved a woman more than I love you. I love your tenacity. I love that other men think you're a ballbuster and that I alone know the truth. I love that you single-handedly want to change the eating habits of Gospel. I love that you know what you're worth. I used to think that if something went wrong in my life, I'd just solve the problem by never making the same mistake twice. But that didn't solve anything. It just made my life lonely as hell. Then you came along and let the sunlight back into my life. And I don't ever want to go back to the way things were before you propositioned me that night in Sun Valley. I love you and I want to be with you forever. I want you to be my friend and lover. Not for today or tomorrow. Not for a year or five years from now.' He wrapped his arms around her waist and lowered his mouth to her ear. 'Kate, be my wife. My lover. My forever.'

After a pause that seemed like a lifetime, she said, 'You're doing it again.'

'What?' He pulled back and looked into her face. Tears rested on her bottom lashes, and his heart beat heavy in his chest while he waited for her to speak again.

'Making it impossible to say no to you.'

He smiled. 'Then say yes.'

'Yes.' She wrapped her arms around his neck and pressed her forehead to his. 'I love you, Rob. I love that you have an ego bigger than mine. I love that you braved the Mountain Momma Crafters for me. I came to Gospel to look for my life, and I found you. You are my lover and my fantasy man.'

He gave her a long, wet kiss, and when he pulled back, he said, 'I was thinking we should go celebrate at the lodge where we first met.'

She placed her hands on his shoulders and leaned back. 'That is not one of my fondest memories.'

He grinned. 'It is mine.'

'You just want me to twist you into a sexual pretzel.'

'You're reading my mind again.'

She chuckled. 'Sometimes it isn't difficult.'

She was such a smart-ass and a trash talker. He held her tight and buried his nose in the top of her head. Those were just two of the things he loved about her.

Epilogue

Kate Sutter raised a hot buttered rum to her lips and took a long drink. Valentine's Day, she decided, was freakin' fabulous. On the 'things that are freakin' fabulous' scale, it ranked somewhere between her husband's naked butt and the four-carat Tiffany diamond on her finger.

Kate looked around the Duchin Lounge, at the shiny heart garlands, roses, and flickering candles. Red and pink hearts were taped up behind the bar and on the big windows looking out at snowcovered pines, groomed runs, and night skiers. She'd been married a total of six hours and was looking forward to the rest of her life.

She and Rob had said their vows at the little church in Gospel, and after the reception, they'd set out for their honeymoon. First Stop, the Duchin Lounge.

Since the end of summer, her grandfather had retired and handed the M&S over to Kate to run. The day he and Grace had driven off in a new Winnebago, Kate had ordered a new cash register that kept track of purchases at the point of sale. Her homemade bread sold out every day, although the jalapeño jelly was still a tough sell.

'Sun Valley Ale,' a masculine voice next to her ordered.

'Draft or bottle,' the bartender asked.

'Bottle's fine.'

Kate ran her gaze up worn Levi's and a blue flannel shirt to a pair of green eyes. 'Wanna see my tattoo?' she asked.

The bartender put the beer on the bar, and Rob raised it to his lips. 'Are you propositioning me?'

'Yep.' She stood and set down her mug. 'We have nine hundred and twenty fantasies we have to get started on.'

He took a drink, then lowered the bottle. 'Nine hundred and nineteen,' he said through a purely lascivious grin. He grabbed her hand and walked with her from the lounge as fast as his boots would carry him. 'But who's counting?'

LORELEI MATHIAS

Step on it, Cupid

Amelie's life is arranged just how she likes it. Well, most of the time.

She has a brilliant job she adores, a great social life and a love life she can take or leave. So it's a shock when she realises that everyone she knows seems to be happily coupled up. Is it time she thought about settling down?

Assigned a nightmarish project in work – writing the ad campaign for Britain's biggest speed-dating company – she is forced into doing lots of market research, very much against her will. But with her best mate Duncan, her annoying boss Joshua and her ex-boyfriend Jack all causing havoc in her life, maybe a speed-dating romance could be her salvation?

Charming, engrossing and very romantic, *Step on it, Cupid* is a modern spin on the oldest story of them all – how to fall in love . . .

0 7553 3272 5

little
black
dress

NINA KILLHAM

Mounting Desire

Jack Carter and Molly Desire are just housemates. There could never be anything between them – they're far too different. **Aren't they?**

Jack, a successful romance writer, is looking for his soul mate. Molly, a fully paid-up sexaholic, views having to lodge in Jack's house as a necessary but very temporary evil.

For a while, it looks as though they're the exception to the oldest rule in the book: **the one that says opposites attract**. But then Molly takes to writing her own instantly successful steamy romances, and Jack is furious. As the sparks start to fly, it appears there's a whole lot more to their relationship than meets the eye. But could it be that two such different housemates could really be . . . soul mates?

'Truly a book to be devoured with relish' Jennifer Crusie, author of *Faking It* and *Fast Woman*

0 7553 3277 6

little black dress

You can buy any of these other
Little Black Dress titles from your
bookshop or *direct from the publisher*.

FREE P&P AND UK DELIVERY
(Overseas and Ireland £3.50 per book)

Daisy's Back in Town	Rachel Gibson	£3.99
The Bachelorette Party	Karen McCullah Lutz	£3.99
My Three Husbands	Swan Adamson	£3.99
Step on It, Cupid	Lorelei Mathias	£3.99
Mounting Desire	Nina Killham	£3.99
Blue Christmas	Mary Kay Andrews	£3.99

TO ORDER SIMPLY CALL THIS NUMBER

01235 400 414

or visit our website: <u>www.madaboutbooks.com</u>

Prices and availability subject to change without notice.